KNUT FALDBAKKEN, one of Norway's leading writers, was born in the small Norwegian town of Hamar in 1941. He studied psychology at the University of Oslo and later worked as a journalist. In 1965 he went to Paris and started his writing career. In fact he lived abroad for ten years – in France, England, Spain, Austria, Yugoslavia and Denmark, supporting himself by working as a bookkeeper, factory hand and seaman. His first novel was published in 1967, and two years later he had his first popular success. Married with two sons, he works as a literary critic in Norway while continuing with his creative writing. So far he has published ten novels and a collection of short stories, as well as writing four plays and a number of screenplays. His work has been published in fourteen countries, including the United States, where his books have recently created considerable interest. Peter Owen will be publishing two more of his novels, *Adam's Diary* and *The Hunter*, in 1989.

# THE SLEEPING PRINCE

KNUT FALDBAKKEN

# THE SLEEPING PRINCE

*Translated from the Norwegian
and with a Foreword by
Janet Garton*

PETER OWEN · LONDON

ISBN 0 7206 0710 8

Translated from the Norwegian *Maude danser*

All Rights Reserved. No part of this publication
may be reproduced in any form or by any means
without the prior permission of the publishers.

PETER OWEN PUBLISHERS
73 Kenway Road London SW5 0RE

First published in Great Britain 1988
English translation © Janet Garton 1988

Photoset by Ann Buchan (Typesetters) Shepperton
Printed in Great Britain by
A. Wheaton & Co Ltd Exeter

· *Foreword* ·

'She could wake him with a kiss whenever she wanted to.'

In *The Sleeping Prince* Knut Faldbakken has taken the motif of the Sleeping Beauty – a passive maiden waiting to be aroused to life and happiness by the bold and handsome prince – and turned it on its head. The central character, Maude, is a mature and idealistic woman who has cherished a dream ever since she was a little girl of discovering her prince asleep in the grass, with shadows playing across his face, elegant and noble in repose. The novel traces her determined attempts to find her prince – attempts that will not be thwarted, despite the clumsy behaviour of other people who do not understand, or the tendency of the sublime to veer towards the ridiculous, or even the seemingly insuperable distance between actual events and the interpretation Maude wishes to place on them.

For it slowly dawns on the reader during the first section of the novel that Maude's account of the rhythms and tensions of life at Clem's boarding-house is capable of a quite different interpretation than the one Maude wishes to place on it; that matters which seem to her to be of major significance – the placing of a serviette, the title of a novel, the intonation of a sentence – may be regarded as completely negligible by everyone else, whereas matters which most people regard as of greater moment – like the actual identity of the man on whom her dreams are focused – are impatiently brushed aside by Maude as irrelevant. Maude herself is aware that she has a special way of seeing things, which she congratulates herself is more subtle and refined than the gross oversimplification of the common view; but she remains totally unaware that her idiosyncratic behaviour is gradually sliding over the borderline into the dangerously perverse. Danger signals are apparent from early in the novel, as Maude reveals that she is forty-seven and still a virgin: she has in fact never been near a man, with the exception of a few Christmas dances, at which the actual contact with a male body aroused rather more distaste than curiosity. Her life has been devoted to caring for her invalid mother –

sickly ever since her father 'ran away' when she was still a child – and since her mother's death, to a reasonably comfortable but extremely circumscribed life at the boarding-house, with just enough money, no work and no close friends. She has nothing to do, in fact, but dream – and dream she does continually, about her 'secret lover'. It is when reality begins to encroach upon her dreams that alarming conflicts arise.

Maude's dream of her sleeping prince has its roots in her childhood, in her memories of 'the summer Daddy went away'. That same summer, when she was six years old, she had found a man lying in the grass early one morning, seemingly fast asleep, pale and noble-looking. He becomes 'her' man, and she refuses to believe it when she is told that he is dead and he is taken away from her. The fleeting glimpse of this beautiful stranger has fed her fantasies and become her ideal, which she later transfers to the ascetic, suffering features of her fellow resident at the boarding-house, Mr Eldmann. So long as he remains the passive object of her fantasies, and takes no active part in the relationship himself, all remains relatively calm for Maude: she ventures further and further, increasingly confident that his passivity can be guaranteed. And when it is ultimately sealed by death, he too has become incontrovertibly 'hers'.

Trouble starts when Maude is actively courted by another resident at the boarding-house, Mr Kønig. Suddenly she is faced with a dilemma; fulfilment as a woman, the goal of all her strivings, is at hand, and she longs to know the pleasures of the flesh and the fabled glory of consummation. Yet at the same time the whole process strikes her as inordinately messy and inelegant: an erect penis is such an unaesthetic object, and her own arousal triggers carefully nurtured reactions of fear and shame. Mr Kønig's urgent pleas to be allowed to make love to her – and his importunate advances, invading her mind and her body – clash with her desire for a sleeping prince, whose sleep bears an increasing resemblance to the sleep of death. Sexuality and death have become inseparably mingled in her consciousness: and the imperative need to act out the combination of the two drives her towards a climax of ultimate fulfilment and ultimate catastrophe.

*The Sleeping Prince* is the Norwegian novelist Knut Faldbakken's fourth novel, published in 1971 when he was thirty. It is an imaginative *tour de force* in which he absorbs the reader in the mental universe of a frustrated middle-aged spinster – for the whole of the story is narrated from Maude's viewpoint -- and yet simultaneously makes us aware that her view is partial, indeed at times plain wrong. The story is recounted in her language, with her obsessive concern for the minutiae of everyday life at the boarding-house, her whole universe: her refined distaste at the vulgarity of so much of social intercourse, and her delicate euphemisms for bodily functions and parts which she dare not approach too closely even in thought. And yet her reactions and reflections are saturated with the sexuality she has denied herself for so long: she need only look out of the window at the rain or go for a walk in the garden to be overwhelmed by the abundant fertility of nature, the heavy sensual ripeness of flowers and fruit, the thrusting, pulsating life force invading her senses and demanding her response.

In this novel, as in most of Knut Faldbakken's other novels, sexuality is the supreme driving force which demands expression; when it is denied an outlet through 'normal' channels, it flows into others, and when it is bottled up too long, it explodes terrifyingly. This is not in itself a new insight, of course; but psychological truisms are startlingly illuminated by the consistency with which Faldbakken follows his characters into the ultimate realization of their darkest fantasies, of homosexuality, incest and mutilation.

Accusations of speculation are rife whenever a new novel by this author is published; the frankness of his erotic descriptions makes some critics suspect a desire to shock and to titillate rather than to write 'serious' literature. And the enormous success of his more recent novels in Scandinavia – and now too in America, where a translation of *The Honeymoon* (1982) has just been published – has done little to mitigate this disapproval. But in *The Sleeping Prince* at least, where so much of the meaning lies in the subtext – behind and at cross-purposes with Maude's words and her conscious intentions – the disturbing finale is not only justified but is revealed to be the only logical outcome of her accelerating flight into another world.

Janet Garton

# I

*The Language of the Bees*

## · 1 ·

Maude had often tried to imagine what Mr Eldmann looked like when he was asleep. She could see in her mind's eye his distinguished face immobile on a pillow, his eyes closed. It was not until she could see him like that, she thought, that she would be able to recognize her prince; only then would she know for sure if it was love. This feeling she had been insistently aware of recently – and not only aware of; she had nurtured it, tended it, watched over and protected it with an eagerness which surprised even herself. It was such a little thing after all. What on earth was it that had got into her? Well, no one could answer that, least of all her. . . . But now and then it became so strong that she was practically forced to dismiss the thought as absurd and unworthy. Good Lord, at her age – what on earth was she thinking of?

But then her anxiety loosened its hold again, and her thoughts drifted back to the other thing, to this feeling that had started to grow; for she was sure that something had started to grow, and kept on growing between herself and Mr Eldmann. Every day she noticed it in so many, many ways, small ways perhaps, details which most people would have paid no attention to, but which were full of significance for her – and for him. It had to be like this in the beginning, whilst everything was so uncertain. They had to be careful, so that none of the others noticed anything; not until the time was ripe, otherwise it would be disastrous. Maude shuddered at the thought of all the stories that people told.

As yet no word had passed between them – apart, that is, from the normal greetings when they met by chance on the stairs and in the corridors, and incidental remarks during mealtimes. Deep down inside she was immensely grateful for all the discretion he demonstrated. They had to think of their reputations, not only as residents of the private boarding-house, but in general. There were well-defined rules about how one should behave in certain specific situations, and she had no intention of breaking them. His co-operation when it came to the observance of this civilized principle left her even more convinced that he was a man of exceptional character. Mature, respectable people. That was something worth holding on to. Name and reputation. Decency. One's responsibility as a citizen.

Maude was conscious of her responsibility: once you gave way to impulses like that; once you had 'fallen'. . . . It could get so bad that she managed to convince herself that she had embarked on something dangerous, something destructive and degenerate, which could well end in catastrophe. At moments like this she thought that she perhaps ought to find herself something to do, like so many women of her age did; a job, perhaps just for a few hours a day. Then she could get out and meet other people, instead of staying around at home and falling victim to such delusions – for they might well be delusions, her own nervous fancies because she just hung around at home, dreaming, and didn't really have any contact with anyone.

But no, there was more to it than that.

Thank God, there was more to it than that. She smiled at her hands and felt a sudden pang in her heart when she thought of the sign he had given her at dinner last night. Only last night. A sign that only she understood: he had pointed at the large painting over the fireplace! In a seemingly casual way, as he raised his coffee-cup to his lips. And she had with studied casualness allowed her glance to wander in the direction of the pointing finger. That was how they exchanged signals. And he had pointed with his ring finger, that was significant! She thought that she could even make out that it was Amor's face he wanted to show her, Amor who was hiding coyly behind the leaves whilst the goddesses danced with the faun out on the open meadow.

What a gentleman! He could have made his point just as well by indicating one of the goddesses, the buxom one, for example, who was dancing in the middle, almost completely exposed – she knew that she herself was what you might call generously endowed – and the thought still made her cheeks burn, for she was not used to being aware of her own body in that way; she was in general extremely cautious when it came to that kind of thing. But there was something about the dancing figures up there on the dully gleaming canvas which had suddenly awoken these feelings; the elegant poise with which they moved, as they almost floated over the little meadow, enjoying their protected freedom in the depths of the forest. And the colours: from a hint of blue in the gleaming white sky the light played on the dancing women, on the delicate, glowing skin, the bold contrast between their abandon and the subtle shadows over the deepest hollows of their bodies. (To dance! To play, to abandon oneself to life's secret sweetness!) The green of the grass on the meadow, in the leaves, in the secretive darkness of the forest which surrounded the meadow and gave that idyllic scene the merest suggestion of sin, which stirred uneasy feelings within her; the wildness in the faun's eyes and his hairy back. . . .

But she had not been frightened, she had just sat there, tremulous, feeling her own mature fullness and her desire to launch herself into the dance: she was ripe and generous! And then Mr Eldmann had a small beard – oh, she wasn't really cross with him for that, actually it quite suited him, *soigné* and greying; it gave him an aristocratic appearance and in addition a slight air of mystique. Forgotten was the lascivious leer on the face of the faun. Mr Eldmann was a history teacher, a real gentleman (and here her observations were supplemented by countless tender dreams); when he raised the coffee-cup to his lips, his ring finger described an arc like the most natural thing in the world.

Of course, none of the others around the table had the slightest suspicion of what was going on, but she knew and she was grateful. Amor was lying in wait, that was what he wanted to impart to her, and she was doubly grateful to him for being so tactful and so discreet, not coming straight out and making references to the goddesses, to their scanty dress – how brash, how dreadfully, embarrassingly brash that would have been! (But how worked up she was getting as she sat there – was that really a proper thing to do?) Almost without thinking she lifted her own cup to her mouth without drinking, and put it down again with a rattle on the saucer so that he would understand that she had seen everything and understood what he meant and was grateful to him. A glance and an almost imperceptible nod as he reached out for the dish of sliced ham had rounded off the episode.

And around the large table sat the other residents and the manageress, eating and dropping chance remarks without any notion of the kind of symbolic dialogue that was taking place right in front of their eyes. She felt like laughing out loud and clapping her hands in sheer excitement like a naughty little girl, but she stopped herself of course; no one was a greater respecter of tact and good taste than she was, and when you took small liberties yourself it was particularly reassuring to think that all the conventions were being meticulously observed. Really it gave her a feeling of security just to be surrounded by the elegant dining-room furniture, when Mr Eldmann sent her signals like that and the liberated dance of the goddesses in the forest seemed to transmit itself to her too. It was as if nothing bad could happen here as long as all the rules were respected, as long as order was maintained at the boarding-house, as long as social intercourse followed its usual pattern, as long as the rooms opened out one into the other, with their tasteful if somewhat old-fashioned furnishings which had not changed for decades.

In this way the house had an important part to play in their relationship. As long as the continuity which existed here, and which they were all a part of, was not broken, she was safe; for within this system only the minutest, most acceptable changes were possible, whilst outside chaos ruled, an anarchy whose consequences were impossible to imagine for decent people. (The things you read in the papers nowadays!) So she took good care not to let her excitement run away with her.

Instead she remained in her place and concentrated on Mr Eldmann's serviette. It was his serviette he used to signal to her when he was intending to select a book in the library before he went through into the lounge. They had already had several secret meetings in the library, but they had of course to pretend that they were completely accidental, and no words were exchanged. Apart from the time when he had politely asked her to read the title on the spine of a volume. He must be a bit short-sighted. . . . But then she was not perfect either, far from it; she did not want to make any such demands on him, not at all; and the book which he wanted to draw to her attention in this way was called *November Rain*, a love story which she had later read secretly, and read again many times. It was a story about two lovers who had to part, and it was so romantic and beautiful it reduced her to tears every single time, for it was clear that the book's evocation of a secret passion reflected their own situation exactly.

But he had laid his serviette down on his left. That meant that he did not intend to go into the library. Oh well. Their signals were so simple: if the serviette was laid on the right side of his plate, it meant that he would meet her in the library. That was because the door to the library was on their right as they sat at table, whilst the lounge lay to the left. It had been a long time before she registered this signal. Of course it did happen now and then that he put his serviette down on the left side and went into the library anyway a little later, but that didn't happen often, and she readily forgave him for such an oversight. Or perhaps he did it deliberately? This manner of signalling between them must not become obvious, nobody was to notice anything; that was almost the most important thing.

Not tonight. Oh well. No doubt it was for the best. But she was almost a little disappointed, just a tiny bit offended. For a moment she thought of punishing him – only playfully, of course – by not offering him the cakes twice as she normally did. But then he had suddenly turned towards her, looked right at her with that mild, almost diffident gaze and said, 'Could you be so sweet as to pass the sugar?' And his words had struck her like a flash of lightning; the sudden surge of amazement and joy took her breath away. He had said 'sweet'! Not 'be so kind' or 'do me a favour', but 'sweet' he had said, straight to her, for everybody to hear! Dear, dear Mr Eldmann! How he knew how to make up for those little disappointments ten times, twenty times over!

And yet it was not what he said or did that was the most important thing for her; the most important thing was the deep understanding which united them, like a stream which carried them both along, which co-ordinated their existence down to the slightest movement and brought them ever closer together. That was the way it felt to her most often. It was ineluctable. It was as if the very hand of fate was directing the process of which they were a part – and all on account of his looks. She felt powerless to resist when she looked at his fine, pale face, his sharp profile, his aristocratic goatee beard (like a prince), and at his hands, slender and elegant as they twisted a corner of his serviette. He was musical as well; a man with hands like his could not help but be musical. The delicious madness filled her breast every time she observed him. Was she in love?

Is this love? she had thought as she tremblingly passed him the sugar-bowl. It was essential to let no one else but him see how moved she was. But Mrs Frank, who sat between them, didn't seem to have noticed anything.

Poor Helena, thought Maude impulsively. It was not long since Mrs Frank had lost her husband.

## · 2 ·

All this had happened yesterday evening. Now she was sitting up in her room, waiting for the clock to reach seven so that the bell for dinner would go. Though it was not quite correct to say that she was just sitting there waiting, for she had plenty of things to be getting on with; she had written a letter, she had attended to her clothes, sewn on a button and darned a hole in a sock, tidied up a bit – actually she had been quite busy, and there were still several little tasks she could turn her hand to before it got to seven o'clock.

Yet again her thoughts returned to the previous day, to Amor's roguish smile as he sat hidden in the branches and peered out at the dancers; the guardian of the pact, who with his unpredictable arrows could strike a tremor into the most timid of hearts. Her own fugitive heart. . . . And yet again she saw in her mind's eye Mr Eldmann's sleeping face, and thought how much it resembled the face of a prince, the prince who had been hers, whom she had found in the garden sleeping, that summer long, long ago; the same summer Father had left them and gone away, the summer Mother had fallen for the first time and had been driven away in an ambulance, the summer she was six years old.

They had told her he was dead, and a tall, serious man with glasses had come to their house and asked little Maude lots of questions, and she wanted to tell him everything, about how Daddy had gone away and she hoped that he would soon come back again. But her mother had interrupted and said that she mustn't say things like that, and she had cried, and Maude had understood that she wasn't allowed to tell the strange man everything anyway, and that when they told her that the prince was dead, it meant in reality that Daddy had gone away for ever.

And the prince who had been hers for a moment there in the garden – they had taken him away from her too. He was dead, they had said; a poor sick man had had an attack in their garden. But she hadn't understood what they meant, for she had thought of the large grey-clad figure as she had seen it lying in the grass, with its white face half turned towards the earth and small white pearls of dew collected in the folds of the dark coat which lay spread out over him and around him like a flapping cloak. There, in their own garden.

A couple of blades of grass were growing between his black lips, a shadow lay over the pale cheek, his eyelids were dark and the morning dew had plastered some black strands of hair to his glistening forehead. White as snow and black as ebony. Maude had never seen such a beautiful man. Immobile as a picture. As a dream.

A prince!

A fly crawled along his jaw, stopped, crawled onwards. She waved it away with her hand.

My prince!

He had come to rescue her. Now he was lying resting after the journey. Soon she could be happy again, together with him, for he was going to stay with her always.

The sun touched her face. It was warm. The flies buzzed. His face was like a white stone in the grass. She still remembered it so clearly; it came back to her like her dreams from the summer when she was six years old, just as vividly, just as achingly: the loneliness she had felt when everything she loved was taken away from her and only the story about the sleeping prince remained.

Then someone had called her and woken her, dragged her out of a secret world where love still existed, and she had to answer the strange man's questions. And they had already taken her prince away from her. He had been fetched and they had driven off with him in an ambulance. The summer that Daddy had gone away. The summer that Mummy had fallen for the first time.

But what was she thinking of, connecting Mr Eldmann with this episode? She cleared her throat. She must pull herself together. Surely this was going too far? A civilized little flirtation was one thing. . . .

She stood up and took a couple of steps towards the window. It had been raining again this morning; the plants, the budding trees, all the spring greenery outside seemed to be thrusting upwards, so fresh and crisp after the last shower. How everything was growing and burgeoning. . . . She felt so easily depressed on days like this.

On a sudden impulse she knelt down by the window, and with her elbows on the sill she pressed her face against the cool pane next to the nearest green bough, as near to it as she could get. Then she fell back as if exhausted: if only everything out there would calm down! She was only human, after all. She felt the quivering growth within herself too. How could she keep her thoughts under control when nature itself was distracting her so insistently?

Carefully she began to touch the skin of her face with her fingertips. It was so soft, so soft; no sign of sagging or wrinkles yet, and her neck – like swansdown. . . .

Forty-seven: the age of maturity, the best. . . .

Her skirt was pulled tightly across her hips and thighs because of her unfamiliar position. She was suddenly conscious of her body, and pressed her hands hard against her breast: herself. The whole of her. Me! All the greenery out there!

Maude, she whispered aloud. Maude. Maude!

She liked the sound of her name. It was like putting a piece of soft fruit in her mouth and slowly crushing it against the roof of her mouth with her tongue. An empty space which was created and slowly filled. Maude! Her mouth was filled with the juice. A feminine name. Eternal feminine. A void which was filled. Woman who enfolded all things, from whom all things originated. Maude! A vacuum, a longing; what shall we fill it with? Have you any suggestions, Mr Eldmann? Hee-hee! How dreadful she was. Really she shouldn't even think such things!

The bough swayed, dashing a hail of clear droplets against her window.

Why didn't he come?

Wasn't that what she was sitting here waiting for? Why play games with herself? She was counting the minutes until he appeared at the front gate. Tomorrow was the last day before the summer holidays, and then he wouldn't have to go off to school every morning. She would know that he was there in the house and wouldn't need to feel so alone any more.

Lonely. It was odd, but she hadn't ever really thought of herself as a lonely person until she became aware of the importance of Mr Eldmann in her life. She had never had many friends, that was true – not even really many acquaintances. She had had her duties, had her cross to bear (in some strange way she found it comforting that woman was born to make sacrifices) – her mother, who had deteriorated, and who in her last years had required constant nursing, a self-denial ordained for her by fate itself; and then there was her natural reticence towards other people. But she had never felt lonely. She had done her duty, done what could reasonably be expected of her, and never given anyone cause for complaint; and that, she felt, entitled her to a place in the 'universal brotherhood of man', where everything functioned so much more efficiently, smoothly and unproblematically than in the private sphere, where there was always a danger of personal feelings becoming involved. In the 'universal brotherhood', people had learned to interact with one another without friction, provided that everyone did what was expected of them; there were rules of conduct in certain situations, and as long as you stuck to the rules you could avoid all unpleasantness. You respected each other, and related to each other on the surface; you let the hidden levels remain hidden. It was so much better to behave like that. You avoided so many problems, clashes and personal pettiness; everything which made life unpleasant. Dangerous.

After Mother had passed away, Maude had moved to Clem's boarding-house. The boarding-house was a kind of 'universal brotherhood'. Here order and good taste held sway, and life was pleasant and predictable. She had never had it so good, for order was as important to her as close personal ties, as friendship, affection, all kinds of more intimate links and relationships which could so easily lead to you forgetting yourself, your place and your duty – so much had become clear to her in the course of time. Order was an essential part of human intercourse. When people didn't keep their relationships in order the result was chaos, unhappiness, despair. She had seen enough examples of that. In order and self-control lay the key to civilization itself!

Order had ruled in her home. Even that summer when Father had left them and she had stood in the window watching the strange men driving Mother away in an ambulance, order had soon been re-established. Mother had come back from hospital and said that Father was dead and would never come back (and later she had even insisted that Maude couldn't remember her father, although that wasn't true; she could remember him clearly, even though it would have been simpler and in a way 'tidier' to have forgotten him). When a stranger had been found dead nearby, this had been like a proof that a new kind of order had entered her existence, an order in which death and the people she was fond of were closely connected. And these thoughts could at times come back to her, just as clearly and insistently as the memory of her dreams from that time.

She looked at the bough which was swaying in the wind, tossing its foliage to and fro, at the path down to the gate (where he would appear) with its white pebbles shining after the rain, the straight, tidy drive; and she straightened up: she had lived her life after all. There had been admirers over the years, and not so few of them either. She had been invited to restaurants and dances. Actually she'd been quite attractive, but she'd always known where to draw the line; there were some things you didn't mess about with. Her own ideas about love were linked to other things, a moist breeze on a summer morning, a face which lay asleep in the grass. . . . Naturally, she didn't believe in fairy-tales any more; yet that picture had remained her guiding principle in affairs of the heart. So subtle and so harmonious was love. So pure. And her admirers' impatient eagerness to become intimate with her had merely made her irritated and miserable. The thought of the practical consequences of love, the dreadful disorder that that kind of behaviour resulted in (for she had read about how it was done, she was not ignorant about such matters), was most upsetting to her; she couldn't possibly see the connection between such chaotic activities and a meeting of civilized people. Besides, she had also had her mother to think of. Their life together had followed a regular pattern: meals, walks – when the weather allowed she pushed her mother around the park in her wheelchair – and nursing. That was the framework of her existence. And the admirers had come and gone.

But I have lived. . . .

She was still kneeling on the floor by the window with her face close to the pane, looking out at the spring garden and waiting for Mr Eldmann.

This morning, quite by chance, she had walked past Number 11 just as the maid was cleaning in there, so the door was ajar and she had seized the chance to peep in. She shouldn't really have done it, and she repented afterwards of her spying, but her heart still beat faster when she thought of the sight of his dressing-gown hanging on its peg, the bookshelf full of books, medicine bottles, glass and jug on the bedside table (a man who kept his things in order – she could see that at first glance!) – and there was his bed, white, spotless, freshly made. And again she had a vision of his sleeping face, his eyes lying in shadow under the bushy brows and his forehead gleaming against the whiteness of the pillow. Why was she so moved by the sight?

But then there was this strange contact which had arisen between them and which was continually unfolding, an almost imperceptible *rapprochement*, understanding without a word being exchanged, considerateness, mutual respect, patience, subtlety (just the way he held his knife and fork told her a great deal about him), everything she could wish for in a man, everything she connected with devotion, with a love which did not involve a threat to order and modesty. . . . And these were the thoughts of a woman who only a few weeks ago had realized that her next menstruation might be her last, and had felt frightened, but also strangely relieved at the thought! It was true, she was approaching the dangerous age.

She had got up. She looked up at the sky. It had begun to clear. The weather would be fine on Midsummer Day. The beach trip. She couldn't wait.

Should she go down and post the letter at once?

The letter to her solicitor was still lying on the table. She'd better go and post it. It had stopped raining. On the other hand, she might as well wait till tomorrow. She would get the money in time anyway. A little surprise for him for the Consul's birthday. The Consul was going to be sixty on the 29th. There was to be a big party, and she was going to wear a red dress, the red dress she had seen in Hoff's window the other day. Perhaps it was a bit youthful for her? But what if it was? He would like it, she was sure he would. It couldn't be helped if she had to spend a bit more than her monthly allowance. She did that at Christmas anyway. You had to splash out a bit occasionally. And she did have the money, the little nest-egg that Mother had left.

Poor Mummy. Twelve years in bed and such pain at the end. Medicine and injections year in and year out. An emaciated white figure in the large bed. She who had taught her that a woman's lot in life is to suffer, to renounce (and that Maude had never doubted, even though she could remember her father well and knew that he was not dead). Fetched home at the end. A happy release. No one to reproach. How time passes – so many years ago already. . . .

Was that footsteps on the gravel? No. . . . She was starting to imagine things, how silly of her. . . .

The little red number in Hoff's window. Just think, red! I'm looking forward to seeing his face. Is there perhaps an Epicurean concealed behind that little beard? Take care, Mr Eldmann, take care!

She hummed a half-forgotten song:

> Love is
> A many-splendoured thing . . .

No, she couldn't remember how it went, but she took a couple of dance steps. Perhaps she should post that letter today anyway?

But that was the gate closing! And then she saw him: dark raincoat, dark hat, briefcase. A fine figure of a man; an academic from a good family (although actually he rarely mentioned his family, he was altogether extremely reticent when it came to personal details, she had noticed), polite and considerate. . . .

Now he'd stopped just inside the gate. Now he was leaning forward with one hand on the gatepost. To support himself? No, why should he do that? Perhaps he had a stitch? She stood there rooted to the spot, following his every movement.

For a while he remained standing like that, half turned away, bent forward with one hand resting heavily on the gatepost. She stood equally still in the window, watching him. What moist freshness was rising from the grass! How the gravel path shone after the last shower! She had to open the window. Get some air. But she must be careful. He could see her if he turned his head. What would he think if he knew that she was standing here watching him?

How the wind was pulling and tugging at the trees out there! Was there going to be a storm?

He was still standing there, with his hand on the brim of his hat. The gusts of wind blew his coat against his back and legs as if trying to reach his body inside his clothes. A bent, slender figure. She suddenly remembered his room, the sparse, grey furniture, the smell of medicine in there. . . . Poor Mr Eldmann, he wasn't ill, was he?

No, now he straightened up, let go of the gatepost and began to walk slowly towards the house. All too slowly, she thought. After all, it was the last day before the summer holidays! Think of the glorious long summer they would have together!

At the same moment she caught a glimpse of his white face as he looked up at the house, straight at her window. Was he looking for *her*? Could he see her where she was standing, a yard – no, a yard and a half away from the window? For a second she was turned to stone, struck motionless by joy, by confusion, for his glance had met hers, privately and without reserve, she was sure, she was quite sure of it! Then he disappeared from sight around the corner of the house.

Oh, Mr Eldmann . . . Mr Eldmann, such boldness!

For he *had* looked straight up at her window, he must have seen her standing there; perhaps he even knew that she usually stood there looking out for him when he came home from school? In that case that little intermezzo down by the gate must have been something he had performed for her sake. Everything became imbued with significance between them. Even that little cough which seemed to bother him now and then, that had to be a sign, she was sure of it. Her heart fluttered like a moth towards the light. What time was it? Two whole hours to dinner time!

She had to go out. Seized by a sudden restlessness she threw a jacket over her shoulders and went out into the passage, past Number 11 (sounds of movement from in there!), down the stairs, through the hall, out into the porch (a couple of wet footprints on the doormat!), and without really knowing what she was after she began to walk down the drive to the gate. She might just as will go and post that letter. Then she remembered that the letter was still lying on the table up in her room. How stupid! How idiotic! How could she be so absent-minded? Letting him turn her head like that.

Just by the gate she hesitated. Really she had nothing to do out on the street. No shopping she needed. . . . Then she got cross with herself again: why was she standing here debating with herself? Why not just go for a walk? Get a bit of fresh air. Such a fine afternoon. Why not?

But she remained standing there. Two small boys on bicycles sped past. The sun peeped out again. The wind. Sounds from the street reached her: high, thin sounds, like the tinkling of glass. Sounds of early summer. A ribbon of smoke curled up from a neighbour's garden fire. Spring had been late this year; rotting autumn leaves still lined the path up to the house.

She drew in her breath sharply, suddenly impatient. What a mess it was! The gardener who was supposed to come, but never came. The path over to the summer-house was almost impassable, full of old grass and leaves. Wet, too, after the recent rain.

She noticed that she had placed her hand on the gatepost as if she wanted to lean on it, but couldn't really make up her mind to move her weight. The same place! The same gatepost! This was exactly how *he* had been standing just a few minutes ago, when she had been standing up there in the window watching him. She let her hand drop, turned and looked up at the house, like a criminal surprised in his act of evil. A window on the first floor closed just at that moment. His? His window which the maid had left open? In that case. . . . She held her breath.

The window nearest to the espalier was his. A gleam of reflected sunlight was all she had seen. The whiteness of the reflected sky could be seen in all the windows on the south side. But didn't it come from there? Precisely from his window? Then he *must* have seen her! Seen her standing there with her hand on the gatepost, exactly where his hand had been lying just two minutes ago! And put two and two together. . . .

Oh, Mr Eldmann!

She stood there in the sunshine, her thoughts in a whirl, unable to move. Just think if he was still watching her! What would he think about such a demonstration? But she had done it unthinkingly, it hadn't really been her fault. And it hadn't been his either. Neither of them was to blame. She took a deep breath, relieved. Suddenly she saw how poetic the coincidence was: first of all him standing by the gate, then her standing by the gate, his hand, her hand, so symmetrical, so ordered; like an involuntary dance co-ordinated by a higher will. Yes, it was like a dance.

How warm it was suddenly, standing in the sun! The moist scents of the fresh grass, of the large garden breathing out after the rain, bombarded her open senses. She sought escape along the overgrown path towards the summer-house, escape from his imagined glance. Can you see me now, Mr Eldmann? Perhaps you can see me now? Wet grass slapped her ankles. Moisture lingered in the undergrowth where the sun did not get through. Crowns, tops gilded by light.

Her hurrying steps and uneven breathing.

There was the summer-house. And the bench. The little fountain. Undisturbed memories of last summer, of the summer before. Countless summers. Here she was safe.

'The park' she used to call this part of the garden, jokingly. Here there stood a couple of maple trees, dripping gold, a broad chestnut tree, there grew rose bushes and other shrubs, willow, alder, a spruce; here they found mushrooms in the autumn. Behind the bench grew three or four overgrown apple trees which no longer bore fruit.

A ray of sunshine had dried and warmed a corner of the bench where she could sit. It was a pity about the summer-house, really. The house was shut up. It was on the point of collapse. The walls were a labyrinthine interweaving of rotting struts and branches of climbing roses and wild vine; the roof a red flame of rust. It would have to be pulled down soon. It wouldn't see many more winters; the manageress had said so. And the fountain was full of rainwater. 'A birdbath', as the Consul had referred to it jokingly during the garden party last summer. Or was it the summer before? It was true, it wasn't very big. The drainage hole was blocked; it was too bad that the gardener didn't turn up.

There was a fresh shoot on a branch of the decaying apple tree. A few white flowers were pushing their way cautiously out from the shadows, dark with age; pink and blushing; just a dozen modest sprays. But it was so pretty! And the bees hummed around them, the scurrying insect legs crawled over the soft petals, a hairy body found its way in to the very heart of the flower, collected the nectar, and then off to the next, laden with golden pollen, dizzy with the heavy scent. She sat there entranced, watching the play; the bees – their intensity – and the defenceless flowers. How often had she not repeated to herself the story of the flower princess, sitting there on her branch and waiting for the prince to come and pick her? It had been the most beautiful fairy-tale she knew; she had read it again and again and told it to herself with small variations, with Maude in the central role as the princess. For she knew that that was how it had to be. She had believed in such things; they had taught her so much about femininity, about what it meant to be a woman. And suddenly she was deeply moved by what she was watching.

Life, she thought. Life – flowers – the eternal feminine! She could find no words. She watched the conquerors, the bees, with thick layers of pollen on their hairy legs, thought about them flying back with their spoils, with their message to the other bees about where to find the honey flowers, their special language which was a dance where each step, each leap, each turn was significant, where even the direction of the wind and the height of the sun had a special meaning, where not the slightest detail was overlooked. It was such a language she and Mr Eldmann shared. The language of love. A veiled reference to the roguish Amor on a painting; her hand on the gatepost where his hand had so recently rested. The dance of love. A wonderful dance! A wonderful language!

She reached out her hand and broke off the green branch. She would put it in water in her room. These old apple trees didn't bear fruit any longer. They ought to be chopped down. Perhaps next autumn. They should plant poplars instead; they grew so quickly and so tall and stately.

The sun went in and it grew cool. The damp had already penetrated her shoes. The garden furniture in the summer-house, which had been standing there now for six years, was the colour of decaying vegetation. A heavy odour of earth, of rotting organic matter drove her back along the path, with the apple branch clutched in her hand and her exaltation of a few moments ago darkened by thoughts of the ineluctable approach of decay, death, dissolution. But only for a moment; for there was the dog, the neighbour's pampered collie, demanding attention, jumping up against the fence, stretching and pleading with shining eyes and wet tongue, enticing her with its yellow belly, asking for a scratch. She gave in.

'Here, boy. Come here, then. Come on. There now.' Her shoes got soaked through as she stood there by the fence. She dug her nails into the loose folds of skin on its neck. It licked her hands, her face. She felt a mixture of pleasure and disgust as it pushed its eager nose against her cheek, making slapping noises with its wet tongue. She could feel the warm breath from its mouth.

'Are you so fond of me then, boy? Are you so fond of me? Does he love his Maude then? There, there.'

No, that was enough now.

Breathless and flustered, she found herself standing by the gate again. Her shoes were soaked through and her feet were cold. She had better not have caught a cold. The low sun cast her long shadow along the path towards the house. But she hesitated for one more moment. Here she had danced the dance of the bees for Mr Eldmann. Oh no, what a thought! What was she standing here dreaming about? Time to get in and change into something dry.

She hurried in.

## · 3 ·

Mr Eldmann came down late to dinner. The others had already sat down and were waiting. Or rather, it was just Maude who was sitting waiting. The meal had already begun; the dishes were being passed round, but she didn't want to begin eating before he came. This little act of loyalty brought them even closer together, she thought, and she was sure he would appreciate it and that he would have thought and acted in the same way in her place. But she hoped he would come soon, so that it wouldn't become too noticeable that she was sitting here with an empty plate. After all, the others mustn't suspect anything.

Exactly opposite her sat Mrs Sebastian, who had her work cut out stopping her small son from smearing marmalade over his little sister's face, whilst all the time keeping up a conversation with the Consul, who was watching the whole episode with forced affability. No one liked Mrs Sebastian's children. Maude herself thought they were two real little horrors, but then she had never been particularly fond of small children, they were always so noisy and messy. Look at the mess they'd made on the table-cloth already. (In order not to look odd, she had to accept some bread from the basket that someone passed her, but she was determined not to eat anything until he came.)

And the mother herself was a disruptive element. Maude couldn't say exactly what it was that she found so offensive about her. It wasn't really any one particular feature, but rather something affected about her whole behaviour. For some reason she always laughed and talked far too loudly, and everything she did became demonstrative and therefore seemed false. She always had to overwhelm the people she was with in some way or other, drown them in her own excesses. Just look how the Consul was forced to keep up a conversation with her at the same time as he had to struggle to maintain a respectable distance between them. (Now he was looking straight at her across the table. Was he asking for help? She had to look away. There was a time when she had thought there might be something special between them. . . .)

Besides, it was really against the rules to let her live in the boarding-house with those two children; it was spelt out quite clearly. . . .

But she was a distant relative of the manageress who had been in a tight spot when her husband suddenly wanted a divorce. It had been presented as a temporary arrangement, but this temporary arrangement had been going on for more than long enough now, and she wasn't the only one who thought that. She bleached her hair as well.

But the Consul was a gentleman, gallant and attentive; he had a way with women, there were no doubt others as well as she. . . . Oh no, what rubbish! It had only been a fleeting emotion, and anyway it was long since over, thank goodness. He wore a gold ring on the little finger of his left hand. He wasn't her type, despite his good side; he was a little too bold, too demonstrative, almost too overwhelmingly attentive, and he was not at all romantic. She had danced with him at the last Christmas party. She had felt small, almost helpless in his arms. He was so tall, and she was not used to being so close to men, even though the conventions of dancing removed the taboo that she usually felt against being touched by a man. He danced well, but she was confused and nervous, and the slight extra pressure that he had let her feel against her stomach had only made her embarrassed. Of course there had been nothing vulgar about it, it had been extremely tactfully done; just a hint which might equally well have been inadvertent. Nevertheless, her feelings for him had cooled, and when he had whispered something into her hair whilst they were still dancing she had answered no immediately, without even being sure what it was he had asked; and as soon as the music stopped she had said that she was tired and had gone up to her room.

But she liked the Consul, even though he had never been a real consul, just employed at a shipping office in Marseilles. The nickname suited him; he was charming, a man of the world. He never lost control of the situation, even though right now he was under heavy attack from Mrs Sebastian, who was laying verbal siege to him in a way the like of which Maude had never seen; whilst the children on her other side were squirming on their chairs and fighting with the cutlery. Really, this was going too far.

Mrs Frank turned to her, holding out a plate of sliced meat. 'You're not eating very much this evening.'

'Thank you, but I think I'll wait a little.'

Why didn't he hurry up and come! Mrs Frank was still sitting there with the plate. She didn't look at all good, thought Maude. She was pale and had dark rings under her eyes. She seldom joined in the social life. She had taken the loss of her husband very badly, so it was said. (In the background the Consul coughed, and Mrs Sebastian's noisy laughter rang out over the table; then her laughter ended in a fit of coughing whilst the Consul cleared his throat. What an exhibition they were making of themselves!)

'Disgusting, isn't it?' whispered Mrs Frank, as if echoing her own thoughts. 'They've no shame at all, carrying on like that, even though everybody knows what's going on in *that* department. Filthy, that's what it is. And her with two small children. . . .'

Here in the boarding-house!

Stunned, Maude turned towards her, making no attempt to hide the bewilderment she felt. Was Mrs Frank really sitting there suggesting that the Consul and Mrs Sebastian . . . ? No, that was just too much to imagine!

'You don't mean you didn't know about it?' Now there was a gleam of life in Mrs Frank's faded eyes. 'The worst thing is that they don't have the slightest regard for other people's sense of decency. They carry on in the garden, in the library – simply everywhere! Believe me, I've seen them and heard them. And she's not even divorced yet! Would you believe that?'

No really, this was too outrageous! Maude did not intend to sit and listen to such talk. In order to put an end to this painful conversation she seized the plate from Mrs Frank and helped herself. Even though she was sure that what the older woman was saying was simply a product of her own diseased imagination (some people said quite openly that her husband's death had disturbed the balance of her mind), the very fact that such inconceivable suspicions had been voiced caused a kind of poisonous fog to spread over the company. It was like a bad omen, a sign that the calm and orderliness which governed all their lives at the boarding-house was in danger of disintegrating; and this was a threat not only to the Consul and Mrs Sebastian, but to everyone, including herself and Mr Eldmann. It was as if Mrs Frank's wild accusations were a warning to her, Maude, to take care, not to let herself be enticed to her ruin. She helped herself to more ham and passed the plate to Mr Adamson, who fortunately was hard of hearing. He thanked her in a loud voice. Poor Mr Adamson. He was supposed to be going to an old people's home soon.

She hardly dared to look at the Consul and Mrs Sebastian. Was there anything untoward in his behaviour? It was so easy for small attentions, even simple politeness, to acquire a dangerous undercurrent of 'something more'. Especially with a man of the world like the Consul. As far as that woman was concerned, you could believe anything of her, she had always thought that. Although she didn't for a moment take her neighbour's vicious gossip seriously, she found herself seeing their behaviour in a new light. She thought of Mrs Frank's crazy assertion, that they were 'carrying on' in the garden and in the library and everywhere else in the house, and she was filled with a strange, sneaking fear of the *illicitness* of the whole thing, at the same time as she could not of course believe a single word of it.

Now little Trine had hit her brother in the face with a spoon and was therefore resolutely removed from the table by her mother. Mrs Moser and the Consul attempted between them to pacify the howling victim. How could anybody eat in such a hubbub? Maude felt suddenly as though the settled existence of the boarding-house was falling to pieces around her.

But there were Mr Eldmann's footsteps on the stairs! And at a moment like this, when she was so upset! She had even taken some food before he arrived. If only he didn't notice how nervous she was, how distracted, how little prepared for their evening communication.

But Mr Eldmann just said good evening and sat down without paying any attention to anyone around him. He looked tired, thought Maude. The last weeks at school, with examinations and all the marking, had taken it out of him. But now the holidays have begun, Mr Eldmann, now you can just relax here at the boarding-house and enjoy yourself – with Maude. Maude. Again her mouth was filled with the juice of sweet fruit. It was such a sensual name she had. She was grateful for that. Shyly she observed Mr Eldmann's thin, pale cheeks and deep eye sockets, and thought she had never seen a more attractive man. His calm movements as he ate completely neutralized all the fuss around the crying of little Johan; the slim hands which held the cutlery were created for other instruments altogether. Forgotten was the recent feeling of threat; she watched him and felt a happy flush rising to her cheeks. First and foremost she loved him for his *orderliness.*

Mrs Frank looked up, and Maude quickly dropped her gaze. She really would have to be careful. That woman had eyes in the back of her head. She just hoped she hadn't noticed anything already.

'Well, Miss Maude.' The Consul's voice rang out suddenly from the other side of the table. 'Have you been out this afternoon? You look as if you've caught the sun.'

'No – I mean . . . yes,' she admitted. 'Just a little walk in the garden.' Why did he have to ask about that right now? Her cheeks burned.

'Just a little walk in the garden. It was really lovely out.'

Had he also seen her brief appearance at the gate? She glanced across at Mr Eldmann, but he was just sitting and looking down at his plate. Poor thing, he really must be quite exhausted after the effort of the last few weeks at school.

'It cleared up. . . .' She stopped, helpless.

'Yes, it did, didn't it?' the Consul called out eagerly. 'At last summer has arrived!'

'Yes, it looks promising for our midsummer outing, doesn't it?' the manageress chimed in from her place at the head of the table. 'The weather forecast said . . .'

'I just hope the water is warm enough for a swim!' Mrs Sebastian had just arrived back after meting out due punishment to her daughter, still with hectic red patches on her cheeks. 'Last year it was so cold that you could hardly . . .'

Swim. So she wanted to swim. Expose herself.

'Well, it's perhaps a little early for that yet,' replied the Consul.

'Not if this weather keeps up,' answered the lady optimistically. 'You know, once I went swimming on the 22nd of May!'

'You're welcome,' said the Consul. 'Personally I prefer the Riviera.'

'Oh, come on – you can allow us to have a bit of fun in these latitudes as well,' said Mrs Sebastian flirtatiously. 'Not everyone can pick and choose like you can.'

'Come, come,' said the Consul, flattered, and coughed behind his hand. 'Don't exaggerate. I can't just take off for foreign parts, you know.'

'Well, I think bathing in the sea up here can be as good as anywhere,' was the categorical answer. 'Not quite so warm, perhaps, but cleaner and more refreshing. Don't you agree with me?' She turned towards Maude.

Maude was aware of the provocation that was concealed behind the seemingly innocent remark. She was to be reduced to a passive bystander, a springboard for Mrs Sebastian in her attempt to win the

Consul's attention and regard once and for all. Perhaps someone had told her that she and the Consul had had a soft spot for each other, round about Christmas time?

'I'm afraid I can't say. I go swimming very rarely.' It was ignominious to have to capitulate to this busybody of a woman. For a moment Maude was quite sure that everything Mrs Frank had told her was true. People like that were capable of anything.

'And you've all got to come,' called out the manageress. 'Every one of you! We're taking lunch with us and something tasty to go with the coffee.' Her sharp glance swept over all those who were present. 'All of you! You too, Mr Adamson!'

'Thank you. I think perhaps I can manage a bit more,' called back Mr Adamson, reaching for the breadboard. Poor thing, he really was hard of hearing now. It no doubt wouldn't be very long . . .

'Oh, won't it be fun?' exclaimed Mrs Moser and dug her elbow into her husband's side. He was always slower to react than she, but he was a solid, reliable man. Retired insurance agent.

'Oh yes!' Miss Leander clasped her hands together and showed a couple of protruding teeth when she smiled. She was so emotional, Miss Leander.

The discussion around the table had become quite lively. All had something to contribute about the weather prospects for midsummer. Dr Lemb discussed sea temperatures with the Consul, and Mrs Sebastian aired her opinion that wearing a bathing-costume to go bathing was really an absurd convention that modern people ought to have long since abandoned. This made the Consul nod and smile at her (and nudge her arm, but in such a way that it was clear that no one else was meant to see it) so that Maude went hot and cold (it was so blatant!); and the manageress planned in a loud voice what they were going to take for lunch on the trip.

Only Mr Eldmann sat still, saying nothing very much. She watched him out of the corner of her eye. Motionless and distinguished, he sat looking at his plate. What a finely shaped head he had. And a long, straight nose. She felt even more drawn to him as the ambiguities in the conversation directly opposite her became almost offensive. Only once did he turn to Miss Leander and ask her something. At least, she assumed he had asked her something, as the girl blushed immediately and said something in reply. Poor little Miss Leander, she hadn't much experience of being in the company of men. She felt almost responsible for Miss Leander, who was so innocent, almost naive really, and so much younger.

'Now then, Eldmann, you're very quiet this evening,' the Consul suddenly called to him. 'Sitting wondering what you're going to do with your holidays, are you?'

'No . . . not exactly.' Mr Eldmann smiled faintly.

'Is anything wrong?' the manageress asked suddenly. 'You don't look too good, Mr Eldmann.'

'Wrong? No no, not at all. I'm in fine form, really.' Mr Eldmann tried to laugh. She noticed that dark strands of hair were sticking to his damp, white forehead. What a handsome man! So noble, so refined. My man! she thought and felt almost intoxicated. Surely they could see that he was in love – that that was what was 'wrong' with him, nothing else.

'It really is rather stuffy in here, isn't it?' Mrs Sebastian joined in.

'Perhaps we should let some fresh air in?' That was Dr Lemb. Somebody opened one of the veranda doors slightly.

'What a lovely evening.'

'Oh yes, that's better,' sighed Mrs Sebastian.

'Do you feel better now?' the manageress asked Mr Eldmann.

'Thank you, I'm really perfectly all right,' Mr Eldmann answered a little shortly. 'I . . . I was actually just sitting and looking at that picture over there.' And with that he pointed right at the large picture over the fireplace so that everyone could see what he meant, and it was as if a shock of joy and astonishment went right through Maude, for now there was no longer any doubt. He had really been signalling to her; he was as preoccupied with the picture as she was, and this was his way of letting her know! Not that she had doubted it for a moment, but now it was certain! She fancied that Amor winked at her from his hiding-place up in the branches, and even the face of the satyr with the little beard seemed more friendly than before. She thought of the dress in the shop window and the letter she had written to her solicitor. Just wait till you see me in red, Mr Eldmann!

'It's a copy, of course,' pronounced the Consul.

'But quite well done,' conceded Dr Lemb.

'It was bought from the estate of someone who'd died. I don't think it's worth very much,' said the manageress.

'It's a common motif . . .' the Consul again.

'Neo-romantic,' was Dr Lemb's verdict.

'It's really dreadfully old-fashioned,' sighed Mrs Sebastian. 'To think that something like that was supposed to be sexually arousing.'

Maude could no longer contain her disappointment. 'I must say that I think it's a very attractive picture!'

And now she had become the centre of attention. It was unusual for her to join in a discussion.

'I . . . I think it's so wonderful the way the goddesses are dancing on the meadow – it's almost as if they're floating . . . and Amor up there in the branches, and the forest so green and lovely. . . . It's all so beautiful!'

'Well, yes, if you look at it like that,' said the Consul diplomatically. Mrs Sebastian shrugged her shoulders. Mr Eldmann didn't look up. She had said it for his sake, but he sat there with his head resting on his hand and didn't look up. But she was sure he had understood what she meant, and just the sight of him as he sat there calmed her anxious heart.

My noble faun!

The evening light from the windows shone through the yellow gleam from the chandelier and gave the faces round the table an ethereal, transparent look. A gentle breath of air could be felt from the open veranda door. The conversation drifted, sounding random and disconnected beneath the high ceiling. Maude felt as if a change had taken place after what had just been said; Mr Eldmann's obvious hint and her own confession; Mrs Frank's spiteful suggestions – all this would have been unthinkable just a few days ago, and she found herself wondering what it would all lead to. She had an uneasy feeling that something was set in motion which none of them had the power to stop. Perhaps such feelings were also a part of love?

But they had cream sponge with the coffee, and everything fell naturally in to the order dictated by good manners and custom, which gave their life at the boarding-house such an atmosphere of security, a feeling that their little society was civilization itself *in nuce*, protected by mutually agreed rules and the responsible behaviour of respectable people.

Besides, cream sponge was Maude's favourite dessert. Every time cream sponge was served she became a little girl again with her own unvarying way of eating it: first the base and the cream, and then the top layer with the icing at the very end. She saw Mrs Frank plunge her fork into her cake so that the cream spurted out on both sides. Really that woman had no sensitivity. How could she have been so mistaken about her?

But Miss Leander asked with shining eyes whether anyone wanted to share the last piece with her. She at least was a sweet little creature, well-meaning, never did anyone any harm. She worked at the library as an archivist. Maude hoped secretly that one day Miss Leander might meet a really nice man. She was the youngest at the boarding-house and it was high time she got married.

Mrs Sebastian was still talking about swimming-costumes. Good Lord, had she decided to ruin their whole outing with her tasteless exhibitionism? The Consul lifted his hand discreetly to his mouth. Mr Eldmann leaned his head on his hand. His serviette had fallen to the right of his plate with the crumbs from the sponge-cake.

On the right! That meant he would meet her in the library.

Dr Lemb pushed his chair back, got up and complimented the manageress on the meal. The others also left the table. Dinner was over. Mrs Sebastian dragged her howling son off upstairs. It was bedtime.

What a lovely evening!

The Consul decided to go for a walk in the garden. Several of the others followed him out on to the patio. Maude hesitated. Mr Eldmann had still not got up. As she passed behind his chair, she whispered 'Gatepost' so loudly in her mind that he *must* feel it. He got up slowly and stood there indecisively. Then he went towards the door to the library.

She would count to ten slowly, and then she would follow him. But as she began to count, she saw that the manageress was beckoning to her. What did she want now? She hoped it wouldn't take very long.

The manageress, an authoritative lady over sixty years old, put her hand on Maude's arm (an intimate gesture which Maude took exception to, but which she could not really object to when it was the manageress) and said in a confiding tone, 'I noticed that you were sitting watching Mr Eldmann this evening. What do you think about him?'

'*Think?*' was the only thing Maude could whisper in reply. She felt as if she were turned to stone and at the same time to jelly beneath the manageress's piercing glance; her lips were tingling, and a numbness was creeping from her feet up to her knees and making her stockings cling together. She was discovered! Lost! She felt a sudden desire to lay her head on the manageress's breast and cry, to admit the whole thing, to beg forgiveness, beseech her to believe that nothing bad had happened. (Oh, Mummy!) The picture of her mother's patiently suffering face haunted her every time she felt a pang of guilt, even though 'that sort of thing' had never been mentioned between them. It was connected with her sense of dignity, with her duty, her fate as a woman.

'Yes, you do know that he's had another attack? I just wondered whether you'd noticed anything particular. He wouldn't hear of sending for a doctor.' A pulse beat threateningly in the manageress's powdered neck. At last Maude could breathe again.

'No . . . no, I didn't notice anything.' She could hardly restrain the tears of relief. 'But is he ill? Does he need a doctor?'

'Well, it's probably not all that serious, but I thought to be on the safe side. . . . After all, it wouldn't be very nice if anything happened *here* – for the establishment, for all of us. . . . You can see what I mean.'

'Yes . . . yes of course.'

'But you didn't notice anything?'

'No, nothing special. He did seem tired. Perhaps it was the change in the weather. . . .'

'Yes, I'm sure you're right. It doesn't do to get too worked up about these things. But please do let me know if you notice anything, won't you?'

'Yes. Yes, of course.'

'Fine. Thank you very much. You're coming on the outing on Sunday, I hope?'

'Oh yes, I certainly am. I'm looking forward to it. If only the weather . . .'

'Yes indeed, let's hope so,' the manageress interrupted her and walked off. Maude saw her well-padded rear disappearing through the doors into the lounge. The Mosers, Mr Adamson and Dr Lemb were already seated around the whist-table in there.

Was he really ill? An attack, she had said. An attack could mean so many things. But she had never heard that there was anything wrong with Mr Eldmann's health, and she found it difficult to believe that there could be anything wrong with so elegant and handsome a man. It must have been a different sort of condition which the manageress was confusing with illness, a different kind of weakness: his fleeing heart, his trembling, uncertain heart; for spring can sow its hopes and doubts in the loneliest of hearts, Mr Eldmann! And its effects were visible. She had seen how his features had become sharper, more chiselled as it were, his eyes had become clearer and shinier, his hands slimmer and more delicate just in the course of the last few weeks; just as she herself had become softer, more understanding, more open to all kinds of impressions, rounder (also in the most prosaic sense of the word, unfortunately, but what did that matter, she would soon lose it if she went on a little diet), more feminine.... No, don't underestimate the powers of the heart, Mr Eldmann! A gentle breeze from the garden moved the curtains playfully. From outside on the terrace she could hear voices. The Consul. Others too. In the hall the grandfather clock struck half-past.

Was it safe to go into the library now? She would really have to be careful. The manageress had noticed her, and Mrs Frank.... But the thought of him sitting in there waiting for her.... She assumed an air of indifference and began slowly to walk towards the door. Just then the girl came in and began to clear the table (his plate with the half-eaten cream sponge!). She hesitated. But a glance at the goddesses over the fireplace, floating there over the meadow, so happy and so free, made her resolute. She also had her reasons for dancing, for floating! She tossed her head and positively sailed out of the dining-room.

But there was no one waiting for her in the library. She stood there uncertainly in the twilight. Surely he had gone in there? Suddenly she was not so sure any more. She had been so engrossed in her conversation with the manageress. Could he have come out again without her seeing him?

A sudden weakness came over her, and without putting on the light she sank down into the deep wing-chair in the corner by the stove (a magnificent piece from Essen, the manageress's pride and joy). The soft cushions gave way beneath her weight with a sigh and a faint smell of dust. Perhaps he would come back? All the irregularities at dinner this evening had made her uncertain and nervous in a different way than before, when she had just been worried that their innocent flirtation might be discovered; the Consul's and Mrs Sebastian's behaviour, Mrs Frank's vicious gossip, the manageress's sudden concern for Mr Eldmann, even Miss Leander's innocent offer to him to share the last piece of sponge-cake – all these things had taken on a deep, almost threatening significance. She felt that she had been surprised by a series of events that she could not have foreseen, that the process she and Mr Eldmann were engaged in had slipped out of their control and was taking a new and dramatic turn which they could only follow helplessly. Into her innermost feelings (and therefore into his too – so complete was the subconscious understanding between them) there had slipped an unsettling sense of unpredictability; and it was all because of the Consul's hand on Mrs Sebastian's naked elbow (did they really meet here in this house at night, soundlessly so that no one should know anything?) and all the other little deviations from rule and custom. Everything she did could have fatal consequences, and at the same time it seemed as if the consequences would come about whatever it was she decided to do.

No. She refused to think like that. With an effort she got up out of the deep chair and went across to the large bookcase, to the place she knew so well where *November Rain* stood, where her fingers found the book and picked it out before her eyes could distinguish the dark spine from all the others. And as she stood there with the book in her hand, looking at it, she noticed a tiny piece of paper which had been placed between the pages as a bookmark. With a sudden thrill of excitement, she opened the book exactly where the paper marker stood and ran her eyes quickly down the page: just a minute, was that not. . . . Yes, there really was a mark in the margin! She held the page up in the fading light: a line, a scar scored in the paper with a penknife or a nail. . . .

'*I am a star prince, you are a star princess, and I love you even though our paths will never cross. . . .*'

She read it over and over again, this sentence which he had found for her and shown her in such a romantic way. A star prince and a star princess; what a lovely sentiment! She was moved and calmed at the same time. She felt like crying. She sank down in the wing-chair again with the book open in her lap. Our paths will never cross. A reassuring distance again. How romantic he was – what a wonderful man! And the mark was on page 18 and 18 was also her room number; there could no longer be any doubt.

But a strange feeling of impatience became mixed with her joy over this first tangible approach on his part, so difficult to resist here in the half darkness. I love you . . . those words were used too. 'I love you,' she whispered towards the silent book spines. He loved her, it said so in black and white, and suddenly she felt an inexplicable desire to do things she knew she should not do, to touch him for example (for she knew well, of course, that the slippery slope towards disorder and excess begins with a touch). She thought of his thin neck with the large Adam's apple, and how lovely it would be to place her soft arms around his neck and squeeze and feel his Adam's apple moving (but I shan't do it, my dear, don't be frightened!). She was tempted to laugh at herself, at such impossible fantasies, but waves of joy and of happiness of a quite different nature were flowing through her. 'I love you even though our paths. . . .' Just think that he was so passionate beneath his calm, almost servile exterior, that *he*. . . .

She took deep breaths. Something within her was demanding to be recognized. Suddenly she felt her body's acute restlessness, a flame which flared up and up. Touching was out of the question. But who would have thought that Mr Eldmann was so passionate. . . . Was this really her? She could feel her breasts against the restraining material of her dress; their secret, reassuring weight, pale shadowy skin; her little chicks. She opened a button at her neck, then another. What would he think of her?

Shadows crept forth from all the corners of the room and condensed into a physical presence. She struggled against it, but in vain; a body that was her own flesh and blood drew nearer and wanted to embrace her, to enfold her. She opened her eyes wide but was incapable of restraining the uncontrollable excitement that had seized her. Through every pore she sensed the appalling nearness. Her hands pressed the precious book hard down into her lap, where it was greeted by a pain full of desire, a flame which flared up and up: is this really me? Is it really you, Mr Eldmann? Who would have thought that you could be so. . . . A second later she had surrendered, powerless, to the temptations of the darkness and the shadows. The spine of the book danced deep in her quivering flesh. Her pulsating powerlessness. The scented darkness against her skin. Her self. Her own scents, own hands. Consciousness contracting like a pupil and waiting for the leap. So passionate . . . so . . . oh my gosh . . . oh *Maude*! And the volcano erupts and empties its accumulated store of suffering; her limbs stretch out to capture an endless fraction of a second. A helpless tear. . . .

The miracle. She felt she was going to float away, weightless, invisible, through shame, through bliss, in the late summer evening light that picked out the window-panes, eerily white behind dark curtains. She fell like dust in there, ceaselessly, silently, nowhere and everywhere, embraced him wherever he was right now, like a cloud, touched every inch of him and at the same time was not there at all. This is how I shall dance for you, Mr Eldmann; this is how we shall dance.

Annihilated by the avowal of his passion, she drifted like smoke upwards towards the first pale white stars.

She must have slept for a while, for she jumped suddenly at the sound of voices. It was nearly dark in the library now. She could hardly make out the outlines of the furniture around her. How late was it? She tried to look at her watch, but as she did so the book slipped from her lap and landed on the floor with a soft thud at the same time as she heard the voice again: a man's voice. It came from the dining-room. The door was slightly ajar. (Oh, why hadn't she closed it properly? Just think if they found her here, whoever they were!) She bent forwards and searched around on the floor with her hand, noticed to her horror that her dress had slid far up over her thighs, and tried as quietly as she could to pull it down whilst she felt around for the book.

'But it won't be much longer now.'

The voice again. The man's voice. Muffled. Insistent. Distorted and blurred by the wall, the darkness. Nevertheless she could make out almost every single word as she sat there bent forward, as if hypnotized, without daring to look away from the door.

'No, thank goodness, it won't be much longer.'

There was a woman with him! They must be standing just inside the door. Perhaps they were sitting on the sofa by the sideboard. What a dreadfully embarrassing situation! Just think if they were to discover her here, sitting listening in the dark. At last she found the book on the floor. The whispered conversation continued behind the door.

'. . . so marvellous not to have to keep it secret any longer!'

The woman again. They must be in the middle of a conversation which she hadn't heard. Was it Mrs Sebastian's voice?

'Yes, it's unbearable like this.'

The Consul's voice. It must be him, surely? It must be those two, the turtle-doves who had no regard for ordinary common decency.

'What do you think they'll say when they find out?'

Were they planning something? He answered something she couldn't hear. It really did sound like the Consul's voice. Then all was silent in there, and the fear of discovery returned; at any moment one of them, or both, might decide to come into the library for something.

But then the woman suddenly exclaimed, 'Oh no, darling, you must be careful!' It was like a laugh which stifled a groan. 'Remember you're not well.'

Not well? What was wrong with the Consul? Now they were both laughing at something in there and the man murmured, 'But they've all gone to bed now anyway.'

More laughter. The sound of movements. Maude became more and more uncomfortable as it dawned on her what was going on on the *chaise-longue* in the dining-room. She rarely got into situations of any intimacy with anyone; it was inconceivable that she should be witnessing something like *that*! Now she could see that the light had been switched off in there; there was no strip of light showing through the crack. No wonder.... Her cheeks burning, she listened to the unimaginable noises which penetrated the pulsating darkness. Now and then an exclamation could be heard from him or her, then she could hear only rapid breathing, then whispering, a word, a plea. The *chaise-longue* creaked, weight was redistributed, positions shifted. Crouched in strange, excited fear Maude sat listening intently in the darkness so as not to miss anything; not a single groan should escape her. She was no longer aware of embarrassment. Before her eyes naked bodies entwined themselves around each other in indescribable contortions, the chaos was irreparable. This was happening here, inside the four walls of the boarding-house, in their own dining-room. How could order ever be re-established and life at the boarding-house return to normal? This would have consequences for all of them. How would she be able to look Mr Eldmann in the eye after this?

A different kind of breathing could now be heard from behind the door, no words any longer, no whispering now, just a determined, purposeful panting, guttural sounds which rose higher and higher (how can anyone keep going like that?). Then there was a suppressed moan from in there, unfamiliar as if it came from a different place altogether, then it changed and became a cry, a hardly audible cry from deep inside a body, not meant for anyone to hear, a cry in itself and for itself: madness! It was madness! Maude clenched her teeth to force back the tears: why did she have to listen to this? Was it because it was in reality *she* who had started it all? *She* who had been the first to transgress tact and good form, the unwritten laws, with her fantasies about Mr Eldmann? Was this a punishment, a sign from him who saw and governed everything in order to give her an indication of the consequences of such frivolity? The disintegration which had started in there would reach her too (now the moaning had turned into a whimpering, as if from someone who was dying), would tear down everything along with it, the madness she had set in motion which already was undermining the stability of their existence.... No! She would not, she *could not* take responsibility for all of them, take on herself the guilt for the horrible crimes that were being committed against morality and decency virtually in her presence. She begged for mercy: couldn't they go away and leave her in peace? Couldn't they find somewhere else to go and carry out their revolting intentions? Couldn't things be once more as they had been, slowly be eased back to normality again? She would forget him! She swore it. She renounced everything.

In despair, she tried to gather together the fragments of her life as tears scalded her cheeks.

It sounded as if it was all over in there. The struggle was over. She could hear voices again. The man's gentle murmurings, the woman's sighs; such different sounds which derived from the same source.

Did she love him? thought Maude. Did he love her? Her fear was receding now.

Thinking of them there on the sofa filled her with nostalgia; she was moved. After all, she had danced with him last year – or was it the year before? – at the Christmas party. He had asked her to dance, placed his right hand between her shoulder-blades and with his left held her right hand high in the air. How tall he was – for after all she was not particularly short, not at all; and even when he had let her feel the slight, importunate pressure, he had been elegant and discreet, and she was grateful to him for that. He was always gallant, always so much the gentleman, so stylish in his dark suit with the cream-coloured shirt-collar against his broad neck; really a man of the world. But she had thought it best to refuse his invitation, even though she had fancied him just the teeniest bit at that time. And in any case the manageress was watching them from where she was sitting. So she had said she was tired. And from up in her room she could hear that they were playing another Viennese waltz on the gramophone.

Not until she heard their stealthy footsteps as they went upstairs could Maude let herself fall back in the wing-chair and give free rein to her tears.

· 4 ·

Sunday on the beach. Scudding clouds. Joy up above, down below. Isolated trees act as a framework for dazzling pictures of summer nature, everything renewed, everything teeming with fruitfulness and growth, with trumpet blasts of light and life: rejuvenation here in the green countryside, up in the air, in the light, far from the clammy shadows of decay which lurk down by the roots, beneath the stones. . . .

The breeze from the sea spreads the sunshine like a flag.

Their beach trip, postponed a couple of days because of bad weather on Midsummer Day. They marched in a convoy from the bus-stop down the dusty path to the beach: first the Consul with the rolled-up sunshade, and Mrs Sebastian sometimes beside him, sometimes at the back keeping the children in order. Then the manageress with the basket of crockery. Then Mr and Mrs Moser, the married couple who had recently moved in, with the food basket between them. After that came Maude and Miss Leander, each carrying a cake dish covered with a tea-towel. Behind them walked Mr Eldmann, alone. Maude counted his footsteps and adjusted her own so that they were together on every seventh step. Not that she was particularly superstitious, but seven had always been her special number. She hoped that he felt that way too. She could hear him breathing heavily. It must be an effort, carrying that bag of cold drinks. She felt for him. He was wearing a light summer suit which looked quite new; he looked more elegant than ever, she thought.

Mrs Frank, Dr Lemb and old Mr Adamson, together with little Trine and Johan, brought up the rear.

Their beach clothes made their steps lighter, they seemed to move more freely, the bright, fluttering colours caught the eye; sun and shade prickled and stroked their pale winter skin. Voices sounded so light and so carefree as they chatted. What incredibly lovely weather. Yes, wasn't it beautiful? What a good thing they had waited; it might not be Midsummer Day, but what difference did a couple of days make? New and changed voices out here in the sun and the wind.

She thought: it will be easier for it to happen out here on the beach, away from the house and from all those familiar rooms which stand there with their familiar furniture lined up in unchanging order! So great was her impatience.

'Have you brought your swimming-costume?' whispered Miss Leander to Maude, who quickly shook her head.

'Neither have I.'

Maude counted to seven and let the sole of her shoe scrape the gravel at the same time as Mr Eldmann's. So much can happen here on the beach. The dust was already depositing a layer of grey on Mrs Sebastian's whitened summer shoes.

'How hot it is! I just hope the water is warm enough.'

'Ice cold, you can bet on it.' The Consul's voice rang out at the head of the procession.

'Get on with you! When the weather's as hot as this?'

'Warm enough for bathing in the middle of June? Not for civilized people. I shan't risk it anyway.'

'Oh, you will always exaggerate!' Mrs Sebastian searched through her bag for something, put out; she didn't find it and turned round. 'Trine! Johan!'

Maude thought: they must have quarrelled. Perhaps last night. Despite the fact that layer upon layer of normality had settled, muffling the dreadful memory of that scene in the library, nevertheless there was something still remaining of the outrage and fear she had experienced. It lay there like a quivering tension, a scarcely noticeable excitement in the whole household, as if a new dimension had been added: the borderline that separated the possible from the impossible had become dangerously thin. Fascinated and repelled, she had watched the Consul's attentiveness towards Mrs Sebastian, correct and gallant as if nothing had happened; and at the same time she remembered the bestial noises they had made as they had held each other in the darkness of the dining-room that night. The impossible had become possible, and she felt strangely elated at the thought.

'You're right, I can remember many summers . . .' the manageress intervened in order to come to her friend's aid.

Mr Eldmann walked along behind them, saying nothing. There was only the sound of his breath issuing regularly from between his teeth.

They decided to settle on a grassy slope, near to a spreading chestnut tree. Then those who wanted it could get a bit of shade, and they would avoid all that confounded sand in their food. That was how the Consul put it. The parasol was planted in the ground.

'Do remember that too much sun can be dangerous on the first day,' shouted the manageress. But the wind took her words and whirled them together with other sounds, cries and clamour from the bathers, the splashing of the waves. It made light of authority, which fluttered like her skirts out here in the open air.

Folding chairs were set up and blankets spread out. The manageress organized the picnic: plates, cups and glasses. Plates of sandwiches. Thermos flasks. Everyone tried to help in the confusing disorder out of doors. Mrs Sebastian disappeared in the direction of the changing-huts, wrapped in a striped towelling robe. The Consul had walked off a little and was standing on the hillside gazing out over the sea. Little Johan had fallen over and bumped his knee. Down on the beach there were crowds of people. It was Sunday.

Maude had sat down on the blanket and stretched her legs out in front of her, a pale winter sacrifice to the summer. She looked at the fine net of veins beneath the hairless skin of her shins and sighed contentedly. Not too fat. No, they were definitely not too fat. Her sun-dress was a little bit tight round the waist, but that was no matter. It's a matter of small importance, Mr Eldmann. The awareness of her own generous figure here in the sunshine, out here in the open air, made her think of the picture over the mantelpiece, of the goddesses, of the carefree dance over the meadow. The sea breeze lifted her shy dreams and made it possible for her to dance herself, across the grass, with the sun and the wind on her body, without a thought for what was proper. She had taken off her shoes and felt the grass tickling the soles of her feet.

In the deck-chair just to her left sat Mr Eldmann, busy trying to get the lid off a jar of marmalade.

'Here, let me help,' called Mr Moser eagerly. He and his wife were trying hard to make a good impression on everybody.

'No, no, it's all right. Thanks all the same.' She could hear how he was struggling. Then, with a grunt, he did it; the top was off.

She breathed out, relieved for his sake, and turned towards him with the intention of saying something – anything – it didn't matter what here under the open sky where the noise from the beach reached their ears in gusts, obeying the changing moods of the wind; but he was sitting so still, staring straight ahead, that the impulse died away.

Was it the sunshine that had changed him so much? His skin seemed suddenly transparent, she thought. Drops of sweat beaded his forehead, and the sun seemed to shine straight through his chalk-white shirt-sleeves. His lips appeared dark over his greying goatee beard. A dark lock of hair curled over his pale temples. (What a handsome man, she thought proudly, my delicate satyr!) His eyes were deep set, almost hidden under the shadow of his hat-brim. Between his sock and the bottom of his trouser-leg his ankle appeared thin and white. Now he really looked like a refined aristocrat, a prince. . . . Her heart swelled towards him, for she herself felt the sun warming her legs, her face and breast. How she glowed, how the eternal feminine in her blossomed here in the brilliant sunlight. She would so like to be able to find an expression for her devotion for him at that moment, to touch him, the inviolable one, to press his face to her breast and comfort him as only she could comfort. . . .

Mrs Sebastian came back wearing a blue and white swimsuit and called out that she at any rate was going to have a dip before the meal. No one seemed to have any desire to follow her example, so she went down to the beach on her own with a towel thrown over her hefty shoulders. The whining children were left in the care of the Consul.

'She's not particularly slim,' whispered Miss Leander, who was sitting just behind Maude. Together they watched with satisfaction Mrs Sebastian's ample backside, emphasized as it was by the closely fitting swimsuit, until it disappeared amongst the other bathers.

A group of five or six young people had settled down on the grass not very far away. A bit too close really, thought Maude, who was slightly nervous of youthful pranks and noise. Youth were so unpredictable. Now they were laughing and joking over there, and she watched as they got changed, with carefree nonchalance, in front of each other; how the girls raised their arms and tidied their hair, examined their smooth faces in small make-up mirrors and rubbed sun-tan oil into their slender limbs, whilst the boys were running about, pushing each other and using their supple muscles. It seemed to her that there was something provocative, something almost offensive in the very way they moved, so elastic, so co-ordinated, but at the same time so aimless, as if their young, firm bodies were floating in a whirlwind of fleeting touch, of sensual stimulation, without reservation and without direction; a dance on a fragile membrane.

It was madness, sheer madness! But she carried on watching them, strangely fascinated by their demonstration of the lawlessness of instinct. And suddenly she had the feeling that she was not the only observer of this remarkable game, that Mr Eldmann, sitting beside her, was also watching the youngsters intently; but when she looked in his direction, he was sitting in the same position with his eyes hidden by the brim of his hat and might almost have fallen asleep. It must have been her imagination. There they went, running down to swim, laughing and shouting. In a moment they were gone, all except one of the girls who lay down on her stomach and opened a magazine, trying to camouflage her condition with indifference.

Someone caught sight of Mrs Sebastian out in the water, and they had to wave. The manageress motioned to her to come back, for they were just about to eat.

So the meal was served on blankets and rugs, cutlery was passed round, and soft drinks for those who wanted them – they wouldn't keep cold much longer. The Consul asked if anybody would like a bottle of beer; he was going to the kiosk to get some. Money was sorted out. Mrs Sebastian came back, cheerful and dripping, and announced that it had been *so* lovely and refreshing; then she ran off to get changed.

Tomatoes, radishes and cucumbers amongst bowls of sliced egg, pâté, a dish of cold chicken from yesterday's dinner, potato salad, cheese. . . . The Consul came back with the bottles and a large brown paper bag: cherries for everyone. Generous handfuls of juicy, dark-red cherries were placed on the white plates. They got hold of the stalks, lifted them and sucked them in, crushed them against the roofs of their mouths. Their mouths were filled with sweet juice. The flesh of the fruit stained their teeth and tongues. They spat out the stones into their hands.

Maude had seated herself as near to Mr Eldmann as she dared. She was like a young girl in love; yes, she was just like a schoolgirl, stealing a glance, a remark, a few moments of attention from her idol. Out here in the sun and the wind she felt neither fear nor caution. She saw him lift a hand to his mouth and bite a blood-red cherry: is he thinking about me now? she thought. Now? Right now? But just then Mr Eldmann bent double in a hectic fit of coughing. 'Here, have a glass of beer,' offered the Consul jovially.

The meal was in full swing.

She made sure that she reached for the butter at the same moment as he stretched out for the dish of chicken, and her hand brushed his sleeve. A glance, a smile and an apology. Always correct. So reassuring. In ancient Rome they used to lie down to eat. Eat and make love and then eat again. But then that was the way things were done in those days. She thought about the purity of the classical statues; they exuded an almost unearthly harmony. Then you forgot about all the other things.

There was a hubbub as the youngsters came back from the beach. They dried each other's backs, both girls and boys; no modesty, no moderation, just excess and outrage. . . . She decided not to look at them any more.

A wasp circled over the food. Mrs Sebastian let out a scream. Someone waved a serviette at it and it flew away. But it came back again, and there was another one.

'Soon we'll have the whole swarm here,' said Mr Eldmann suddenly to Miss Leander, who was sitting on the other side of him. 'They have a kind of language, you know, a system of movements, a sort of march or dance so that they can communicate with each other.'

'How amazing!' answered Miss Leander, immediately entranced.

Maude felt the blood rise to her cheeks: he knew about the dance of the bees! He was initiated in the meaning of the signs, in the subtlety of the tiniest movements, just as she had hoped, had known all along! Nothing had been in vain; he had understood everything every smallest signal, and he was using this opportunity to let her know!

'Is it really true that one of them can tell the others where to find food just by doing that?' Miss Leander wanted to know more.

'Absolutely. It's been proved scientifically.'

'How fantastic.'

She had to say something on the subject as well, to let him know that she was with him every step of the way. 'Yes, just think if we humans also had a language which was so . . . so subtle, so *poetic*!' Her heart was hammering. Now it was said. Now they turned towards her. Now she had to go on. 'Well, I mean, there's so much you can't express in words. . . .'

'Do you really think so?' asked Mr Eldmann after a short pause. His voice did not sound in the least embarrassed. He looked straight at her, and the glance from his deep-set eyes made her feel quite giddy. Did he want her to say even more?

She felt that she was losing even the slender thread she had been holding on to. 'Well, yes, there are things, moods for example, delicate nuances between people which we just don't have words for. Or rather, the words we use in such situations are too clumsy, too ordinary to convey . . . well, what they need to convey.'

She noticed that she had raised her voice. One or two people around the white table-cloth laughed a little.

'What kind of situations are you thinking of, then?'

His glance still rested on her, friendly but neutral, as if it came from a long way away. But, my dear man, why do you have to ask about *that*? Did he want her to give them away? Did he really not understand what she meant? That it was *them* she was talking about, her and him; that words, the banal symbols for everything, would tear a hole in the fine net of tenderness and understanding they had spun between them, that love as she and he experienced it was too fragile, too vulnerable, too unique for expressions for it to be found in the vulgarisms that sprang just as easily to the lips of the common herd? That that was why she had sought refuge in the language of the bees, to tell him what she felt? But now they had all stopped eating and were waiting, their hands had stopped reaching out to the dishes. Her glance moved hastily from one to the next; not from face to face, her fear prevented that, but from plate to plate. She knew that all they were waiting for was an admission, a false move, the slightest slip of the tongue which could provide a little hint for their ever-suspicious minds.

'Oh . . . there are all sorts of situations. . . .' Her voice was barely audible.

'Fancy that, there are all sorts,' remarked Mrs Sebastian to the manageress.

Everyone seemed to be waiting for the answer still. She felt a surge of desperate defiance: she would show them, especially that monstrous Mrs Sebastian. 'I was thinking of love for example!'

Now it was said. She felt relieved, transported, whirling freely like a feather in the summer breeze.

Mr Eldmann looked away. 'Oh well, that's rather a special case.'

After yet another slight pause, the manageress said in a loud voice, 'Do please help yourselves. There's plenty of chicken left.'

'Yes, it is a little difficult to make general statements about something as personal as that.' Mr Eldmann tried again. They were sitting there to one side with the conversation they had started, Miss Leander, Mr Eldmann and Maude. She was crushed: how could she have been so irresponsible, so egoistic, putting him on the spot and making herself a laughing-stock in that way?

'I think I understand what you mean,' said Miss Leander thoughtfully.

'Yes, love needs more than one language,' came from the Consul.

If only they could let the matter drop! Mr Eldmann had fallen silent again. She was aware of Mrs Frank sending her a searching glance from her place in the shade of the chestnut tree. What a blunder she had made! How stupid she had been!

The cakes were unwrapped and the manageress served out coffee from the flask. A shadow passed over the cloth, a mere streak: a bird. The subdued murmur of sea and voices reached them in rhythmic gusts from down on the beach. Time and a thousand details interposed themselves, merciful and protective, between her and her tactless outburst.

'More than one language, so it does,' repeated the Consul, and patted Trine's pink bottom. The children had been given permission to play on the beach, and Mrs Sebastian was helping them off with their clothes (she would do it just now, whilst they were eating!); but they were not to go anywhere near the water. Otherwise they would go straight home.

Finally lunch was over. The cloth and plates and all the leftovers were packed away. Rugs and deck-chairs were rearranged. Now the sunbathing could begin. Maude lay down on her rug with an inflatable cushion under her head. Beside her the Consul was given permission to rub cream into Mrs Sebastian's back. On the back of her thighs too; it seemed they were friends again. She saw how his fingers kneaded the soft flesh. Now she asked him to pull down the zip on the back of her sun-top. Evenly brown. It really wasn't right. They were simply going too far, those two, she thought vindictively. And then the Consul opened his shirt and exposed his vast chest. Maude closed her eyes. She found all this nakedness so importunate. Really she wasn't all that fond of trips to the beach. The sight of all those undressed bodies lying side by side like slaughtered animals, or running around looking unattractive, enjoying themselves demonstratively, had always stirred her dislike. It was so unnecessary to expose yourself like that, so far from what she associated with comfortable, unforced companionship.

'Why have you got hair under your arms, Mummy, and that lady hasn't?' Little Johan had come back and was standing looking sceptically at his mother's body. Miss Leander jumped and blushed. It was her he was pointing at. So Miss Leander shaved under her arms? The trouble-maker was shushed and sent away.

Mr Eldmann was sitting beside her on a folding chair, reading the newspaper. Fortunately he had not undressed. He was a real gentleman. The Consul, on the other hand, had settled himself down with his head resting on Mrs Sebastian's ample behind. How could they take such liberties, here in the presence of everyone? How could she allow a thing like that, when she had two small children? Maude's indignation grew. Had she not, if not exactly seen, at least heard them *in flagrante* only a few nights ago? How would it all end if the provocations continued like this? They were simply trampling underfoot all that was beautiful and sacred! It was people like them who debased the universal expressions of love and put difficulties in the way of decent people when they wanted to express their devotion for another person. It was corrupting, that was what it was!

A breeze wafted away all guilt from her forehead, all memories of her careless outburst a short while ago, of her immodest dreams, her secret licentiousness, and the sun cast its soft blood-coloured light through her trembling eyelids.

Her fellow lodgers were sitting or lying around in a half-circle on the gently sloping hillside, with expressions of patient suffering, whilst the sun attacked areas of skin that were exposed for tanning. Only Mrs Frank preferred the shade under the chestnut tree.

'In France you get the sunbathing over before you eat,' sighed the Consul, and wiped the sweat off his face. 'After the meal you relax in the shade. Too much heat straight after a meal is bad for the heart.'

When he moved his head it had a ridiculous effect on the proportions of Mrs Sebastian's bottom half.

'But they have a hotter climate in France anyway,' objected Mrs Sebastian in a drowsy voice into the rug. 'People don't die of heatstroke round here.'

Maude caught a glimpse of the white of her breasts as she lifted her upper body slightly in order to change position, and this strip of defenceless skin, together with the sight of the Consul's bald pate pillowed on her rear, all built up into an overwhelming impression of unacceptable intimacy. She had to look away.

The warmth of the sun had penetrated beneath her skin and played like a flame over her shoulders and arms, and up and down her legs. Her face felt swollen. She raised herself up on her elbows. Mr Eldmann was sitting on his folding chair with his hat pulled far down over his forehead and his hands folded in his lap. The newspaper lay spread out over his knees. What was he thinking about? Just beyond him lay Miss Leander with her skirt pulled up well above her knees. The heat and light had struck them all motionless.

    Suddenly Mr Eldmann wobbled on his chair, seemed to tilt to one side, tried too late to recover his balance by waving his arms about in a panic, and tipped over. For a moment he lay unmoving on the ground just next to her, and then he began to struggle confusedly to raise himself into a sitting position. Numb all over with shock and fear, Maude was kneeling beside him before she knew what she was doing, trying to help. She grasped hold of his arm and lifted and pulled, her breath coming in gasps like his own. How heavy he was! He was practically pulling her over! And it was all she could do not to lose her balance and fall on top of him, the way he was pulling at the arm she held; and whilst they were both flailing to regain their balance, he kept trying the whole time to say something to her which she couldn't quite make out. It sounded as if he was saying 'It's all right', but that must be mistaken, for it was obviously not all right, far from it. He needed help, he needed *her* help, and she held on grimly to his arm as they got more and more hopelessly entwined in each other, as if their limbs were acting of their own accord, independent of any will. He came so close to her that she was aware of the smell of him (when they bumped heads), a smell of washing-powder and after-shave (fortunately he was a non-smoker) that she found very clean and inviting. It suddenly occurred to her that they were in a kind of embrace as they half sat and half lay entangled in each other (she could even feel the warm wetness of his armpit); and this made her even more determined to help him (for now there was no other respectable way out of this), whilst he panted in her ear, 'Nothing . . . it's nothing . . . nothing to worry about . . .' and a long, bluish-red vein stood out sharply in his neck, all the way from his ear until it disappeared under his collar. But she for her part saw only the fine blush which had spread over his neck and jaw, and that his eyes had speckles of green in the brown, and she felt all her strength and warmth flow across into him whilst she repeated over and over: 'It's all right, Mr Eldmann, now you must just . . . look, now we'll just . . . now . . . here . . .' as they wrestled around on the green grass and he kept trying to free his arm, which she was holding in a grip of iron.

    This idyll lasted perhaps ten to fifteen seconds, and then fortunately some of the others intervened, and he regained his balance.

'No really, it was nothing. No harm done. I must have dropped off for a moment. Damn stupid. . . .' Red-faced, Mr Eldmann was standing brushing greenery off his light-coloured trousers. She understood him so well; she didn't like being the centre of attention like that either. His hair was standing out at all angles. His hat had rolled a little way down the slope and stopped forlornly next to the oil barrel which served as a rubbish container. His face was quite pale now.

Maude sat on the rug, in a daze, trying to straighten her hair. So much had happened today, but it was as if the wind and the sun had neutralized everything, and nothing seemed to have the significance that rightly belonged to it. She thought of her indiscretion earlier, of the smell of his hair-tonic, of the moisture in his armpit, the stiff shirt. . . . Her head suddenly felt as heavy as lead.

'Perhaps it's not a good idea for you to sit right in the sun in this heat?' The manageress looked solicitously at Mr Eldmann, who had still not quite got his breath back after the incident.

'No, too much sun is no joke at your age,' called the Consul, attempting to give the whole episode an innocent air of comedy. 'Sunstroke can affect the best of us.' He laughed.

'I just dropped off,' Mr Eldmann murmured again, still upset about all the fuss. 'It's nothing worth bothering about.'

Mr Moser helpfully retrieved Mr Eldmann's hat. The manageress withdrew with a searching look at Maude, and she remembered their conversation of a few days previously and at once felt strangely guilty – although she could surely not be blamed for his queer turn and, anyway, who said it was a queer turn? He had fallen asleep and fallen off his chair, that was all.

A cloud passed in front of the sun, spreading a slight unease amongst the sunbathers. Little Trine came back from the beach in tears, saying that her brother had been naughty. Mrs Sebastian dealt with the matter at once, and soon the sinner's piercing cries resounded through the sleepy hum of the afternoon. A sudden wind ruffled the glittering surface of the water, pulling black clouds after it. Clouds were gathering in the west, a deeper blue against the blue sky. In the mouth of the fiord the last gleams of sunshine shone white against the threatening sky. Was the wind getting up? Someone wondered. A piece of paper came fluttering through the air.

'There's going to be a storm. Mark my words!' The Consul had got up and was standing with his hands deep in his pockets, gazing out over the fiord. He expressed what they were all thinking.

'Do you really think so?'

'Oh, how annoying, just when we're starting to get brown.'

'Well, according to the weather forecast. . . .'

The sun went behind the clouds for good.

'Heavens, I think it's starting to rain!' Mrs Sebastian arrived, dragging her red-eyed miscreant by a thin, reluctant arm. 'I think we'd better find some shelter!'

'Yes, I think you're right!' The manageress was already busy organizing baskets and bags. Again everyone rallied round to help: rugs were rolled up, lilos let down, rubbish was carried off to the bin. But it was as if they were still feeling the effects of the sunshine, which made them heavy and slow. The cool shade seemed pleasantly mild and refreshing, and the clearing up proceeded at a leisurely pace. The storm came nearer. The first heavy drops were greeted with loud cries of surprise.

Maude kept her eyes on Mr Eldmann as she hastily packed up her own cushion and rug, worried that they would lose each other in the confusion. Several of the company were already fleeing down the slope in the direction of the restaurant and the bathing-huts. She pretended to be looking for something on the ground as the manageress shouted the last instructions and set off as well. Mr Eldmann was still struggling with his folding chair.

'This way!' shouted the Consul as he hurried past. 'Before the restaurant gets full.' Then he disappeared down the hill.

The rain was falling faster now, blotting out all sound. Miss Leander was still standing undecided and looking in their direction. She shouted something Maude could not hear. She waved to her, still bent double, and pretended to be searching for something in her beach-bag. Miss Leander waved back and ran off. She was the last.

Then they were alone. The haze of falling rain, like a mist of dust and glass which grew thicker and thicker, separated them from the others. Moisture spread out in a pattern across the back of his white shirt, as dark roses of water spread and merged into each other. He was holding his jacket bundled up under his arm whilst his thin hands struggled with the folding mechanism on the chair. Suddenly she acted, driven by an irresistible urge to help him and by the mounting feeling of discomfort as she stood there motionless, getting slowly drenched and with her eyes fixed on the figure that was so dear to her, only a few paces away. Suddenly she was standing beside him, grabbing his arm.

'Come on, you'll get soaked!' she shouted at him and began to pull him towards the chestnut tree. He followed her without protest, his jacket clutched firmly in his free hand. The storm was raging around them now. She could feel water running down her face. Her hair was plastered to her head. What must I look like! Side by side they ran the last few steps over to the tree, to the accompaniment of his gasping breath.

Then they were safe. The thick panoply of leaves let through no more than a few scattered drops now and then. They stood close to the trunk and gave way to an impulse to laugh.

'Well, have you ever seen anything like it?' he said, breathless and excited. 'We only just made it. What a storm!'

'Dreadful,' she replied without meaning it. Here they were standing close together, just the two of them alone, with a torrential summer shower protecting them against all distractions, against the intrusion of the outside world. Nothing could be dreadful now. She looked down at herself and had to laugh: her summer dress was spattered with rain and her shoes were stained with earth and grass.

'What do I look like?' she said, out loud this time. She turned towards him in order to be reassured that she really didn't look that bad after all, but he was standing with his head leaning against the tree trunk, watching the rain that was gusting in from the sea in wave after wave, and didn't seem to have heard what she said. A drop of blood had oozed from a scratch on his cheek.

'You're bleeding,' she said. 'Look. . . .' She wet her index finger with her tongue and wiped away the evidence of the recent struggle. She had to lean over towards him a little, and felt his upper arm against her breasts; a distinct resistance met her fruitful abundance, firm but tender. His skin was rough where he had shaved. She sucked in the drop of blood which had coloured her fingertip. Your blood, my blood. Her knees felt like jelly.

'Thank you,' he said somewhat tonelessly.

I must help him, she thought, he needs someone who can look after him. . . .

So they stood there, the two of them, watching the rain and feeling how more and more of it penetrated through the covering of leaves. They even had to move now and then to avoid an ice-cold trickle.

'Have you ever seen anything like it?' he muttered again. 'But no doubt it'll stop soon.'

No, she didn't want it to stop! It had to go on like this, she thought, with him and her here alone, sheltering under this tree, like two shipwrecked sailors, the first and the last people. . . .

'Have you ever seen anything like it?'

'November rain!' It came on an impulse, too strong for her to be able to hold it back. It had to be spoken between them some time: his signal. His secret passion. Too late to regret it.

'Yes, you can say that all right!' He seemed cheerful. 'We soon turn the corner once we've passed midsummer.' He peered towards the sea. 'Have you ever seen . . .'

The sound of laughter reached them before she had time to wonder about his reaction (after all, it was just the two of them here, a rare opportunity . . .) – carefree laughter through the monotonous drumming of the rain, and soon after figures came into view, first as shadows, then as human figures, jumping and laughing in the rain. It was the youngsters who had been sitting close to them, smooth, brown and dripping, hand in hand, arm in arm in the rain, completely unconcerned in their carefree happiness. How attractive they were, and at the same time how repellant! How she envied them, at the same time as she thanked God that she lived in a different world, an older, better, above all more sensible world where order ruled, where you were in control of your own being and felt responsible for the consequences of your acts. Look at them, barefoot on the wet grass! One girl was riding on the back of her boy-friend. Her broad hips had not yet achieved their mature fullness; her knees stuck out shamelessly under the boy's armpits as he irritatedly pushed her long wet hair away from his face. Now they were falling over. Shrieks of laughter. He helped her up again, one arm round his neck, then a push, a kick. . . . What do these slender nymphs know of woman's unfathomable tenderness? And the boys, what do they know, with their taut stomachs, their swimming-trunks, their open eyes and open mouths, about women's needs, about women's hidden depths? She thought about the little intermezzo just now; Mr Eldmann and her capsized on the green grass. . . . Had not that been something else? The scent of his shaving-lotion and of his shirt, his hair so near to her warm cheek; all awkward and clumsy, of course, but something else, something greater nevertheless?

She noticed that he was moving. He waved. One of the young girls had stopped and stood waving to them, shouted something through the rain. And Mr Eldmann was waving back! She was speechless. Did he know her, that half-grown girl? As far as she knew, Mr Eldmann didn't have any relations. Had he no idea of what was right and proper? Or perhaps he had affairs with young girls? Indignantly she moved away from him. Had she been mistaken about him? Was he too one of these old libertines who . . .

'One of my pupils. . . .' He was standing smiling after them, one hand still half raised in the air. 'Very promising. . . . In the final year. Top results. . . .'

She melted at once; more than that, she felt sorry she had been so suspicious and moved a little closer again (but not too close, she didn't want to seem too forward), reassured and grateful. How considerate of him to provide her with an explanation. *He* knew what was due to a woman. Her heart swelled and overflowed.

'Marvellous youth,' continued Mr Eldmann. 'Strong and healthy. It almost makes you wish. . . .'

Oh no, my dear. She moved a little closer still, almost touching his sleeve with her shoulder. He mustn't say things like that. *They* were the ones who had the maturity and the depth to realize their genuine feelings fully without exaggeration and vulgar provocation; *they* were the ones who knew the true meaning of love. She gazed with him after the group as it disappeared in the rain. She could feel only pity and regret for all that happy beauty which was thrown away.

'But we old ones can comfort ourselves that each age has its charm. Its charm, yes,' he repeated, pulling out a handkerchief.

'Yes, that's true,' she said, happy that they were once more in accord (although neither of them could be called 'old'). 'One's soul matures as the years pass.'

'One's soul, yes – you're no doubt right,' answered the apple of her eye, in the intervals between blowing his nose energetically.

And as he put his handkerchief in his pocket, his arm brushed against her breast, so close together were they; and she blushed like a rose as he begged her pardon.

Nothing more happened beneath the tree.

It was clearing up. The breeze came and pulled the heavy curtain away, and hung up a light veil of drizzle which shone silver and steel through the gaps in the clouds. The resurrected landscape stretched itself cautiously in all directions and eventually lay there as before, resting and breathing out after the shower.

Someone came hurrying up the slope towards them, running awkwardly with one hand on her headscarf and the other holding her skirts: Miss Leander.

'Mr Eldmann! Miss Maude! Thank goodness, there you are! We didn't know. . . . We were so worried. . . .' She was quite out of breath, and smiling uncertainly; her glance shifted from his face to Maude's, and back to him again.

'Thank you, we're perfectly all right,' Mr Eldmann parried jovially. 'It's the best shelter there is,' he added, pointing up towards the branches, which were still releasing light cascades on to them now and then. He seemed cheerful and lively, thought Maude. My dear, dear man.

But Miss Leander suddenly went quite pale and had to lean against the tree trunk. Wasn't she well? Maude watched with rising irritation as Mr Eldmann offered her his arm (he was not the sort to leave a woman in the lurch!) and asked if everything was all right. Yes thank you, she'd probably just been running too fast. What was she thinking of? Coming galloping up like that and forcing herself upon them. . . . Perhaps she had been sent along by the manageress to spy on them?

But you couldn't for very long attribute evil intentions to Miss Leander: she was so naive, poor little thing, and goodwill shone out of her face, even now, though she did actually look a little the worse for wear, and still had to lean on Mr Eldmann's arm, and had nearly been sick a minute ago. No, Maude forgave her everything (with a glance at Mr Eldmann's calm, noble face, with a lock of rain-soaked hair clinging to his forehead); she had really been worried about them, little Miss Leander.

'The others are leaving,' she said. 'Since the weather is so unsettled.' She was feeling better now. 'We're taking the half-past four bus back.'

A cascade of sunshine washed over sand and sea and warmed the back of her neck as she walked along behind Dr Lemb and Mrs Sebastian, who were each carrying a folding chair as well as a basket of beach things. Behind her she could hear Mr Eldmann breathing in time to his steps. He had given his arm to Miss Leander, for the grass slope was slippery and the ground was soft and treacherous in places. On the gravel path their steps fell into time as before. Together on every seventh step, her lucky number.

Back home in the tidy and secure surroundings of her own room, in front of the mirror, she inspected her face, upper arms and shoulders:

yes, there were two white stripes from her shoulder straps – she had caught the sun. She took a deep breath. What a day! She thought as she stared straight into her own open eyes that it had perhaps not been such a bad thing that she had mentioned love whilst they were eating. On the beach so much was possible. She could still feel the weight of him where he had fallen and leaned on her arm, the intimate smells of clothes and soap. And her warm spit against his cheek. . . .

She sighed happily and smiled at her figure in the mirror. She was a dream, a vision as she stood there with her hair flowing loose, in her silk underwear with real lace.

## · 5 ·

Maude came home from her trip to town in a state of high excitement, with the red dress in an elegant parcel under her arm. It was Thursday the 29th, the Consul's birthday. The dress fitted her like a glove after a couple of small alterations. It was rather low cut, but tactfully so. . . . Well, after all, she had kept her good figure, so why not?

As the wrought-iron gate swung to behind her, she found herself suddenly standing face to face with Mrs Frank. Although there was not the slightest reason for it, she realized that she was feeling embarrassed and awkward. The fact that she reacted as if she had been caught *in flagrante* although she had the clearest conscience in the world made her so annoyed with herself and her own lack of independence and self-confidence that she burst out spontaneously, 'I've been shopping in town!' – as if she owed her an explanation.

Mrs Frank, who only now seemed to notice the fatal parcel (was it too low cut after all? And red at her age!), asked without a great deal of interest, 'Oh? You've been making some purchases, have you?'

'Just a dress. A little thing for the party this evening.'

'Oh, that. . . .' Here Mrs Frank clearly saw her chance to talk about what really interested her. The dress was forgotten. She lowered her voice and fixed her sick eyes on Maude with a malicious gleam. 'You know, I really haven't the slightest desire to join in with this beanfeast of theirs.'

'But, Mrs Frank, you must! Everyone's going to be there.' Maude waited anxiously for what was to come.

'The way they carry on!'

What should she say to that? That she had also heard them (to put it mildly)? That it didn't interest her? Try to calm this sick creature down and maintain that she must be imagining it all?

'From morning till night!' continued Mrs Frank. 'High and low! Do you think I haven't noticed it? And this is supposed to be a respectable house! It's her fault, mark my words. Divorced people are the worst.'

'But don't you think they might be really serious? That . . . that they're going to get engaged?' Maude remembered the conversation she had overheard; it sounded as if there was something they were both waiting for. You shouldn't judge people before you knew their motives (although it was true that the Consul and Mrs Sebastian were often incautious in their behaviour).

'Get engaged!' Mrs Frank snorted. 'Do you think I'm going to believe that? But the worst thing is . . .' she lowered her voice even more, 'the worst thing is that those two aren't the only ones at it.'

'What do you mean?' Now she really had gone crazy, thought Maude, at the same time as she felt a shiver of fear. Perhaps she had been a bit irresponsible, the way she had got close to Mr Eldmann on the beach that Sunday?

'They've poisoned the whole house with their brazenness. Do you know, the other evening I came across a couple on the sofa in the dining-room! And it was *not* the Consul and Mrs Sebastian!'

'Who was it then?' Maude's heart stopped beating. Was she talking about the same evening when she herself was sitting in the dark library? But no one had come then.

'They had put out the light, so I couldn't quite make them out, but I know it wasn't the Consul, because I'd heard him in the bathroom five minutes earlier.' Mrs Frank's room was next door to the bathroom on the first floor.

'What did you do then?' Maude couldn't help herself. She had to find a way out of this labyrinth of slander and suspicion that the spiteful widow had led her into.

'I let them get on with their filthy deeds. Do you think I want to get involved? Oh no! And what do you think I saw this morning? Somebody had been sick all over the place in the downstairs toilet!' She said it as if the two occurrences were intimately linked, although Maude could not see that there was any logical connection between them at all. Anybody could feel a bit ill one morning and be sick.

'You know what that means?' Maude just looked inquiringly at her, but she didn't wait for an answer. 'Filth breeds filth! They'll not escape the consequences of their disgusting acts, you'll see! No, you can thank your lucky stars, Miss Maude, that you have avoided such disgrace, that you've avoided the shameful things that happen between men and women.'

No, that was going too far! Maude felt a surge of defiance. She didn't have to stand here listening to this in broad daylight. Flushed with indignation, she muttered an excuse and fled past the astonished

Mrs Frank, up the sun-flecked garden path. Why had this malicious female chosen her of all people? Was she secretly hoping that she might 'fall'? That she too might become a victim of the 'shameful things', as she called it? She was assailed by doubt. Perhaps she had sinned (although Maude was far from being what you would call religious, she frequently used the word 'sin' in connection with actions that offended her acute sense of decency and morality, and, on the other hand, she found that the word 'holy' could be applied to sentiments that fulfilled her strict standards in that area, and the Heavenly Father had more than once helped her across a slippery patch). Perhaps she had let herself be carried away at an unguarded moment? Mrs Frank's words rang in her ears like an echo of the voice of conscience. The sight of her sick mother came back to her: an elderly woman in a wheelchair with thin hands beneath her rug. The birth which had ruined her health. The husband who had run away. The strokes.... And little Maude who had hidden her first love away, in a place where no one could break in and destroy it for her; for it was far, far too fragile for her to be able to take it out and look at it, or share it with anyone. Then it would crumble away. She was fully aware of that. Even then.

No, no one had a more elevated understanding than she did of the holy alliance between man and woman, of that she was sure; and this certainty made her invulnerable to spiteful gossip and innuendo.

But wasn't it a beautiful day? She could still feel the slight sunburn from the beach trip on Sunday itching beneath her dress. She thought longingly of her room, where she could take off her clothes and lie down on the bed, rest and day-dream. She loved to lie down on her bed in the afternoon.

And tonight, Mr Eldmann, we shall dance! she thought as she laid her hand on the front door-knob. Tonight I shall feel your arm around me! A sudden feeling of gaiety. Her caution, which was really laughable. The dangers, which no longer existed. The steps, which carried her unperturbed into the forbidden no man's land of love. A fleeting moment whilst the summer caressed the hand she had laid on the door-knob, and the wrapping-paper around the box with the red dress in it rustled under her arm.

The Consul himself served the champagne. Large and jovial, with a stiff shirt and a flower in his buttonhole he walked round with the silver tray and gave everyone a glass. After two small mouthfuls, she could feel the little gold cross on her breast rising and falling on its thin chain. Music flowed from the radiogram. Black Negroes in dinner-jackets glided around, flattering provocatively with their instruments. Dance. Breast to stomach. Thigh to thigh. She had been to a dance restaurant once. A long, long time ago a gentleman had leaned over the table, over the remains of the meal, and taken her hand. What had he said? She couldn't remember. She had looked up at the dance band, at the woolly-haired saxophonist who pursed his blue lips around the mouthpiece and twisted his powerful shoulders beneath his jacket. She had danced with her perspiring Oliver and thought of deep forests, wild shores, flight. . . .

And then she had danced with the Consul once, at a Christmas party two or three years ago. The lounge had been prettily decorated, as it was now, and some of the furniture had been moved to one side to make more room. He had asked her and they had danced. Christmas parties at the boarding-house were always fun. They had danced a Viennese waltz. It had been such a pleasant atmosphere. But she had felt tired and had gone upstairs before the others.

'Well, cheers, everyone!'

As they raised their glasses, they all exchanged glances full of high spirits. Goodwill nodded to friendliness, tolerance acknowledged self-restraint. Maude loved the social intercourse of civilized people. She looked round over the edge of her golden glass, caught his glance and lost it again. Cheers, my beloved! He was sitting on the sofa talking to Mr Moser. He was wearing a dark suit with discreet stripes. He was more elegant than she could ever remember seeing him.

'Cheers! Congratulations!'

They drank to the guest of honour. The Consul laughed heartily. Something reminded him of other celebrations, in other places, many years ago. Oh dear me, yes, time does fly. A complaint full of satisfaction. They were preserving themselves in this room where each piece of furniture, each detail had its past, deposits of their own lives and those of others, friends, former residents. This was a boarding-house full of tradition, the manageress did not let them forget that, and this very fact gave them all a certain importance, a little pride, greater self-respect, perhaps just a feeling of solidarity, of belonging to a place that it was good to belong to, where other people you could respect also belonged. Clem's was not just an ordinary boarding-house; its standards appealed to one's ambitions, its order became one's own order. It was just this which gave them a feeling of security, of permanence; as if misfortune could never strike in this house – and that made it easy to ignore an unpleasant detail, a small oversight, such as the fact that the Consul and Mrs Sebastian. . . . In a way it was not important after all. Not now anyway, when they were all sitting and standing around in their party clothes with raised glasses, drinking to a dear fellow resident, thought Maude. She took another sip from her glass and tasted the sharp bouquet on the roof of her mouth. Now everything was happening exactly as it should, now nothing could disturb the tastefulness and warmth that was the hallmark of the boarding-house.

All the best!

Suddenly she noticed that someone was missing. Mrs Frank had not come down.

'What a lovely red dress!' Mrs Sebastian looked her up and down as she walked past. She was wearing a fashionable ankle-length dress with a top so transparent you could see her underwear, of course. 'It's charming! Is it new?'

She smiled broadly, showing her gums. Her blonde hair seemed even blonder. Her thin arms hung down from broad shoulders. She was about a head higher than Maude. She had managed to get brown that Sunday on the beach – unless that colour was also the result of chemicals. Maude felt ashamed of her thoughts for a moment and smiled back, shyly grateful. The red dress suited her, she knew that; it was cut so low that you could just glimpse the hollow between her breasts where the cross was palpitating gently in time with the butterflies in her insides. She had experimented with perfume, and with lipstick. Even a little eye-shadow. Her hair was fastened up on top of her head. Around her wrist her platinum bracelet caught the light. And all for him, all for his sake!

'Cheers!'

She smiled and nodded to Dr Lemb, who had raised his glass, together with the manageress, and was nodding and smiling at her. Mr Eldmann was sitting talking to Mr Moser. She wondered whether it would look too obvious if she went over and sat down on the sofa in the empty place beside him, but decided it would be best to wait. There would no doubt be an opportunity later on. Instead she followed Mrs Sebastian with her eyes. Now she was going over to the Consul and interrupting him in the middle of a conversation, standing close up against him so that she touched him with hand and hip.

'Well, aren't we going to dance?'

Yes, they were going to dance. Someone changed the record. Someone coughed, a little embarrassed. The carpet was rolled back even farther. The gramophone struck up a Viennese waltz. The guest of honour and the divorcée were already swaying in each other's arms, moving seriously and purposefully across the creaking parquet floor. Just look how she was thrusting her thighs against him! The music and the strange sight of a couple dancing here in this room made Maude feel in a Christmas mood. Now he could come. She was ready to dance as soon as he liked. She was standing on the same spot, just inside the broad dining-room door, exactly where she had been standing when the Consul had served her a glass of champagne.

Suddenly Mr Moser was standing in front of her, blushing slightly and bowing. So she would have to dance with Mr Moser. She said thank you and put down her glass. He clasped her around the waist and twirled her around energetically.

Everyone was dancing now. Dr Lemb with the manageress; Mrs Moser was conducting a reluctant Mr Adamson round in circles. In a glimpse she saw Mr Eldmann get up and bow to a blushing Miss Leander. Mr Moser was breathing in her face. He wasn't very tall. She was relieved when the record finally came to an end.

Fresh drinks were served. She knew that she ought to be careful, because she wasn't used to alcohol; but she accepted the glass that was offered to her and drank the bitter mixture. Cheers, Mr Eldmann! The manageress had got hold of him and was standing giving him a lecture. Poor man, she was always fussing over him. What was the matter now? She peered up at the chandelier through her glass and let it dance a little in front of her eyes.

The music droned on. Now the Consul was dancing with Miss Leander, and Mrs Sebastian with Dr Lemb. So that was how things stood. The lion and the lioness. The others were sitting down, having a rest and a drink. She observed the Consul's concentrated tango. Would he try it with her too? Not that it mattered to *her*. . . . She was just interested – well, a little excited at the thought that he perhaps did it to everyone (like with Mrs Sebastian just now, that had been positively embarrassing, but there she was just as much to blame as he was). The excitement she felt was wellnigh indistinguishable from the indignation that filled her when she thought of the concealed little penis beneath his stomach which made itself so strongly felt when the dance music started to play – an indignation which was directed at him, at herself (she had behaved ridiculously that time) and not least at Miss Leander at this moment, letting herself be enticed into this. No sooner had the thought occurred to her than Miss Leander took a false step, almost stumbled and hung in her partner's arms whilst a high, thin heel slid helplessly across the floor as she struggled to regain her balance; and this little misfortune of course gave the Consul an excuse to draw her even more closely towards his body, as if his closeness was sufficient guarantee against a repetition. Poor little thing. She was no great shakes at dancing either. Maude suddenly felt a surge of pity for this no longer young girl who was so helpless, so vulnerable, and who had furthermore not looked all that well these last few days. Had she put on weight too? She would so much have liked to put her arm around her waist and teach her the difficult steps (just as she herself had learned them at the dancing-school in the small town where most of the pupils were girls), hum the tune close to her ear, count the beats in a soft voice. Then they could have danced together, she and Miss Leander, head to head, breast to breast, and no treacherous attacks would threaten them from the depths of a suit.

But what was she thinking of? It was Mr Eldmann she was sitting here waiting for (and really, the concoction in her glass was beginning to taste rather good). Where was he? Now when he had the chance. . . .

But just then the music stopped. Someone called for refreshments. Around the table they discussed the good weather in loud voices. The manageress came past. 'Well, are you enjoying yourself then?' But Maude was not frightened any longer. She remembered how her skirt had blown about wildly on the beach, and her old, anaemic legs without stockings. . . .

What was Mr Eldmann doing? Then she saw him sitting in an armchair. He looked as if he was about to drop off at any moment. But it was only ten o'clock. What was the matter with him? She hardly noticed that the Consul took her empty glass away from her and replaced it with a full one, making a friendly remark and stealing a bloodshot glance down into her cleavage. Was he not in party mood perhaps? Oh, she must find some way of bringing him back to life again. The impatience that had niggled at her like an itch these last few weeks now demolished the last remnants of reserve. The bitter whisky and soda gave her courage; all she needed was the opportunity. So when Mrs Sebastian out on the dance floor clapped her hands and announced the ladies' waltz, and someone put on a dance record, before she realized what she was doing she was standing in front of him, in her youthful, pretty red dress with its flatteringly low neckline, which she had bought for his sake, with her bracelet, lipstick and gold cross, all for his sake, and asking him to dance. And when he hesitated, she stretched out a hand in admonition. Now he was going to get what was coming to him, and no excuses would be allowed to disrupt her calculations any longer. So he gave in, sighed, got up from the chair (as he did so she noticed that he was not quite steady on his legs and had to take a small step to one side), said, 'Thank you, I'm honoured', buttoned his jacket and followed her on to the floor. And then Maude and Mr Eldmann were dancing.

He held her gallantly, half an arm's length away, and danced soberly and with effort, looking down most of the time. At intervals their knees touched. He was not the man to force his lewd intentions on an innocent dancing partner, she thought; and had to repress a sudden urge to laugh. What was the matter with her? Was it the drinks that had made her so incautious? Her hot right hand was resting in his dry left one, and the firm fingertips on her spine sent their small Morse signals through the material of her dress. Yet it was as if there was still something missing, even when his beard at one point brushed so closely past her warm cheek that it could almost be called an attempt to kiss her. She could have stood so much more this evening, especially this evening when they were at last in each other's arms, their bodies close together, moving in time to the waltz. Even a certain little pressure against her stomach she would have accepted with pleasure. She suddenly needed so much more of him than before, she didn't know why. It was so easy to let oneself go at a party; the external orderliness, the attractive clothes, the refined manners, the festive spirit were so reassuring. She felt so sure now, the way things had been developing between them the last few weeks, it was high time. . . .(Yes, she had drunk too much! She was a little too bold now, but it was their night tonight! Tonight she could dare!) Mr Eldmann had to become the man to whom she could admit all her fears, on whom she could try out all her tender dreams. Their individual orbits would cross soon, she was certain, a first, holy meeting, and then melt together for all time. Yes! There was no doubt in her heart as he guided her around the smooth floor of the lounge at a rather strenuous tempo.

So certain did she feel that she decided to pretend that she had stumbled. She lost her balance and let herself fall against him, at the same time as she moved her hand, which until then had rested so decorously on his shoulder seam, and with a quick grasp around his slender neck pulled his face towards hers. She thrust her thigh in between his legs and let all her opulent, inviting warmth flow across to him at the precise point where she could feel the swelling of his groin through the layers of clothes that separated his skin from hers. Now! Now he was hers!

But the result was not quite what she had hoped, for Mr Eldmann stumbled too, in sheer surprise or by coincidence; and together they slid along the dance floor, she clinging around his neck and he flailing desperately for something to hold on to, a wall, a piece of furniture, one of the guests; until they finally crashed into the piano, let go of each other and were safe.

He was breathing heavily, holding his hand protectively against his chest. She giggled guiltily, the roundabout still whirling round in her brain. 'Oh my goodness, I'm terribly sorry. I must have stumbled. . . . So stupid of me. . . .'

'Not at all,' he protested weakly. 'A gentleman's first duty is to stay on his feet.' Someone laughed in the background. Beads of sweat collected on his forehead, ran down his pale cheek and dripped on to his jacket collar. (My lover, my dark knight, you are dancing with a tear in your buttonhole.) He got out his handkerchief.

'It is dreadfully warm in here, isn't it?' She was repentent now, realizing that she had perhaps gone too far and made him feel unwell. She wanted to make up for it. 'Even though the veranda door is open.'

'Yes, isn't it?' he agreed. 'Very warm.' He glanced longingly towards the armchair where Mr Adamson had fallen asleep. The others were dancing. Maude fancied that Miss Leander kept looking at them from where she was dancing with Mr Moser. She was no doubt thinking about her own accident a little while ago.

'It must be lovely and cool out there,' she said tentatively. The garden was the ideal place.

'Yes, it must,' was all he said.

He was leaning on the piano. He still kept his hand against his heart beneath his jacket (a signal?). His suit with the fine pin-stripes was so becoming. He was more attractive than ever, she thought, and as they had been dancing together only a moment ago, she dared to ask him, 'Wouldn't you like to come out on to the terrace for a while? We could walk a little.'

'Yes, if you like,' he muttered and mopped his face. His thoughts seemed to be elsewhere. But he wanted to walk in the garden with her. He had given his consent!

'I'll just get my shawl,' she called happily, and moved away.

On the way she had to walk past the guest of honour, who was standing indecisively watching the dancers, with a glass of whisky in each hand.

'Hey!' he called. 'Hey, Miss Maude!'

She had to stop.

'How red and beautiful you are tonight.' His voice was slurred and affectionate, and he stared down unabashed at her lovely breasts. 'Wouldn't you like to dance?'

'No thank you,' she said, laughing; though right now, in this moment of happiness, she could have been tempted – just a little bit, anyway – to waltz around with this mountain of a man. 'I'm just going outside to get a bit of air.' Behind her back she heard Miss Leander saying something to Mr Moser. She didn't feel too well, she said, she couldn't dance any more, he must excuse her.... Naturally he excused her.

'So, you're going out for some romance under the stars, are you?' the Consul teased her. 'Well, I'm sure it's a good idea. You never know what might happen on a starry night. Here, look, you'll need supplies....' She had to accept a full glass from him, even though she had already drunk more than enough. 'But you'd better be quick,' he continued, winking confidentially, 'otherwise he might not wait for you!' He pressed her arm in friendly fashion. She giggled, although she was really deeply shocked that he had seen through her (and at the thought that perhaps *everyone* had noticed, and known it the whole time, and was waiting to see what came of it, as she herself was waiting); but she forced herself not to turn her head to see if he was still standing there, because she didn't want to give the Consul that triumph, and anyway she trusted Mr Eldmann.

Her shawl was hanging over the back of a chair. She seized it, turned round and saw that he was gone. There was no one standing by the piano any longer. No doubt he had gone out in advance so that it didn't look too obvious. How considerate he was, the dear man. As discreetly as she could, she slipped through into the empty dining-room. There was no one there either, but she thought that she saw the door to the little parlour close just as she came in. Miss Leander? She had gone in here just after she had broken off her dance with Mr Moser.... But what would she be doing in there? The parlour was a kind of study, but it was now used almost exclusively as a store-room for unwanted things, furniture, boxes of various cast-offs, journals and magazines. It must have been her imagination.

She stole out through the hangings on to the dimly lit terrace. There she remained standing motionless, letting the stillness and the space around her slowly overcome the churning noises in her own head. She could not see him anywhere. Taken aback, she sat down on a chair on the veranda and waited, took a sip from her glass, shivered, peered up at the stars which whirled around each other high up there in the cold, never-ending space. . . .

But wait: what if he had gone down into the garden, across to the bench perhaps, and was sitting waiting for her? Hardly had the thought occurred to her before she was hurrying down the veranda steps, across the grass, on to the gravel path that stretched out white and unfamiliar in front of her, level and still between the trees in the pale evening light. The gravel crunched with each step she took and echoed in her aching head. The way he held his hand on his heart as he stood by the piano; like an old-fashioned courtship, a declaration of love – her gallant suitor of the old school. . . .

She turned off and stole along the garden path, moving silently over the soft earth, so quiet suddenly. There was a ringing and singing in her ears. In front of her loomed the summer-house, looking dark and unfamiliar now. Was there a figure on the bench? No, no one. She was out of breath. Walking so quickly had exhausted her. A sip from her glass. Not a soul out here. She'd better sit down, and then he would soon come. He'd just been held up a little.

The fountain was splashing away, sending its thin stream of water down into the black pool in the marble bowl. The water had been turned on for Midsummer's Day. The gardener had finally arrived and tidied up the garden. Ah well.

A bird fluttered up from the bushes just behind her. She jumped, terrified; then she realized what it was and relaxed, drank a little more and felt the nausea rise at the back of her throat. She knew that she was tipsy now. She giggled and breathed on her glass to make it misty. Up above little bits of sky were sailing about between the branches and the leaves. Down in the garden, beneath the trees, the darkness was thick, impenetrable. The complete stillness overcame Maude as she sat there on the bench. She turned into glass, she was at one and the same time herself and everything else around her. A flower blossomed inside her. Now he should come and put his arm around her; an easy conquest now that she could be his at the same time as she was not here, was everywhere; two loving words were all it would cost, or perhaps only one? A kiss, a touch of a tongue on her temples. . . . So long we have been waiting! She could confess that now that she had turned into glass, now that she was sitting here waiting for him and at the same time was a part of the darkness around her, now that she could give herself to him and be in all other places too. . . .

So long, too long! She had to cry. A short, almost soundless sob escaped from her breast. It sounded lonely and hurt, so miserable that the very sound made her cry more; and suddenly tears were streaming down her face, warm and liberating, and she abandoned herself to her confusion and her boundless longing.

When she next looked up, she could see the sky revolving slowly around the star that she had chosen as her own. Mr Eldmann and herself up there, separate and united from eternity to eternity. How beautiful it was, how overpowering and how melancholy: two small people in the great void. She leaned her head against the hard back of the seat. Faint waves of nausea came and went. The firmament pulsated and rotated and Mr Eldmann was all at once so close, yes, closer in body and soul, in the flesh as well as in the spirit, than he could have hoped to come if he had actually materialized. Here she became his, fully and without reserve.

And this lovers' pact, concluded in drunkenness and loneliness, was not dissolved until Maude fell asleep, as she so often did when she was exposed to strong emotion or drank too much alcohol, curled up on the rotting wood of the bench with her thumb in her mouth and the melancholy stripes of tears down her carefully applied make-up.

She woke up shivering with cold and with a headache that she could feel in her whole body. What time was it? It must be late. She could feel that she had to go to the toilet. From the next-door garden she could hear a bird already beginning its morning chorus. There was a faint gleam of light in the sky. The trees and bushes around her stood lifeless, as if they were turned to stone in the twilight.

Unsteadily she hastened back. She had fallen asleep. He had not come. What had happened to him? Had something stopped him? Had someone demanded his assistance? Had he misunderstood her invitation? Her head ached. They must surely all have gone to bed. What had they thought when she just disappeared like that?

The house lay in the grey early morning light with dark, dead windows. The front door would be locked, of course. She stopped to think. Perhaps the veranda door. . . . Fortunately the veranda door was still open a crack. She left a wet trail across the flagstones of the terrace, sneaked back in again the way she had come out so full of delicious expectation, entered the dining-room, listened, heard nothing, tiptoed in the direction of the hall and the blessed toilet, but stopped short at the door to the parlour. What was that? A movement, a sound from in there?

She could not resist; she peeped in. She had no idea what she expected to see (and was painfully aware that she needed to move pretty quickly to answer the call of nature), but felt herself nevertheless shaking with excitement. Perhaps she could not quite forget her hope that something would happen tonight, something big, something transformingly wonderful that would make all her days and all her nights different from now on; something which would give that nameless, feared, indefinable thing called love a place in her life, turn it into something legitimate, not, as it was now, an obscure fog full of fear and doubt and unacceptable impulses that seeped around and in between everything she said and did, and made her nervous and shy and afraid of other people, even afraid of herself and her own ungovernable thoughts.

She leaned forward cautiously and peered through the half-darkness. There was a figure asleep in shirt-sleeves in the armchair. Mr Eldmann! Yes, it was he! She could make out his dark beard against his shirt and the pale skin of his face. So it was here he had waited for her. Now there was no obstacle between them any more. Driven by a desire that she neither wanted to nor could suppress, she entered the room silently. There was a smell of dust and old furniture, and Mr Eldmann was asleep. He slept. He was half sitting, half lying in the chair like an impatient Sleeping Beauty. He was sleeping with his mouth open, showing a set of false teeth. But his forehead shone white and pure, and some strands of hair had formed little curls at his temples. Something not quite proper was trying to surface in her consciousness. What was it about a sleeping man? Something she had heard and forgotten again, something she had found remarkable, almost improbable when she had heard it, which had made such an impression on her that she had ever since had a strange feeling whenever she thought about a sleeping man, and now she recognized the feeling again. . . .

He was breathing quickly and uneasily, making sharp noises in his throat. His jacket, waistcoat and tie were draped over the arm of the chair. In the half-darkness in here his eyelids looked like half-moons in their dark hollows. What are you dreaming about now, Mr Eldmann? And at the same moment she knew; at that moment it came back to her that she had once read that men always had erections when they were asleep! She didn't know where she had read it; perhaps someone had told her it, but she had remembered it ever since. She did not even blush as she leaned over, as near to him as she dared, and laid a finger as light as a feather on his belt buckle. He was breathing quickly, raspingly; he was sleeping sweetly.... My darling! Her fingers moved, crept downwards along the vertical fold of his flies, her heart thumping so that she was afraid he would hear it. What if she fainted now? Then she was right down there, and could feel what she was searching for under her fingertips. She placed her whole hand, gently as a wing, like a covering over his male pride as it lay there, spread over his thigh, waiting in its cocoon of clothing.

A breathless second which was an eternity. It was moving under her hand! The tickling sensation in the palm of her hand transferred itself to her whole body. She was aware only of this, had no other clear thoughts at that moment, but something was pushing and pushing inside her as if it wanted to impose new and different formations on her fantasy. The fear that she had felt at her impropriety was drowned in heedless exultation. She felt dizzy. The pressure did not cease. She did not know what it would drive her to, but she capitulated, gave up all thoughts of herself, the last remnants of resistance. She prepared for the cataclysm, the void that must be the only thing which would be left, all for that little swelling under her fingers. Something broke somewhere at the back of her mind and she let the warm stored-up liquid run free. It scalded down over her thighs and down her legs, darkened the colour of her dress, collected in her shoes and trickled down on to the carpet. What a relief!

And the horror at the same moment. She sprang back, squeezed her legs together with her hands on her stomach, ground her teeth, fought like a mad thing to stop this unimaginable shame. But she could not staunch the flow, it ran out independently of her will, regardless of her cramp-like movements and the guttural noises in her throat, until it stopped of its own accord, leaving its victim and its source on the verge of hysteria, pierced by the cold steel of panic.

*Get away!* was the only thing she could think. A lukewarm, numbing feeling of discomfort originating from between her legs penetrated her consciousness. The soiled dress clung soggily to her silk stockings. He slept on undisturbed. Thank God for that! She was holding his waistcoat in her hand (why? where from?) and pressed it against her mouth in order to muffle the groans that emerged from her throat and threatened to turn into loud cries. Then her legs obeyed her and she fled.

But by the time she was running up the stairs, at a reasonably safe distance from the dreadful scene of her disgrace, she was already aware of what that night had meant for her: now he was hers, hers alone and for all time. Her voice sang the same words again and again for a solitary listener.

She could hardly bear to wait the few hours until it was breakfast-time.

## · 6 ·

But Mr Eldmann did not appear at the breakfast table next morning. He was feeling a little unwell, so it was reported. The maid had found him in the parlour earlier that morning when she went in there to clean and had helped him to bed. He was going to have breakfast in his room today.

'Let him sleep it off. He must have been hitting the whisky bottle last night!' This came loud and clear from the Consul's place. As for him, he looked to be in fine form despite last night's festivities.

'Well, you're only sixty once. And not everyone makes it as far as that!' He laughed.

They talked about the successful party. Everyone had had such a marvellous time. Some people said they thought it was strange that a gentleman like Mr Eldmann had not gone steady on the strong drink. It was whispered that there had been a terrible mess in the parlour. . . . But then, on the other hand, accidents will happen.

It became overclouded, and by lunch-time the rain was pouring down. The air in the lounge was heavy and stale after last night's jollities. There was a general feeling of sluggishness amongst the residents. There didn't seem to be much to talk about except the fact that the weather had taken a turn for the worse.

At three o'clock the maid came running down from Number 11, calling for the manageress. A telephone call was made at once, and the doctor came. It was a stroke; but the situation was not critical. An hour later a nurse arrived to keep an eye on him overnight. Everything was made ready for him to be admitted to hospital the next day.

The evening meal was eaten in silence. Most people said good-night and went to their rooms earlier than usual. They were no doubt still feeling the effects of last night's party. They whispered in the corridors, and the doors were closed as silently as possible.

At a quarter to eight the next morning, whilst the toast was burning in the kitchen and the manageress herself, still in her dressing-gown, was ticking off the housemaid for not closing the window in the library, Mr Eldmann passed away, peacefully and without pain, without having regained consciousness. The ambulance was there almost immediately. Two men came in and placed him on a stretcher, calmly and efficiently. Then he was carried out.

Maude stood in the window watching the ambulance drive away.

# II

*Transformations*

· 7 ·

The Inspector came and wanted to ask a few questions. Purely a matter of routine. There were one or two points that were a little unclear; it wouldn't take a moment to clear up the little misunderstanding. The manageress showed him into her office and closed the door.

In the meantime his room had been cleared out. His clothes and his few possessions had been packed in cases and boxes labelled with his name. Now they were just standing there, forlorn and unwanted, waiting to be sent off.

The Inspector would be grateful if he could be allowed to inspect the room. Permission was naturally granted. The maid was instructed to unpack again. His possessions were subjected to a thorough examination. The Inspector did not seem entirely satisfied. The manageress fussed around him with excuses and an apologetic expression (it was bad enough that a policeman should have cause to visit the house at all). She had of course inquired into Mr Eldmann's background; she didn't accept just anyone. . . . He had had excellent references. No, it had never occurred to her that there was anything to be suspicious about. He had been the ideal resident, a gentleman, popular and totally reliable. This must all be due to some inexplicable coincidence, some oversight or other for which she could not be held responsible.

'I see,' said the Inspector. They would have to investigate matters further. She would be hearing from him.

No one knew really what to make of this strange episode. Rumours were buzzing around, guesses were hazarded, but no one had anything definite to go on. And you couldn't really ask the manageress straight out. The general opinion was that Mr Eldmann had committed some irregularity or other which had only now, after his death, come to light. But what on earth could a high-school teacher have done that could be discovered in the middle of the school holidays? No, the most likely thing was that it was all a mistake on the part of the authorities; after all, that kind of thing was not unusual.

And in any case, it wasn't a very tactful thing to do, sitting around so soon after Mr Eldmann's death and speculating as to whether he had been an out-and-out scoundrel.

But the speculations did not decrease as the days went by and the date for the funeral was postponed. The manageress, who had written to Mr Eldmann's sister, had the letter returned stamped 'Not known at this address'. The Inspector visited them once more to inquire about something. The whole boarding-house suffered in this state of uncertainty and confusion. It was not possible for the residents to acclimatize themselves to the changes that Mr Eldmann's death had brought about whilst none of the many questions that had presented themselves in that connection ever received an answer. Why was the funeral taking so long to arrange? (Why couldn't they get it over and done with? someone asked quite openly.) What had Mr Eldmann done that was of interest to the police? And what did it matter anyway, whatever he had done, since he was dead after all?

Concerns such as these, and this artificial hiatus in the ordered pattern of existence, from life to sick-bed to the grave, left the residents with an uncomfortable feeling that there was something mystical, something positively unreal about Mr Eldmann's death. It was as if Mr Eldmann could not be properly dead, since the dust, as it were, would not settle on him; and this sense of outraged decency at having constantly to revive one's relationship to a deceased friend and fellow resident in an atmosphere of suspiciousness and scandalmongering – this disrupted the familiar rhythms of boarding-house life for everyone.

For Maude, this disruption of an order which she regarded as inviolable was almost incomprehensible and hurt her deeply; at the same time, this little suspension of the inexorable progression of events functioned as a breathing space in the merciless reality, and allowed her at times to forget that Mr Eldmann, her dearest love, was gone for ever.

In the end, it turned out that matters were both more simple and more complicated than any of those involved had dreamed of. One day they were all informed that doubts had arisen as to Mr Eldmann's true identity. He had not left behind any identification papers, his name was not to be found in the town's public records or on the census lists, the address which he had provided for his so-called sister did not exist, and a telephone call to the island where the school superintendent was on holiday had established that no one of that name had ever been employed as a teacher at the town's high school. As matters stood at present, there was no shred of proof to substantiate the claim that Mr Eldmann had in fact been Mr Eldmann.

· 8 ·

The days immediately following Mr Eldmann's death remained in Maude's consciousness like a progression of vague moods that swung from one extreme to the other.

She had stood there, watching them drive away with him; but she had not felt any sudden rush of sorrow or despair. It was rather more like reliving a dream in waking life; something that she had foreseen, and had almost hoped would happen, had happened, and in the melancholy mood that filled her as she stood by the window, watching the red back lights on the ambulance disappear down the drive, the heaviest feelings which had moved her to tears were nostalgia and sweet regret. What did it matter that they were driving away with her prince, now that he was hers, now that the love for him which she had borne and nurtured finally lay, safely and indestructibly preserved, in her heart, removed from the sphere in which it was vulnerable to other people's unpredictable actions and impulses? She felt that she possessed something, as she stood there, that nothing and no one could take from her: that both she and he were safe now, for ever.

But then there were the mealtimes, with his empty chair and the glances that seemed almost to be drawn to it, even though they made strenuous efforts to behave naturally, in an everyday fashion, as though there was nothing wrong.

The practical details connected with Mr Eldmann's decease had perhaps upset her less than most of the other residents. After all, she was accustomed to being in the presence of sickness and to the subduing effect which the pointing finger of death had on the living. The years spent with her mother shrivelling up in her wheelchair had made her familiar with that barren land of shadows on the other side, beyond facile hope and optimism. But his empty chair at the table was a concrete symbol of his absence that she could not rationalize away. She joined in when the others discussed the Inspector and Mr Eldmann's past, even though it upset her to do so, in order to weave as many threads as possible between him and the everyday world, to reduce the distance and postpone the inexorable departure, to keep him alive amongst them. She could play games in her thoughts, to the extent that she could make herself believe that he was still alive and moving behind the closed door of Number 11, and at night he and she still talked together and he was especially good and loving towards her and whispered a tender good-night when sleep came and carried her away. But nothing of this could compensate for the sight of the empty chair, this gap in the familiar table arrangement which more clearly than anything else demonstrated that he was no longer amongst them; the nervousness that this irregularity created in all of them; the irrefutable witness of the empty space. And then, when glimpses of a reality that could not be denied broke through her dreams, when she grasped the enormity of the concept 'dead and gone' (with Mother it had been different, she had gone away from her that summer long, long ago; after that, life had simply continued for a few years, had just slowly ebbed away); when it was brought home to her that the empty place would never be filled by Mr Eldmann's beloved form, and she thought how near they had been to each other through glances, signals and secret touches – then it was as if she lost her senses and just sank and sank in sorrow and hopelessness. More than once she grabbed hold of the nearest person she could find, as if in a rage, in order to break through their indifference, their superficial speculations, in order to express *something* at least; and she repeated through her tears how dreadful it was that he, he of all people, a man like Eldmann, should be torn from them; in his best years, in the midst of life, so much still to do, such a loss. . . .

And on all sides her complaints met with understanding and warmth, for death legitimizes outbursts of emotion; and many people, indeed most of them, assured her that they were just as upset as she was. Miss Leander, poor girl, was inconsolable; she could not even bring herself to come down to meals for the first few days but had to have them taken up to her room. She was so sensitive. Maude herself took a tray with afternoon tea up to her once, to show her how grateful and moved she was by her sympathy. She had forgiven her for the fact that she had danced with Mr Eldmann with her underarms shaved.

She heard the news about Mr Eldmann's mysterious identity as they were sitting eating the evening meal. Suddenly she had the feeling that they were all turning towards her, as if this was of particular concern to her, as if the manageress's brief information or the Consul's remark were directed at her rather than to the others; but she made no response. She just sat and stared down at her plate and tried to take in this new attack on everything that was precious and sacred.

If Mr Eldmann was not Mr Eldmann, by what name could she call love? Who was it who filled this dreadful emptiness within her? She tried to picture him as he had been in life, but under a different name, and she felt a sudden shock: all at once it was as if his face disappeared! She could remember details – his pale skin, his hair, his beard, the melancholy brown eyes, the thin lips – but when she thought at the same time of a different name, the features refused to fuse together and form the face she knew. Mr Roth, Mr Adler, Mr Borgen? No, it was as if a hollow, empty suit was sitting there eating dinner on the empty chair next to Mrs Frank. Suddenly her grief was nameless.

The others had immediately begun to discuss this new turn of events. This was a sensation indeed: if Mr Eldmann had not been Mr Eldmann, who could he have been? And what had he been doing all these years if he had not been at the school? She had to get them to stop talking like this; it was threatening to deprive her of all her dearest memories, to rob her of the last remnants of a happiness which she could no longer enjoy. She tried to join in the discussion, to suggest that it must all be a fabrication, a misunderstanding, a bureaucratic mix-up; but around the table opinions were already being aired about what kind of swindler this 'so-called Mr Eldmann' had been, and what had made him choose to hide away here at the boarding-house under a false name. Just think how cleverly it had all been done: up and out every morning, back after the end of school, keeping such a close check on half-terms and holidays. What bold-faced cheek! What nerve the man must have had.

Some people were more cautious and thought that as long as there was no *proof* that Eldmann, or whatever his name was, had been a criminal, one ought to be careful about leaping to conclusions; but one thing at least was certain – that he hadn't been the schoolteacher he had claimed to be – and that was enough for most people. The sensation had given an edge to their voices. They needed to let themselves go a little, after all these days of uncertainty and gravity. They were already discussing who might possibly move in to Number 11. A new resident, someone said. Let's hope it will be someone respectable!

Suddenly she couldn't bear it any more. She felt as if this heartless conversation and the thought that she was now alone, hopelessly alone and lost amongst these vindictive people, would ultimately poison every fibre of her being and destroy her reason. She gripped the edge of the table and shouted to them, screamed at them, losing control in her despair. 'But you know who he was! He sat here – didn't he? – and ate with us! He walked about in these rooms! He was a resident here like we are! And . . . one of the girls on the beach knew him . . . was one of his pupils! What you're saying is all lies! There just isn't anything . . . anything mysterious about Mr Eldmann. . . . Leave him alone! Please!'

She ran from the table. Blindly she stumbled through the hall, up the stairs, into her room. She had his waistcoat, at any rate. No one knew that. The waistcoat from the Consul's birthday party; the only proof she had that he had been the person he was for her, for them all. The anonymous garment lay in her drawer, right at the back, rolled up, stained by the bitter tears of the one who was left behind.

## · 9 ·

Uncertainty drove her to act. Next morning just after breakfast she went out. It was a cloudy, misty day with a warm, moist wind. She got on the bus at the usual stop and got off at the hospital. An efficient receptionist explained to her where she should go. Her footsteps sounded loudly in her ears in the long corridor, making her quicken her pace nervously. She was already regretting her decision.

She found the door and went in. In the waiting-room there was a writing-desk and a couple of filing cabinets, and around the wall there were some tubular steel chairs. Behind the desk sat a little bald man, writing. She mumbled her request in a low voice.

'What was the name?' said the man.

She didn't understand which name he meant, so she repeated what she had just said.

'And your name?'

She whispered her name.

'Are you a relative?'

'No, we weren't exactly related, but. . . .' How could she explain that she had been the person closest to him? That she had a right to see him?

'And authorization? Do you have an authorization?'

Authorization? Where should she get that from?

'No. . . . I didn't know . . .'

'I'm sorry,' said the little man. 'Then it's just not possible.'

'Not possible? Do you mean that I can't . . .'

'I'm afraid you can't, no. We have our regulations. You must understand that we can't just display our – what shall I call them? – clients to anyone who asks.'

Maude thought she saw the ghost of a smile flit across his expressionless face at this flippant remark and was even more outraged. 'But isn't it possible . . . ? Is there no way I can . . .'

'I'm sorry. Not without authorization. Unfortunately.'

'But you *must* let me see him!'

He made no answer, just shrugged his shoulders almost

imperceptibly. What a repulsive, self-righteous little man. She turned her back on him to walk towards the door. All her arguments had evaporated, but she was still determined to get her way. She had to see his face one last time, so that she would have *that* at least. . . .

'I *must* see him,' she repeated with her back to the little man. She could almost see the sneer of disdain on his mouth. She walked indecisively to one of the chairs and sat down. She had to think about what she could do, how this unsympathetic person could be persuaded, tricked. . . . But her knees were already shaking beneath her, and deep inside she knew that she had lost. The little man had gone back to his writing and was taking no more notice of her.

She remained sitting on her chair, vanquished, without the initiative to embark on a new attack or even to gather herself together to make a sweeping exit. Even the purpose of this fruitless visit was no longer clear to her. What possible connection could there be between her beloved and this room? These dead white walls? That ridiculous little man, sitting over there behind his desk? She had wanted to see him in order to be able to preserve more clearly her memories of the way he was, to protect them against this namelessness and give herself the confirmation she needed in order to be able to carry it through. But could it happen here, in this room? Or even worse, in the cold store, where the dead lay in numbered drawers like anonymous entries in an archive? How stupid she had been to come here!

But just a short time ago she had seen it so clearly: the Prince in his sarcophagus. As she walked down the drive this morning, she had seen his image clearly imprinted before her inner gaze; the moisture on the fresh grass reminded her so of the hair on his white temples, the clouds of the shadows on his cheeks, and a tear-shaped leaf of his eyelids.

To be able to hold this fast.

'Is there something I can do for you?' The little clerk perhaps thought something was wrong with her, since she remained sitting there for so long.

'You must let me see him,' she simply repeated automatically, obstinately, although she did not wish for anything any more, and certainly not for admission any farther into the recesses of this sterilized waiting-room for death. Through the dry, cool breeze from the ventilator she fancied she could smell the air around her, heavy with the stink of corpses.

'You must understand that I have to obey the regulations.' He was talking persuasively now. 'We're just not allowed . . .'

'Oh, in that case. . . .' She interrupted him pettishly, pouting like a little girl, and remained sitting where she was. He went back to his work, but kept on looking up nervously, as if he was going to say something.

Serves him right, she thought, but without malice or triumph. Why can't he talk to me like a normal person. She felt unspeakably lonely and empty, sitting there. The thought of Mr Eldmann was no longer at the front of her mind. Now she was aware of herself as others saw her: insignificant, timid and middle-aged, colourless and ordinary with her handbag on her lap; she could have cried at the thought of her own ordinariness and at this man who couldn't even treat her like a human being, like a woman.

He kept looking up nervously.

Serves him right, she thought. Sitting there hiding his teeny-weeny penis behind the desk. That's just what he's doing, isn't it? The thought cheered her up, made her feel superior.

'You . . . you can't stay here!' said the little man suddenly. Determinedly. 'It's not allowed.' He didn't seem sure about his position any more. Perhaps he suspected that she was sitting there gloating about what a little one he had.

'Yes, I suppose that's against the rules as well,' sighed Maude; but she had the feeling she was gaining ground.

'Well, not exactly,' – he hesitated – 'but it's not usual for people to sit here for ages like this. . . . It'll be time for my lunch break soon anyway!'

'Well, you can talk to me for a bit, and then I'll go,' said Maude innocently. Every time he hesitated she felt stronger. She was a woman after all, she knew how to take advantage of a situation like this. What if she were to faint, for example, so that he had to carry her up to the rest-room?

'*Talk* to you?' It actually looked as if he was blushing. Was he already a little in love with her? He was looking at her the whole time now. Automatically she smoothed her skirt down and took a firmer grip on her bag. It wouldn't do to seem too inviting.

'But what do you want to talk about?' Complete capitulation, and all just because he had to sit there hiding his teeny-weeny penis behind his desk, because it was so little – just as little as he was himself. She curled her little finger slightly. If he was observant enough, he would see what she meant.

'We could talk about why you have to sit here and refuse me permission to go in there.'

His expression changed, became sympathetic and concerned. 'Was he a friend of yours? A close friend, I mean?'

'He was my closest friend.' She could say it now, open herself to him; she knew a good deal about him too. . . .

'Oh, I see,' he said. He decided that he would reveal something as well. 'Well, you know, there's supposed to be something funny about him. No one knows for sure who he was. . . . I mean. . . .' He realized that she didn't want him to say any more.

'I know who he was,' she said. 'He was my closest friend. More than a friend.'

'Oh yes, of course.' He was very meek now. 'All I know is, he was the muscular type all right. I have to lay them out in there.' He obviously thought he ought to contribute his version of events. 'A real hulk with ginger hair, a great mane. . . .'

'Yes,' she said. 'He was a powerfully built man.'

What difference did it make that this little funeral director's clerk was mixing Mr Eldmann up with someone else?

'But do you have to go already?'

She had muttered her thanks and was walking towards the door. Everything in here seemed so unspeakably horrible. She heard him half rise from his chair behind the desk.

'Do you have to go?' But she had already gone.

## · 10 ·

She stood for a moment uncertain, aware of what she wanted to do but at the same time a little bit hungry too. She felt so much like something to eat that she went into a café and ordered a coffee and a slice of cream sponge. Immediately she regretted it: it would remind her so much of Mr Eldmann. She remembered the last time, just a couple of weeks ago, when they had eaten cream sponge together and she had seen him take the iced top layer off before he ate the cream (and had it proved to her yet again what a cultivated and sensitive man he was). But perhaps in this way he would come to life again within her, a little bit of comfort whilst she was eating, she thought. She hoped so. Too late to do anything about the order, anyway.

The peaceful sweep of the main street looked grey and anonymous through the large panes of the café windows. The sky arched above it, white and impenetrable as far as you could see. There were few people in the street, and there were no customers in the café except her. The only visible movement was someone walking in the direction of the little harbour. A quiet time of day. Plants in pots on a stand in the window. A gentle humming from the coffee-machine. Her eyes were filled with the white daylight and she wished that it could flow into her quietly, healing and assuaging the pain that was within her, just as it embraced the dead street, houses, people and cars and softened all the sharp corners, all edges, all points. A hazy day.

She drank her cup of coffee and ate her sponge-cake and thought about that embarrassing episode at the mortuary. Well built and ginger-haired, the little man had said. How grotesque that sounded when you thought about Mr Eldmann. But of course he was just a little pygmy of a pen-pusher who couldn't tell his nose from his elbow. Nevertheless, she was disturbed by such comments in connection with her beloved. It was as if her memory of him was threatened yet again, was being attacked from a new quarter. She decided to forget the whole thing as quickly as possible.

The last spoonfuls of cream and cake, and then the iced top layer, the best bit of all. She really would have to keep an eye on her weight.

She looked at the clock. No lunch for her at the boarding-house today. Tra-la-la. She knew what she was going to do. She had been feeling restricted for a long time, bundled up in all these confounded clothes.

The bus roared away behind her. The gravel path down to the beach seemed untrodden today. You could hear the waves washing on to the narrow strip of sand from right up here. It wasn't quite deserted, though; some children, three boys and two girls, were running along the water's edge. They stopped, stared, crouched down and examined something, ran on farther, called to each other.

Gusts of wind brought drops of warm spray on to her skin. The sea lay like oil over quicksilver, completely ignoring the little strip of surf that ran along the edge of the beach. Sea and sky met where thought ceased and dreams returned from whence they had come.

She walked over to the kiosk where various kinds of swimming equipment were for hire. The young girl looked her up and down unsmilingly: yes, they had swim-suits. For an hour, or the whole day? Size? She got a swimming-hat too, and the key to a bathing-hut.

In the little changing-hut she freed herself with a gasp from all her tight-fitting garments and pulled on the swimming-costume, a simple, black sheath of tricot which fitted snugly over her well-rounded figure. She stretched and smooth the material a little, ran her hands over her warm and ample curves and felt much better already. Once outside she stood still, shivering as she felt the wind on her bare skin; but it just felt unfamiliar, not unpleasant. The stiff grass tickled her toes. How long was it since she had last run bare-legged through the grass?

She ran down the gentle slope, feeling her own weight swing and quiver. It was a marvellous feeling of freedom: all alone by herself on the beach, released from all trivial constraints (this feeling was bound up with a weightlessness, a vacuum in her which had been present ever since he had departed and which made her feel that more than anything else she wanted to flee from everyone and everything, from the boarding-house, her friends, the daily demands and duties, just run away, become air, disappear into nothingness out of the reach of searing grief). So she ran, her arms swinging, her breasts bouncing, with round, white, woman's thighs. . . . Ah – she had to stop for a moment, that little jog had made her quite breathless. The group of children in the far distance. She had the whole beach to herself.

The sea lay there, smooth and impassive. A chilly gust was borne towards her at the water's edge, but it was as if she was hypnotized: to float, to rock, to drift; to let oneself be carried far, far away.... She was standing up to her knees in the water, shivering a little. The little wave splashed and slapped against her frozen thighs, came back again and again, like a cool, impatient tongue. Yes, yes, she said to it, yes, yes, just wait a moment, just a little moment.... The swimming-hat magnified the sound of the sea in her ears, as it painted its thin stripe of foam along the sand. Her feet were deathly pale, crippled on the hard sea-bed, already numb, they didn't belong to her any more.

She took a sudden decision, stumbled a few steps, plunged her arms in, and let the cold creep up to her waist. A few steps more. It's not really cold, not extremely, not like I thought! The little wave, stronger now, embraced her, lifted her, pulled her towards the shore. But she wanted to go farther out and fought it, losing her footing; she panted, struggled, swallowed water and was suddenly swimming with neck craned and head held high. Ha ha! Like Mrs Sebastian. There you see, you're not the only one!

Swimming with short, concentrated strokes she conquered the watery element. When did she last swim in the sea? Ten, fifteen years ago? She remembered the trips to the beach with her mother on warm summer days, the problematical manoeuvring of the wheelchair, the sick woman's demands for shade, cool drinks, comfort, as if the overheated restlessness around them had crept in behind her rug and made her crippled body itch and tingle; the sudden decision to return home earlier, complaints, tears, recriminations....

She rolled over on to her back, turning a mouthful of salty water into a warm fountain mixed with saliva. Look what I can do! She caught glimpses of her white knees, her bent toes, and kicked with her feet. The splash was hardly audible beneath her swimming-hat.

Then she lay still, floating on her back with her breasts just breaking the surface of the water, feeling the numbness from the cold water slowly creeping into her body. But it was good, a blessed feeling nevertheless: to freeze away the doubt, the indecision, all distractions, and leave behind the essential, clear and purified. She felt for the bottom with her feet and was alarmed to find that she couldn't reach it. She swam a few strokes towards the shore, wary of being out of her depth.

She waded slowly towards the white strip of sand. The wind and the cold water had cleared her mind. Now she could recall Mr Eldmann, no longer as a human being encumbered by the base qualities of mankind (those barbs that so easily become a part of normal social intercourse if you don't take care), but as a state of mind, the highest and the best, which she would always treasure as her most precious possession, and she thanked him for that. At the same time she noticed with satisfaction that the contours of her body were unashamedly outlined by the material of the hired swim-suit.

Overcome by this new and elevated feeling, she sat down and graciously allowed the waves to lick her toes. She leaned on her elbow and gave a deep sigh of well-being, then lay on her side with her cheek resting on the sand. She remained lying like this, staring out into the nothingness between sea and misty sky whilst her thoughts became more and more peaceful and the spicy scent of the ebb tide tickled her nostrils. Finally she became a piece of driftwood washed up on a lonely shore, at one with the sea, the sky and the sand, slowly disintegrating into her original elements; and she experienced such a great, such a boundless feeling of contentment that she did not even notice the cold which sent regular shudders through her body – and indeed she even ignored the slight pangs of hunger in her stomach that reminded her about the good lunch (Thursday, lamb chops) which she was now sacrificing.

She remained lying there for a long time.

Footsteps approached out of nowhere and stopped. A voice asked, 'Are you unwell? Can I help you?'

She looked up, startled, and became aware of an elderly man in an overall, a refuse collector with a spiked stick in his hand and his bag of rubbish slung over one shoulder.

'Are you hurt?' He looked down at her with an expression of concern.

She suddenly remembered her revealing costume and curled up, embarrassed. Whilst one hand shielded her breasts, she tried with the other to brush the sticky sand off her face. 'No. . . . No, not at all,' she heard herself say. 'I was just resting a little. I swam quite a long way out.' She nodded vaguely towards the water.

'Oh, I see. Well, I'm glad there isn't anything wrong,' the man went on, speaking slowly and carefully. His hand looked like a gnarled piece of bark hooked around the worn handle of his stick. 'You never know.'

'No, you never know.'

'It's chilly today,' he continued, making conversation. How could she get rid of him and make her escape to the changing-hut?

'But the water isn't too bad.' She looked around helplessly. She couldn't stay sitting in this uncomfortable position for ever.

'It's seventeen degrees, so I heard,' said the man. The spike found a sweet paper and made short work of it. 'There's not many here today, but you should see it at the weekend when it's sunny.'

Despite the neutral tone of his comments, Maude had the feeling that his gaze did not leave her body for a second. She shrank from this molestation, but didn't know what to do about it, had no defence against it.

'Take the other Sunday for example. . . .'

The sand prickled and irritated her. She felt her legs becoming numb. She was shaking with cold now.

'I think I'll go and get dressed,' she began, hoping that he would depart tactfully; but he remained standing there, obviously determined to make the most of his chance.

'That Sunday, yes. It was beautiful weather in the morning, warm and sunny, but then there was a sudden downpour. . . .'

She struggled to her feet, trying to turn her back on him without seeming too demonstratively unfriendly; after all, he had only wanted to help. At the same time she racked her brains to think of something light and straightforward to say that would round things off. 'You must have your work cut out on days like that.' In profile now, stomach in. Far away she could make out the safety of the changing-hut.

'Work cut out? I should say so. And that day was worse than most. You see, when it started to rain, people just dropped everything and ran. You should have seen the mess! There was a group up on that slope. . . .' He pointed towards the little hill that she remembered so well, all too well (was it only a fortnight ago? The air was so pure! The sky so high!). 'Elderly, respectable people they were too, but the things they left behind them! Rugs and packets of food and sun-tan lotion and goodness knows what else! I'd never seen anything like it. I can tell you that it took some doing, clearing up. I took the food home for the dog.'

She could see them all in her mind's eye, a colourful and variegated **group** up there on the slope in their sun-dresses and sport-shirts and **sun-hats**. But *elderly* people . . . ? The thought struck her painfully. **Had she become old?** Suddenly and for no reason? Without any **warning?** No, she wouldn't stand here any longer, listening to this silly old man.

'A strange lot they were,' continued the rubbish collector, rubbing his brown chin with his hand. 'You'd think that people of that age – I mean, they were elderly, respectable people – you'd think they'd know how to behave, if you see what I mean, but the things they got up to, you just wouldn't believe it!'

Got up to? What did he mean?

'There were two of them especially, a woman and a man, and they couldn't have been married either – married people don't carry on like that at that age. . . .'

'What did they do?' She couldn't restrain her curiosity, at the same time as she felt an irresistible gaiety rising within her. She was a stranger, anonymous as far as he was concerned, safe and inviolable from the speculations of this old gossip.

'What did they do? You might as well ask what they didn't do!' The old man nodded meaningfully and looked at her sideways. 'When it started to rain and everyone else ran for shelter, those two decided they would stand under that big chestnut tree you can see over there. . . .'

Of course she could see the tree! Their chestnut tree!

'And I can tell you they were at it! I was sheltering under the boat-house over there' – he pointed – 'so I could see them clearly. I mean, I see all kinds of things down here on the beach during the summer, but such decent, elderly people. . . . She stuck to him like a leech. You'd almost think she was going to rape him on the spot. They looked like a couple of newly-weds who couldn't wait till they got inside.'

'Oh no, you're exaggerating!' She had to protest. Her feeling of superiority had dwindled away. What the man said opened such vistas for her, such overwhelming possibilities. . . . She felt almost dizzy as she imagined the two of them up there under the tree in an abandoned embrace.

'Exaggerating? That I'm not, I can tell you. I was standing behind that boat-house watching them, just as sure as I'm standing here talking to you now. The Sunday after Midsummer's Day. It couldn't have been more obvious what they were up to if they'd just laid down and got on with it! And in full view of anyone who went past.'

'Were they . . . really intimate? Was she really so forward?' She couldn't hold back the question.

'Intimate? I'll say they were intimate! She was all over him. She knew what to do with her fingers, that elderly little miss. Excuse me, but you understand . . .'

'Of course.' Her voice was almost inaudible. She just wanted him to go on talking. She could see them now with her own eyes, how they grabbed at each other greedily, voluptuously, only just hidden by the branches, her and Mr Eldmann.

'She wasn't bad looking either, the little lady.' He was aware that he had captured her interest and made the most of this rare opportunity, tried to engage her complicity. 'A bit on the plump side, but she carried it well. As far as I could see anyway.' She felt his eyes on her swim-suit and blushed.

'What about him?' she whispered, quite shameless now, roused by the man's forthrightness and her own wild dreams. Yet were they just dreams? He must have seen *something* under the tree, something bold, something exceptional.

'Him? Oh, he was a lad who knew how to get what he was after. A fine-looking chap too, tall and well built, the manager type with a beard and glasses.' (*Glasses?*) 'He was the crafty sort as well, I'm sure I saw him fiddling about with one of the other women in the party whilst they were all lying sunbathing; a younger one, quite pretty she was. . . .'

No really, she'd had enough of standing here listening to the fantasies of this old peeping Tom. She was frozen through as well. 'You really must excuse me,' she said, 'but I've got to get changed. I'm getting cold standing here like this.'

'Oh yes, of course,' he said at once. 'It's chilly today.' He'd got the story off his chest.

'Yes,' she said. 'Cheerio, then.'

'Bye. Nice talking to you!'

She went off, leaving him standing there. She could feel his eyes on her as she climbed up towards the changing-hut. What a tale.

'What a tale!' she exclaimed half aloud. The dirty imagination of a randy old man. Revolting! But on the other hand he *had* seen something. A sweet memory was pushing its way through: they had stood close together beneath the tree and she had been aware of the strong, clean scent of his shirt, of his hair, the taste of his blood on her tongue, the moisture under his arms. Who could say exactly what had happened? Memories, dreams and visions melted together.

I wonder if he's still looking after me? Suddenly she felt gay and cheerful. I'll give him something to look at all right! She tried to wiggle her bottom provocatively as she walked the last few yards to the changing-hut, but wasn't sure if she had managed it.

Inside in the sheltered half-darkness she took off the swim-suit and delivered up her nakedness to the stillness, which was broken only by the sound of her own breathing. Salt and sand made her body tingle all over and she became conscious of an itch in her lower regions, which she found her way to, blushing, with her fingers.

But as she passed the chestnut tree on her way back to the bus-stop, she was once again floating in the clouds, safe from her own little sensual indiscretions. It seemed to her that the tree was standing there like a monument to their sacred, inviolable devotion in this world and the next. And in the bus on the way home she sat with her hair gathered under her hat and her bag safely on her lap, feeling the sand trickle between her toes inside her stockings, and thought about the last time, the Sunday after Midsummer's Day, when she had been sitting here in this very place travelling back home from the beach trip with the others. Mr Eldmann had been sitting there on the seat just behind her, together with Miss Leander, and she had heard him laughing and breathing just behind her back and seen his reflection in the window, broken up by sudden flashes of sunshine and by splashes of rain into joyful, blind spots. And she thought romantically that that was surely the highest moment for her, his face in a halo of sunshine after their experience together; and nothing, not even peeping Toms on the beach or malicious speculation about identity, name or behaviour, could destroy that moment and that memory. She was once again so happy and secure, and so grateful for all the times they had had; she was certain that in the realm of eternal life they were already standing at the altar as bride and groom.

But that evening at supper, when she was to her great surprise placed beside a Mr Aleksander Kønig, a large and well-built man who had that very day moved into Number 11, and when Mr Kønig, no less surprisingly, placed his hand on her knee beneath the table-cloth, just after coffee had been served, she let it happen without making any fuss, without making the slightest attempt to protest at such shameless behaviour. Not even a flicker passed over her face as she watched the Consul, who was sitting opposite her, and who at that moment placed his hand on Mrs Sebastian's shoulder, whilst she felt the sand from the beach in her stockings trickling between her toes.

## · 11 ·

Rumours had already been circulating for several days about the new resident who was to move in after Mr Eldmann. The most widely differing speculations had been aired, but no one knew anything about him for certain. The question had been of little interest to Maude, as she was unable to conceive of a stranger moving in to Number 11 just like that. With a feeling of irritation she had watched the preparations, the cleaning and sorting out, the removal of Mr Eldmann's earthly possessions; but she had not really grasped the possibility that it might be happening soon, and her heart still, as it had always done, fluttered with devotion and missed a beat every time she had to walk past the closed door with the faded number 11 painted in black on the stained wood.

The first thing she noticed as she walked up the drive after her morning's excursion was a large, black motor cycle parked by the front door. In the hall she came upon Mrs Sebastian, who whispered, 'The new one's arrived!' before she vanished into the lounge, from where loud, merry voices could be heard.

At that moment the manageress put her head out and called, 'Oh, Miss Maude, you must come in and say hello to our new resident.' It was as if she had been lying in wait, ready to pounce on her the moment she came in the door.

So she was introduced to Mr Aleksander Kønig. He was quite tall and ruddy, stout and almost bald; but his eyes were friendly and kind and his handshake was warm and hearty. He was dressed in greyish-brown tweeds and smoking a cigar. A glasses case showed in his breast-pocket. The circle of hair around his round pate was reddish, with touches of grey. Maude could not conceive how they could let a man who looked like that move into Number 11, and she was filled with revulsion at the thought that this man was to lie in Mr Eldmann's bed, between Mr Eldmann's sheets. It was sacrilege! But she smiled politely and said hello and felt that he held her hand for an unnecessarily long time, at the same time as she was aware of the sand in her shoes (and suddenly remembered in all its details her conversation with the refuse collector), and because of that got a strange feeling that Mr Kønig was a part of what had happened to her that morning.

'Well, where have you been all day? We missed you at lunch-time.' The manageress was the soul of friendliness and seemed warmly interested; but it was obvious that she was not merely asking in order to make conversation. The others were also standing around smiling, as though they knew something. Or perhaps they were just curious. After all, it was a a rare event for Maude to go out all alone and stay out for most of the day.

'I had some errands in town. I told the maid in advance.' That was the usual thing when you were going to be away for a meal.

'Oh, I see.'

That seemed to satisfy them. She hoped that they had not noticed the blush which betrayed her. She remembered how the Consul had seen through her motives at the party. She had better be careful; they had eyes in the back of their heads. She hoped that they would forget her now and return to entertaining the new resident, letting her escape unnoticed. She was longing for her room, to be able to lie down on her bed alone with all her thoughts and impressions after this remarkable morning.

But they were just about to drink a glass of sherry in his honour. She was drawn into the circle once more; she even felt as if the others were deliberately putting her forward, almost pushing her into Mr Kønig's grasp, as he stood there so genial and flushed, with his cigar and glass in hand, chatting to the people around him.

'Miss Maude is our guardian angel,' someone said. The Consul of course.

'One of my oldest residents, and my very favourite one,' confided the manageress.

'Our little sweetheart.' It was Dr Lemb who came out with that – a man she for some reason hardly ever exchanged a word with. What did they all mean?

'Well, that's quite a recommendation!' said the newcomer, who was feeling expansive as a result of all the kindness and the strong drink. He took a step towards her. 'Look, you've got a little bit of God's nature on your shoulder.' He deftly picked a little piece of straw from her jacket. Everyone laughed. She felt hopelessly compromised.

'I . . . I went for a walk in the park.' She could still feel the sand between her toes.

'Here's to the park!'

'Here's to God's nature!'

They didn't believe a word of what she said. The sherry was passed round again. Suddenly she felt quite remote from the whole company and from all their gaiety. It was as if Mr Kønig's arrival was being used as an excuse, so that they could noisily put to flight the last still shadows left by the visit of silence to the house. They were all exerting themselves to manoeuvre Mr Kønig's portly figure into the gap left by Mr Eldmann. That was the reason why they had to encourage her to like him, and vice versa. And that was the reason why she constantly found herself in his loud-voiced vicinity, regardless of how silent and still and invisible she tried to make herself in order to be able finally to escape and be alone: in order that she together with Mr Kønig should restore the symmetry and the order of the boarding-house. At that moment she realized that they had all known it, they had been aware of her and Mr Eldmann's secret love but been too polite and too civilized to let it be apparent; and this thought was dreadfully upsetting to her, at the same time as she was deeply grateful to them. She looked around, but could not see Mrs Frank. Then she remembered that someone had mentioned that Mrs Frank was going to visit some relatives for a few weeks. She was relieved at the thought.

Now they were showing Mr Kønig some pictures from a distant event, a trip on which she had not been present, and were challenging him to identify the people he could see.

Well, he wasn't sure about that. He had to get his glasses out. He discovered the Consul and Dr Lemb, each on a bicycle, but was less sure of the others. Maude also gazed eagerly at the grey and white photographs, even though she had seen them countless times before. For some reason Mr Eldmann was not on any of them. She found herself standing beside Mr Kønig and could not understand why the fact that he wore glasses (or had red hair, for that matter) should be so distracting.

But the lively mood of the others finally penetrated even Maude's confusion and reserve. She allowed herself to clink glasses with the newcomer (at the Consul's suggestion), heard him explain that he was a sales representative and had been educated in England (and with a name like that he must come from a good family), and even dared to ask whether the large motor cycle which was parked by the steps belonged to him. The answer was in the affirmative, and Mr Kønig himself was generous enough to invite her immediately to allow him to take her on a trip around the neighbourhood. But he would never be a *real* resident of Number 11, said a voice within her again and again.

Later, when she had finally escaped and was lying resting, exhausted by the day's impressions, she dreamed about his voice and his warm hand, and his face, which was looking down at her smiling and cheerful with a large red beard. She felt as if she was falling and falling.

She heard him moving about inside Mr Eldmann's room, and her heart fluttered with devotion and missed a beat before she collected her thoughts together and realized that it was someone else now, a large and loud-voiced person by the name of Aleksander Kønig, who had demonstrated that he was happy to flirt a little, but who was almost as tall as the Consul and really rather vulgar despite his name and his English education.

However, at the evening meal she was to her surprise placed next to him. It was natural enough, considering that he was obviously given Mr Eldmann's empty place and Mrs Frank was away; but she couldn't help feeling that they had all had a hand in this clever arrangement and were now sitting and awaiting the result of their treacherous plan. Her consciousness of this made it impossible for her to concentrate on her food. She sat there keeping an eye on them just as she knew they were sitting there keeping an eye on her and Mr Kønig. And when, just after coffee was served, he leaned back in his chair and unbuttoned his jacket and in doing so dropped his serviette on the floor, and placed his hand on her knee as he bent down to retrieve it she took no notice whatsoever of his complete disregard for all good manners. She allowed the infringement to occur without the slightest change of expression, as if it was happening to her in a dream; for the action was so unbelievably vulgar and offensive (especially here at table!) that the whole thing seemed totally improbable. At the same time her anguished mind registered that this was precisely what everyone was sitting waiting for, that this was why they had manoeuvred them together here at the table. In defiance of those who were sitting there smiling and observant and were to blame for everything because they were in such a hurry to replace Mr Eldmann by someone else, she behaved as if nothing had happened as she watched the Consul, who just at that moment laid his hand on Mrs Sebastian's shoulder (as she offered him the tray of cakes for the second time), and her as she leaned towards him and smiled toothily.

For when you thought about it it *was* possible, she reasoned, when the dropped serviette had been safely gathered up and the intrusive hand had released its grip (had it really happened?), that it had been inadvertent, an accident. It wasn't easy for fat people to bend down, and one had to admit that Mr Aleksander Kønig was stout.

## · 12 ·

The Inspector came and wanted to interview them one by one. Nothing as serious as an interrogation, of course; no one was suspected of having done anything illegal. He just wanted to have a little talk with them, a private conversation with each of the residents in order to discover whether anyone might know or remember anything that could help the police with their investigations into the 'Eldmann affair'.

Maude felt almost feverish as she sat waiting to be called in. With a heart full of fear, but also with a thrill of danger, she felt that in the presence of an Inspector she could be tempted to confess everything; but she also knew that she must pull herself together. Just think if it became known (she completely forgot about the strange feelings she had had on the day that Mr Kønig had arrived); how meaningless, and how embarrassing now that it was all over. Though she would dearly love to show them. Wouldn't she just!

It was a reassuring thought also, that there was an Inspector in the house. After all, he was here in order to solve the mystery, to bring clarity and truth to them all, to re-establish order in the chaos that had arisen after the departure of Mr Eldmann. She felt that the simple fact of his presence here, the knowledge that all the loose threads were now gathered into the hands of authority, gave the impression that everything was under control. She at least would do all she could to help.

Then it was her turn, and she went in and closed the door after her. The Inspector was sitting at the manageress's desk (he was younger than she had expected, hardly over forty, no age at all for an Inspector, she thought – and realized immediately that he must be exceptionally good at his job). He offered her a chair. She sat down and answered his introductory formal questions stumblingly whilst she tried to accustom herself to the proximity of this very special man. He was wearing a well-cut grey suit, his thick dark hair fell forward over his forehead in a boyish way, his face was already sunburned and the blue eyes behind the attractive glasses were impartial but friendly.

He asked her if she had know Mr Eldmann ('the deceased') very well.

She had to answer yes to that.

Would she say particularly well?

What did he mean by 'particularly'?

Well, had they spent much time together, talked together a lot, had what one could call a 'private friendly relationship'?

Well, yes, one could certainly say that. She herself was one of those who had been living longest at the boarding-house and Mr Eldmann had been living there for several years as well, five if she remembered correctly. Of course they had had a relationship. Besides. . . . It slipped out involuntarily, because she knew that it was this other thing he would be interested to know about and she felt that she had no right to hide it from him any longer, in fact she longed to confess everything to him.

Besides what?

Besides, there was something else. . . . She wasn't sure whether it was of any interest to him, but actually the fact was that recently. . . . Well, recently they had had a very close relationship. (If she told him about it, then their love would be confirmed, would be immortalized with the help of this representative of order!)

Oh really? He was interested now, she could see that clearly.

Yes, actually she and Mr Eldmann had been engaged. As good as.

'Aha,' said the Inspector, taking notes. Then he looked at her with interest through his glasses, and Maude swallowed her shame and her pride and was happy and relieved that she had dared to say it. She felt so safe now. The Inspector was a man to whom one could tell everything.

He asked her gently if their engagement had been official, but she had to admit that it had been a secret; as far as she knew no one had known about it – that was the strange thing about living at a boarding-house like this. And she would be very grateful if it could remain like that, after what had happened. . . . Here she was overcome by tears, more to her surprise than to that of the Inspector.

His next question disappointed her, for she was prepared for anything now, ready to reveal all the details of her intimacy with Mr Eldmann if it should be necessary in order to serve the law; in fact she was positively looking forward to revealing her secret depths to this attractive man who was sitting there so calm and reassuring, and by his very presence restoring equanimity and peace in her and in the whole house. But all he said was: 'And during this time, did he say anything to you, or did he show you anything that you think might give a clue as to his real identity?'

At first she did not understand what he meant. For her, Mr Eldmann was Mr Eldmann! She could have described in detail his features, his habits, the whole of his person; neither well built, bespectacled nor red-haired (and now he was so clearly visible to her that she could almost smell the scent of that dark hair with its becoming hint of grey, of his aftershave, of the freshly starched shirt), but *Mr Eldmann*, the man himself, just as he had been, *her* Mr Eldmann, her lover. . . . Her bewilderment must have been clear from her face, for he added, 'Of course I can understand what a blow his death must have been for you, but it is nevertheless my unfortunate duty to try to clear up the question of your fiancé's identity. And if you think about the matter, I am sure that you will agree that it is in your interests too to get to the bottom of this. You see, the results of our investigations have demonstrated that Mr August Eldmann actually never existed.'

Never existed? But didn't he understand . . .

'And therefore it would be of the utmost importance for us if you, who must have been in his confidence, could remember a name, a chance remark, a letter with an address on it, anything at all that he might by chance have left with you.'

With this it finally became clear to her that the Inspector also represented the other side, this new 'order' which contradicted her own, and which they all were trying to trick her into accepting. The other residents at the boarding-house, the clerk at the mortuary, the peeping Tom on the beach – they were all trying to make Mr Eldmann into someone else, into a man she did not know and whom she certainly could not love, a stranger who fitted in with their own preconceptions, their sensationalism, their censoriousness, their lack of finesse and their filthy imaginations. She was the only one who really knew who and what he had been, and for that reason they were all doing their utmost to confuse her, to make her waver in her convictions, to get her on to their side, to obliterate all remaining traces. But as long as she resisted, her love was inviolable, she was sure of that (for it had also become obvious to her that it was that they were all striving to soil, to trivialize and destroy; they could not endure that which had existed in their midst, and yet at the same time so completely beyond their grasp). And she would resist, even though the Inspector's authority and self-confident charm made it a little difficult for her just at that moment.

'No,' she said finally. 'He left me nothing. We couldn't give each other anything. . . .'

'I understand.'

She observed that his interest was waning and felt isolated and unhappy because she could not explain to him what it was he had left her, the most wonderful, the only thing that mattered: himself as he had been, as he lived on in her as Mr Eldmann, unassailable as love itself.

'But I would nevertheless be most grateful if you could give the matter serious thought. Even the slightest hint might cast light on the matter. The solution to a mystery is often concealed in a seemingly trivial detail.'

She remembered something: the girls on the beach. The one who had waved. She stuttered, 'There – there was one thing. . . .'

He looked up.

'A girl he said he knew. She waved to him one day when we were on the beach together.' (Should she tell him about the embrace beneath the tree? Dare she?) 'It was apparently one of his pupils . . .'

'Really?' Renewed interest. 'Did you know the girl? Did he say who it was?'

'What? Oh, no, I'm afraid not. She was just a perfectly normal girl. Long brown hair. Pretty . . .'

'Right,' he said and made notes. Then he looked up and said in a different tone of voice, 'I've heard that – let's call him Mr Eldmann for the time being – was quite an authority at the boarding-house, that he was very popular and outgoing, you might almost say the life and soul of the place. Does that accord with your view of him?'

'Well, yes, I suppose so,' she said hesitantly. All at once she felt so uncertain; that was the sort of thing that was always said about people when they had passed away. She could remember clearly several occasions when Mr Eldmann had entertained them all with a story from the staff-room. Yes, he could be amusing sometimes. . . .

'Right,' he said, and wrote something again.

Then it was over, and she could go.

'Thank you very much for your assistance,' he said. 'And if you happen to remember anything, or come across anything, then please ring me or come and see me at my office. Here is my number and the address.' He gave her his card.

'Thank you very much,' she said, and almost curtsied to him. She went towards the door.

'Would you mind asking Miss Leander to come in? Thank you.'

But he *had* left her something else, something extremely concrete! Gripped by a sudden eagerness, she hurried up the stairs after having signalled an all clear to a nervous Miss Leander. She did have something of his, something significant that could perhaps provide a clue.

His waistcoat was still lying in her drawer. She pulled it out, unfolded it, held it up and studied it from all angles. Dark blue suit material with discreet white stripes. The silk of the back was a little worn and the half belt at the back was broken. On the shoulder seam there was a little pink cleaners' label fastened by two or three careless stitches. How typical of him not to remove it. She had to smile, even though the waistcoat reminded her so painfully of that last evening, how elegant he had looked in dark blue with stripes, while they were dancing together.... The number on the label was so worn that it was illegible, but she was happy and excited nevertheless. It demonstrated a concrete link between Mr Eldmann as she had known him and the outside world. Probably the cleaners in Balder Street.

The waistcoat had pockets too: a breast-pocket and two fob-pockets. In one of the fob-pockets there was a primrose and in the other a hairpin. But she hardly had time to register this important find, for her fingers had already located a folded piece of paper in the breast-pocket. Shaking with excitement she smoothed it out. After a few moments' bewilderment she realized that it was a restaurant bill, with the restaurant's name half torn off: '. . .ern Restaurant' it said. It could be the Lantern, a well-known restaurant in the town centre! She sat there overcome, looking at these new pieces of evidence. Not for a moment did it occur to her to run down to the Inspector with what she had found. He would simply confiscate the objects, send constables to the restaurant and the cleaners, and ask hundreds of questions, all for the purpose of proving that Mr Eldmann had really been someone else. For her, on the other hand, these two or three insignificant objects represented invaluable links between Mr Eldmann as he had been and his surroundings. A flower, a hairpin and a slip of paper from his own waistcoat with the cleaners' label and the illegible number – wasn't that proof? Did not these things constitute a system of co-ordinates that yet again assigned him to her, definitively and unambiguously?

She picked up each object separately, examined it and imagined its history. A primrose whispered of May, changeable weather and wind, a stroll in the park. Look at the flowers, the bees, how they dance over the flowers, which hardly dare to open themselves shyly. She can see his straight, slim figure with a hat and a light overcoat, with a cheerful primrose on his dark lapel. He walks along as if he is intoxicated by the new scents, the unpredictable weather, like a man in love. Then suddenly it starts to rain, a green and golden rain which filters down through the fresh leafy crowns of the avenue in the park; his fingers fumble with the awkward umbrella, then he gives up and takes shelter from the downpour beneath a chestnut tree. . . .

Then he is sitting in the Lantern Restaurant, eating dinner at a quiet table in the background. At the table just next to him he becomes aware of a woman. She is in her forties, a little plump with brown hair, which is fastened up (the hairpin), but still extremely attractive. He thinks she looks like a goddess. 'What weather! Have you ever seen anything like it?'

His voice.

'November rain.' She is sitting there so chaste and dignified at her table, but indicates to him that she is just as entranced by the marvel of this May day as he is himself. He leans back on his chair and opens a button on his jacket, his serviette falls on the floor and, as he bends down to pick it up, he places a hand gently on her knee. Then they are sitting at the same table drinking coffee and eating cream sponge, and his knee touches hers under the cloth and he says that she makes him think of a nymph, the way she holds herself, her attractiveness, and she lets her hand rest on the white cloth where his hand has just rested. And in the taxi on the way home her hair becomes ruffled and she lets him pick up a hairpin that has fallen out, lets him keep it as a little souvenir because he is so polite and so attentive and does not try to kiss her, just tickles her a little with his beard, and she is happy, so happy. . . .

But on the back of the bill from the restaurant there was something she had overlooked: an address. She was jolted out of her dreams: *c/o Holder, 82 Strandgaten.* It was written in a clear hand (his? She didn't know) and bore unmistakable evidence of a past that she did not know and could not imagine. What was the meaning of this unknown address? Was it a place where he had once lived, before he came to the boarding-house? Was it the address of someone he knew, a girl-friend perhaps? At once the hairpin also appeared to her in a new light. She was losing him in this way as well! The man for whom she had felt such tenderness in the taxi was instantaneously transformed into a Casanova with a moustache and glasses, a man about town, a leading light of society, the life and soul of the party. Perhaps he was red-haired and well built into the bargain! How could she hold on to him when there was so much of his past that she did not know about? All at once she had the feeling that she was faced with the enormous task of unravelling and absorbing all this, if she did not want to lose him for ever. And at the same time she became aware of the need to tell someone about them both, even more strongly than she had felt it during her conversation with the Inspector a little while ago; everything about their love affair, their secret life, in order to hold this fast, to imprint a picture of them both, him and her, on something outside herself and her own memories, in order to rescue their love from the deformation of oblivion, the tacit conspiracy of her surroundings. She had to find someone she could confess to, in order to confirm to herself once and for all that she had sinned, in her heart at least. And she knew to whom she had to go, the only person who would not dismiss her with incomprehension or, worse, with condescension: Miss Leander.

· 13 ·

She had no plan, did not even really know how she was going to manage to express what she wanted to say, but she felt nevertheless extremely determined and, in a strange kind of way, confident as she knocked on Miss Leander's door. She could hear a faint sound of radio music from inside the room, which was turned down before a voice answered, and immediately afterwards the door was opened nervously, just a crack.

'Oh, it's you!'

'Yes, excuse me for bothering you, but I wonder if I could come in for a moment? I. . . . There's something I should like to talk to you about. Something important.'

'Oh yes, of course, do come in. But you'll have to excuse me. . . .' Her hand indicated that not everything was in perfect order in the little room.

So they sat down opposite each other, and Maude noticed for the first time how ill and worried Miss Leander looked. It was so noticeable that she burst out, 'But, my dear, whatever is the matter?'

And when the girl opposite only shook her head and looked down without answering, she repeated, 'Are you not well? Is there anything I can help you with?' And she laid a reassuring hand on the arm across the table.

At this touch it was as if something melted in Miss Leander, as if she sank down a little. Her face seemed to grow rounder, her features softer, like those of a child, and it seemed to Maude that her eyes were all at once filled with tears, and her mouth opened as if to cry out. But she merely whispered, 'That dreadful Inspector!'

Then she just sat there, staring down at the table miserably. Maude did not understand anything. Was it the Inspector from this afternoon she meant? That nice, straightforward young man? What had happened?

'What was the matter with him?'

She had to question her as patiently as a mother, for it was clear that Miss Leander was on the verge of breaking down. 'Did he do anything to you?'

'He kept asking questions, wanted to know everything . . . just everything! As it if was something criminal!'

'Criminal? What? That poor Mr Eldmann died?' Maude had completely forgotten what she had come to talk to her friend about. She just had to get to the bottom of this and find out what had happened to Miss Leander.

'No, not that he died. . . .' Miss Leander shook her short, brown, permed curls and could hardly answer. Heavy tears dripped down on to the table-top and she held on with both hands to Maude's comforting one, making her into an accomplice. She felt the pressure of her own melancholy grief, which urged her to join in with her friend's.

'But you must tell me what it's all about! Perhaps I can help you. What was it the Inspector did to you?' Her voice shook. She was begging. She was on the point of tears herself. 'You know that you can depend on me.'

'Oh yes, I do know that, Miss Maude, and I've thought several times that I should have told you all about it, but it was so difficult. . . . And now there's no one who can help me any longer!' The words came from a long way away, lonely and despairing, one by one.

Maude felt the suffering in her own breast, mixed with pity and misgivings, for this must be something to do with Mr Eldmann's death, it had to be some terrible detail she didn't know about. And in an imploring voice, as if she were asking more for her own sake than for that of the friend she was supposed to be helping, she repeated, 'What did you mean by criminal? Was it the way he died?'

'No, not that.' It came out as a whisper, monosyllabic, from the other side of the table. 'He just asked questions, had to know everything, cross-examined me as if I was nothing . . . nothing but a . . .'

'But why on earth should he do that?'

'Because we were engaged!' A cry so full of sorrow and loss that Maude did not at once grasp its meaning.

'Engaged? Who? To whom?' And her own voice rose as she gradually realized what it was her friend was saying.

'August and I! We were going to get married! This autumn. . . . At the end of the holidays!' She hid her face and abandoned herself to her grief.

At that moment there was a curious displacement in Maude's understanding of what she had just heard. As the full consequences of her friend's announcement dawned on her, she realized simultaneously that this was just a new tactic, a trick on 'their' side to shake her faith in everything that was precious and sacred. The fact that poor Miss Leander seemed to believe the tale she was telling, indeed seemed beside herself with grief at the loss of her beloved 'fiancé', simply went to show what power 'they' had, these ideas against which she was struggling and which she must not let herself be vanquished by if she wished to keep alive the flame of love which burned so brightly and purely in her heart.

But at the same time she was conscious of the fact that this too was a part of Mr Eldmann's past that she must absorb, forgive and understand and make her own if she was going to preserve her picture of him, of the triumph over loneliness, their indissoluble union.

Strangely enough, these opposing impulses did not create any conflict in her consciousness. They were both justified and completely necessary to her balance and peace of mind, and in addition they had a mutually neutralizing effect, with the result that her reaction was muted, giving rise to a lesser feeling of shock and revulsion than each on its own would have done. Therefore it was with a strange feeling of calmness and detachment that she squeezed the hand of the unhappy woman and exclaimed, 'Oh, you poor dear! How dreadful! I really had no idea! Were you really engaged?' – in order to discover more about this matter which she had for the sake of clarity to get sorted out. At the same time she was careful to convey the correct impression of sympathy in her voice and in her expression, so that Miss Leander should not notice that she did not believe a word of this tissue of lies spun by an unbalanced and hysterical female.

'No, no one knew about it.' Miss Leander pulled herself together and tried to restrain her tears, grateful for the opportunity of talking about it at last. 'We kept it secret because we didn't want too much talk here at the boarding-house. I'm sure you can understand that! We were going to get a flat this autumn. . . . Oh, Miss Maude!' She burst into tears again, then pulled herself together after a while and carried on talking, whilst Maude sat there taut, at breaking point, like a bow drawn back to shoot, and struggled to keep her thoughts in order, maintain finely drawn boundaries, evaluate hair-fine nuances, preserve established categories.

'It really all started last Christmas party. He danced with me. . . .

But we had been interested in each other for a long time, or at least I had in him. . . . We simply fell in love, I don't know if you can understand that, but it was the first time it had happened to me.'

Maude nodded; yes, she could understand that. She felt more and more pity for that poor misguided creature.

'But this Inspector had to know everything, of course. Every little detail. He kept asking and asking. . . . He made me feel like nothing better than. . . . Well, I know we didn't behave as we should have done. . . . We took liberties, we couldn't wait, we were so much in love with each other. . . . You can't imagine. . . . We were almost discovered several times! That awful Mrs Frank. . . .'

It was as if these indiscretions made her sorrow easier to bear, at the same time as they increased the scepticism of the listener. Now it was clear that the unfortunate woman was making it all up.

'And I told him everything, everything he wanted to know, except that. . . .' And at this point it was obvious that a recollection occurred to her again and made her voice anguished and her face swollen and ugly as if it were damming up an unbearable flood of grief: '. . . except that I'm pregnant. I'm going to have his baby! What shall I do, Miss Maude? What shall I do?'

'Have you got morning sickness, then?' Maude thought aloud in a flat, toneless voice.

'I did the first few weeks. We were so happy about it, you can't imagine. . . . But now – what shall I do now? An unmarried mother. . . . I'm desperate!'

Maude studied her stomach, but couldn't find any sign of a swelling, as expected. Miss Leander's imaginary pregnancy did not interest her particularly; it was simply a consequence, unappetizing but logical, of her other fantasies. She thought with a shudder of Mrs Sebastian's ill-behaved brood.

But at the same time she had to try to accommodate this new ambience of drama and seduction to the picture of her Mr Eldmann. Reluctantly she had to admit that he had been a ladies' man and had had a way with the weaker sex; although this admission bore of course no relation whatsoever to Miss Leander's sick fantasies. Despite all this, she had to ask, 'But are you quite sure? I mean, a hundred per cent sure that you're expecting this child? Mr Eldmann's child?'

A startled glance back. . . .

'Am I sure? I tell you, I've never even looked at another man. He was my first. I've always dreamed about someone like him, all my life. . . .' She was on the verge of tears again. 'And you wouldn't believe how good he was. . . . He made it so easy for me. . . . Oh, I'm sorry.' She fumbled for her handkerchief.

Maude felt for her in this, deeply and sincerely. The deflowering of a virgin had always seemed to her to be a moment of eternity, filled with poetry and pain. The irreplaceable vanquished by the irresistible. The very thought – and how often had she not thought it? – brought a lump to her throat. Why was it woman's fate to have to suffer like that? And she wasn't just thinking of the physical side of it, of the brutal assault, the bitter pain (how often she had imagined the pain, how it must hurt!), but of the degrading messiness of the whole affair. Just to think of another person so close to you in bed (or on the sofa, or on the grass, or wherever it was that you were overpowered), of the embarrassing, inelegant undressing, of immodest caresses, of the respective positions of the limbs (which she had worked out for herself originally, long before she had discovered the facts from books). The whole thing appeared to her to be ugly and undignified, and she could not understand that such degradation had anything to do with love. So she felt sorry for the poor girl who was sitting there still holding on to her hand, in despair because she had had to submit to such a fate, and now you could see the result. Even though she did not for one moment believe the story about the child, of course!

So deep and genuine was her sympathy that she got up from her chair, and suddenly found herself on the other side of the little table, beside her friend, sitting on the arm of her chair and with her arm around her narrow shoulders (as Mr Eldmann had perhaps sat once in a distant past that did not concern her in the slightest, but which she had to know about in order to know him fully), comforting her with her closeness. And this warm, generous contact released a flood of tender feelings in both; the rape victim cried openly with her face against the soft material of Maude's blouse, whilst Maude let silent tears fall on to her friend's permed hair. She had always cherished maternal feelings for that defenceless little girl.

Afterwards there was not a great deal they could say to each other.

Maude repeated automatically that she was so sorry for her friend, at the same time as she concentrated on avoiding focusing on the mental image of the supposed cause of the misfortune. Concrete mental pictures of their intimacy (which was in any case the invention of a virgin's morbid fantasy) had to be resisted at all costs, as they would only bring confusion and disruption to her own clear-cut perspectives. On the other hand, she had already forgiven him his small amorous adventures from the time when she could not have had any claims upon him; more than that, she almost felt pride on his behalf, that he had been so sought after, so passionate (and at the same time so loyal, tender and considerate towards her, and above all so romantic, as she was), and she felt a deep gratitude that she was the one who had owned the fullness of his love.

As she left, Miss Leander stammered out her thanks. It had been so good to talk to someone about it at last; she had been thinking for a long time that she should have come and told her the whole story, but it had been so difficult, and now she was so grateful to her. Maude must forgive her for making such a scene about it, but she surely understood how dreadfully upset she was. And she must beg her not to breathe a word about it to anyone; because if this came out now it would be the end for her. She couldn't even bear to think of it.

And Maude gave her assurances and promises and pressed the girl's trembling body to herself one more time before she whispered farewell. She felt so secure in her own memories, in her own world where no facile lies, no ambiguities would be allowed to intrude and destroy the ordered calm, her own harmony, her and Mr Eldmann's harmony, the only thing she possessed in this world.

But on the way back to her room she was nevertheless seized by unease, as if something was not as it should be; and she stopped in the corridor, hesitated, then turned around and walked back, down the stairs. She was still not really sure of what she wanted to do (but was spurred on by a muffled cough from Number 11 just as she went past. These noises he made, just as if he'd always lived there! Her heart trembled and danced). She went through the hall and into the dining-room, from where she could hear voices in the lounge; women's voices, Mrs Sebastian. She snapped up a fragment, a sentence, like an accompaniment to the thoughts that were whirling around in her own head, just as she slipped past.

'. . . and now she's going around imagining that she was having an affair with him, that they were actually *engaged*!'

Of course! She realized at once that it was Miss Leander they meant; it was clear to everybody that she was in a highly nervous state and that she was making the whole thing up. So it had all come out after all, poor little thing. . . .

But there was still a faint unease at the back of her mind, for the idea had suddenly seized her that it could just as easily have been her they were sitting talking about. She didn't know why she felt that. Was it just her imagination? Something which had been said just before or just after what she had overheard but had only half taken in? The tone of voice? The whole atmosphere? She didn't know what it was, but she could not dismiss the thought until she was standing in the soft light of the library, looking along the shelves for their book, the book with the secret mark of their liaison. . . .

*November Rain.* There it was. She pulled it out and turned over the pages (from the dining-room she could hear that the table was being set for the evening meal), found page 18, searched, read, but could find neither his mark nor that particular passage, the formulation of his undying love for her. She had to hold the book up to her eyes. She peered at the white margin: this was where the mark had been, so neat but at the same time so clear, from him to her, without any doubt, and yet. . . . She searched the pages before and after (could she have been so wrong about it?), read and searched, to no avail. But it had been on page 18, the number of her room (seven numbers from his own!). Could she have pulled out a different book in the half-darkness that time? Would she ever be able to find that section again? Would this little straw also be snatched from her grasp?

Suddenly she felt she was losing him. For the first time she was really frightened: the memory of him was being slowly distorted, one detail after another grew fainter, then became hazy, disintegrated. . . . So much had happened these last few days, so many distractions, so much confusion. . . . His face! She had his face. That she did have. The little beard, the eyes, the high, pale forehead, the hair. . . . Was she for a moment in doubt about the hair colour? Rubbish! He had dark hair. Mr Eldmann had dark hair with a becoming hint of grey. Of that she was certain. But his voice could no longer be isolated and distinguished, and his figure seemed to stretch and overflow in all directions, now shorter, now longer, now fatter, now thinner. . . . Until she insisted that he was on the short side and rather slender; then it stopped and immediately filled out the correct proportions to her inner eye. But it could not be retained like that and shifted out of focus again, to her sorrow and horror.

She stood there, lost, staring at the unmarked page, her fading memories undermined by the lack of certitude.

Then she was sitting at the dining-table and everything was different, was lighter and more cheerful around her, calmer and more optimistic inside. She sat eating egg and ham whilst the Consul and Aleksander Kønig (still wearing the same boring tweed jacket) discussed the climate in France and England, and after that their wartime experiences. When she sat facing forward in this way, and at the same time watched him out of the corner of her eye, she could when he sat in a certain way or moved in a particular fashion suddenly have the feeling that it was *him* sitting there close beside her, enjoying his meal; as if a film were being played superimposed on a photograph, so that outline, colour or perhaps just a detail occasionally matched up and was identical. She both liked and was put out by this double vision, for Mr Aleksander Kønig was not Mr Eldmann; the very comparison was odious. But it was perhaps precisely because the difference between the two men was so great – and that fact was incontrovertible – because not the slightest blending of their two figures was possible, even in the smallest detail, that these innocent little optical illusions aided her, in a perfectly innocuous way, to fill the chasm of emptiness that at times threatened to engulf her, and allowed her to tolerate this weakness, this somewhat disrespectful game from which she distanced herself at the same time. And the fact that they were sitting at table helped as well. The formality of the mealtime endowed the relationships between the residents with the static calm of a controlled setting. This allowed the possibility of fantasy and escapism without any risk attached. (In the lounge, where they were occasionally present at the same time, she hardly glanced at him, and if they chanced to pass each other, she hardly dared to greet him.)

So long as one kept within the bounds of good taste and tact, she thought; and she realized from the suppressed smiles on the men's faces that the conversation must be touching on a rather risqué subject.

Mrs Sebastian laughed out loud with her mouth open and cheeks flushed, and asked Mr Kønig across the table, 'Do you really mean to say that all dead men have . . . ? And she gestured with her finger in a way that made her meaning abundantly clear, as she giggled once more, leaning against the Consul.

'What is it, Mummy?' asked little Trine, and was shushed.

'Well, I can't actually guarantee that they *all* do, ma'am,' replied Mr Kønig with a self-satisfied air; 'but I can assure you that it is quite common. I had opportunity enough to observe that during the war.'

'Yes, there's certainly something in that,' parried the Consul, not wishing to be outdone. 'I once witnessed a car accident on the motorway to Lyons – a dreadful affair, one of the cars burst into flames and the petrol tank exploded before anyone could do anything.'

'Oh dear, how gruesome,' came the manageress's voice.

'Yes, it was terrible, but as I said, there was nothing that could be done. And when the fire had burned itself out and we could get close, we could see a man sitting in the driver's seat, stone dead of course, and half charred. . . . To tell the truth, he was the colour of a grilled chicken.'

'Oh come, really!' Half laughing.

'But what I was going to say was that the way he was sitting – because his clothes had all been burned off him, of course – it was quite clear that he had . . . you know.'

'Exactly!' concluded Mr Kønig.

'How gruesome,' repeated the manageress.

'What does the doctor say?' Mrs Sebastian turned to Dr Lemb, who had also listened attentively to the conversation. 'What is your opinion of this . . . *theory*?'

'Well,' began Lemb, 'it's not easy to say. . . . We do know that it happens, but it does of course depend on the cause of death. I think it quite likely that a so-called violent death, a way of dying that involved fear and pain for the dying person, and therefore activated the adrenalin reflex and thus the heart and muscular activity . . .'

Maude listened to the conversation with rapt attention. She completely forgot that this was a most unsuitable subject for the dining-table. She felt that it concerned her in an inexplicable, almost mystical way, concerned her relationship to the deceased. It both moved and appalled her that death could give a man an erection. All in all she found it poetic (and at the same time most unpoetically exciting – she could feel a strong urge to go to the toilet) to think about a lifeless figure, a handsome man with the gleam of sweat on his brow over dark sunken eyes, and with his lance of desire at the ready; as with men who slept, but a sleep from which there was no awakening. She thought of her last meeting with Mr Eldmann, in the parlour that night after the birthday party; she thought of the thrill she had felt at her minor infringement of his modesty, a man already marked by death, a prince who was returning home to the land of dreams. How beautiful these figures appeared to her, how desirable in death when they could no longer inflict their own desire upon a woman's body, and yet. . . . In that state, 'it' was no longer dangerous or threatening, then 'it' was almost moving, a symbol of love's aspirations to defy death. . . . How it touched her, all this. . . .

Coffee was served and the subject of discussion was dropped.

Mr Kønig suddenly leaned over towards Maude and asked her in a low voice if she realized how much she resembled that woman in the painting. The similarity was striking, he asserted: the same distant, refined charm, the same elegant figure too incidentally. . . . Really a most remarkable coincidence.

Although she was both bewildered and embarrassed, Maude was not particularly surprised that he should so casually intrude into the secret territory she shared with Mr Eldmann. It suddenly seemed to her that she had heard him comparing her with a nymph before, though she was unsure whether it was reality or a dream; and besides, it was a consolation to hear Mr Eldmann's words, even though they were formulated by the lips of this man who had no business to say them, and in the vulgar flirtatious accents of the primitive male of the species. She half expected him to nudge her with his knee under the table, and thought irritatedly and half reprovingly that it would have been better if he had had a little beard, or at least some hair on his head (even if it was red). However, this time it was his hand, as it took a piece of cake and afterwards remained lying next to hers, which was holding the fine porcelain cup (the coffee was still rather on the warm side); his hand, which was lying so dangerously close that she could not avoid the thought: now he's going to try *that* trick; so near that it was unavoidable (and what was more, both of their hands were half concealed by the flower arrangement and by the serviette, which he had already laid down). And just as she expected, she felt a little finger against her own, a slow, intimate movement (which one would hardly have believed a man like Mr Kønig capable of, so large, so loud, so entirely lacking in finesse), which lasted far too long for there to be any question of chance or accident. And just like his first assault on her, that time he had laid his hand on her knee, she was left with a feeling of unreality. This could not be happening to *her*; it was too demonstrative, too obvious, yes, too banal to be able to happen in real life, and in addition an unheard-of transgression against all decent table manners and common politeness. So she pretended that she had not noticed anything and turned towards him and thanked him prettily for the compliment (for he had remarked that she was so like one of the goddesses, the most beautiful one), and he looked at her, friendly and cheerful as he always was, and said, 'You are a funny little thing.' And raised his coffee cup to empty it.

Just think, a funny little thing.

But no more was said, to her grudging disappointment.

A glance from Mrs Sebastian over the empty cake dish made it plain to her that their stolen tête-à-tête had been registered, and confirmed that they were all waiting for developments. But instead of feeling indignant about their manipulations (for she was no longer in any doubt that the others were aiming deliberately at propelling her and Mr Kønig into each other's arms, on the basis of some crazy logic about the vacuum left by Mr Eldmann), she was filled with defiant pride at the knowledge that they were being observed. She had not forgotten the comment about the imaginary affair and engagement, which she had overheard from Mrs Sebastian recently. Although that had of course been intended to refer to poor Miss Leander.

## · 14 ·

Number 82 was an ordinary five-storey block of flats with a grey façade decorated with crumbling ornamentation and projections which bore witness to a different age, a better age when architects still had time and energy left over to concern themselves with such luxuries as pleasing the eye and builders still had resources enough to splash out on unprofitable aesthetics.

Actually the style suited Mr Eldmann, thought Maude, who liked such old buildings, but this particular house was in a state of some decay, so it was hardly credible that. . . . She hesitated, despite the fact that she had made her decision; she knew that she had to find the address and find out what she could about Mr Eldmann's past in order to find peace, to re-establish some kind of order, sort out her turbulent thoughts, gain control over her impulses (a couple of minutes ago she had seen Mr Kønig coming out of the house and had almost fainted with surprise and shock, until she saw that the man was nowhere near as tall as Mr Kønig, and anyway he was slimmer; she had been deceived by a tweed coat). She was not herself, she suffered from this uncertainty, which was not even a genuine uncertainty but an artificially induced one, a false feeling that things were changing, that nothing was remaining constant, that the passage of time was distorting and obscuring everything uncontrollably; and yet she knew that nothing could change her love for Mr Eldmann.

There was the number, 82, on a dilapidated board. So it was this house. No further doubt was possible. She walked resolutely up to the entrance. Holder, the name was. None of the labels by the row of battered bell-pushes was legible. She would have to go in.

On the stairway, daylight filtered in fitfully through filthy window-panes, and she had to bend down every time she wanted to read the name by a doorbell. It was an effort, and she felt extremely awkward. She jumped when a dog suddenly reacted to her presence and began to bark behind a door with the name of Peterson. A baby yelled. There was a faint rustling of water in pipes. Stone steps worn by feet, wooden banisters worn by hands. She carried on half-heartedly. She no longer knew what she had thought of achieving by coming here; it was impossible to connect this dusty staircase, these peeling walls, these battered doors with Mr Eldmann. What had her beloved been doing here in this house? How could he have been Mr Eldmann and at the same time have lived here, in conditions like this? She suspected that it had been a mistake to try to find clarity and help in these strange surroundings, to move the mystery associated with Mr Eldmann's existence away from where it belonged, namely at the boarding-house. What could she expect to find here, if not greater distance, more questions, greater uncertainty?

But it was not certain that he had lived here, even though the address she had found did suggest that. Perhaps it was an acquaintance of his? Perhaps a girl-friend? The thought impelled her onwards from door to door, with and without sounds from inside, with and without smells, scratches, traces of people who had nothing to do with her lover.

Then she found the door, at last! J. Holder it said on the brass plate. There weren't many brass plates on this staircase; perhaps it wasn't that bad after all. Out of breath, she pressed the bell. What was she going to say now?

A thin, elderly woman opened the door. 'Yes?'

'I should like to know. . . . I have a question I must ask you!' She blurted it out to stop herself from becoming completely tongue-tied. Then nervously, 'You *are* Mrs Holder, aren't you?'

'I am Mrs Johanna Holder, yes.'

'Yes, well, you're the person I need to talk to.' She knew that she was making a rather ridiculous impression, but that did not bother her now, now the only important thing was to make herself understood. 'It's about a man you knew, I mean, you perhaps. . . . Do you take in lodgers by any chance?'

'Yes, I rent out two rooms.' The thin woman looked at her with suspicion in her sunken features. 'Why, is there anything wrong?'

'Oh no, not at all, you mustn't think that. . . .' Her voice broke in despair. 'You mustn't think that. . . .' She looked pleadingly into the other woman's stern face as if to assure her that she was not in the habit of imposing on people she did not know with her own problems, but that this was a special case, and that it was of vital importance for her, a matter of her peace of mind, of life and death.

Life and death. The moment she thought the thought, she could see the image of Mr Kønig before her eyes; his importunate size, his weight, his large, flushed face, his voice, the whole of his offensive *vitality* appeared to her inner eye without her being aware of what it was that had caused her to think of him; perhaps it was just that these surroundings seemed to go with someone like him.

'It's to do with Mr Eldmann,' she interrupted herself, fastening her gaze on Mrs Holder's apron buttons. 'Mr August Eldmann. I just wanted to know if he had rented a room with you.'

The thin woman pondered for a moment.

'Eldmann. . . . Yes, there was a Mr Eldmann who used to live here. But it's a long time ago, about four years. Let me see. . . . It must have been in . . .'

'So he did live here!' exclaimed Maude. 'You had him living here, Mr August Eldmann?'

'Yes, August was his his first name, that's right. . . . But what of it?'

But not even her suspiciousness could stop Maude now. 'Then I must ask you to tell me everything about him, everything you can remember, what he said and did. . . . *Everything!*' Here at last was something to hold on to, an individual who had known him and who could have no interest in casting doubt on his person, on his very existence.

'But what on earth is the matter?' exclaimed the thin woman in alarm. 'Why have you come here demanding that I should tell you all this? What right have you? Who are you anyway?'

Maude realized that she would have to be more careful what she said, but she was too overwrought to be upset by the woman's unfriendly tone.

'I am his next of kin,' she lied breathlessly, and introduced herself. 'You see, Mr Eldmann passed away recently. Yes, it was a big shock for us all. Nobody was even aware that he was ill.' It didn't really disturb her to take such liberties with the story of his death, since nobody would be able to doubt her good intentions.

'Oh, but, my dear!' exclaimed Mrs Holder, and for a moment her pinched features lost their stern look. 'I had no idea. You must forgive me. . . . You get some strange people knocking at the door sometimes.'

'Of course.' Maude was only too happy to agree with her about that. 'But you do understand that it's important for me to get to know as much as possible about my dear . . . cousin. Unfortunately we had very little contact with each other in recent years.'

'Well, there's not all that much that I know,' said the woman defensively. 'It's not so easy to remember everything. . . . I've had so many lodgers over the years. But won't you come in?'

The living-room was rather gloomy, with windows facing out on to the backyard and the dark grey back wall of the next-door flats. There were potted plants in the windows behind light, flowered curtains; a crocheted cloth lay on the shining mahogany table with carved legs which stood in the middle of the floor, and on the cloth stood a heavy crystal vase with an inscription. Three armchairs and a pouffe, a little table with an ashtray, magazine and reading-lamp, a modern wireless, a bookshelf with more ornaments than books on it, a sideboard, a corner cupboard, a cold fireplace, a clock under a glass dome and a chandelier constituted, together with the table, the main furnishings of the room. Landscapes hung on the flower-patterned wallpaper.

Maude sat on the edge of one of the threadbare armchairs.

'What do you want to know about then?' the woman asked, in an attempt to make up for her unfriendly attitude a while back.

'Oh, anything. . . .' Maude was not so sure any more. She looked around the room, and could not, with the best will in the world, connect Mr Eldmann as she had known him with one single detail in here. Seized by a sudden fear of what she had set in motion, and of what she was going to hear in a moment, she said quickly, 'Just whatever you remember. What he did whilst he was living here with you, what habits he had, what sort of impression he made on you.'

'Well, now, let me see,' said the woman thoughtfully. 'He lived here for fourteen months, came in June and moved out in September of the following year, that must have been over four years ago.' That could be right. Mr Eldmann had come to the boarding-house nearly five years ago, a miserable wet day with a biting wind. She had heard the bustle in the corridor, looked out of the window and seen him carrying his suitcases up the drive. There was a taxi standing at the gate, and it was already getting dark. Later, at the table, she had noticed that his hands were shaking. That was all there was. He had said so little. But you always noticed the little details when a new resident arrived. . . .

'I had no reason to complain of him as a lodger. Always up to date with his rent. Always friendly and good-humoured, he was, he could be the life and soul of the party when he was in a good mood. You should have heard him – all those stories of his from England.'

'England?'

'Yes, he said he'd been in England. Studied there or something. He was a salesman for an English firm.'

Mr Eldmann a salesman?

'But wasn't he a teacher? At secondary school?'

'No, not whilst he was living here anyway. He wasn't the type either, if you see what I mean. He was far too full of life. He would never be able to sit at a desk like some dry old stick. . . . Well, of course, there are all sorts of teachers, and I don't mean to say anything against them, but Mr Eldmann would never have suited a job like that. Besides, he wasn't all that fond of children as far as I remember.'

'But are you *sure*? It is August Eldmann you're talking about? It's not possible that you're mixing him up with someone else?'

Maude felt as if she was sliding into deep water. What the woman was sitting there saying couldn't possibly be right. She had never heard that Mr Eldmann had been in England (though why not? Teachers often went on study trips. . . . There was a slight hope there), and the fact that he was a *salesman*. . . . The very suggestion seemed to her to be repellent. She didn't know many salesmen, but everybody knew that they were common people, not respectable at all. Mr Kønig, now, he was just the type; *he* was a salesman, and it was obvious from his lack of manners, his absence of refinement, all the vulgarity and pushiness of his behaviour. But to think of Mr Eldmann going from door to door with his suitcase of wares. . . .

'Are you *sure* it was him?'

'Of course I'm sure,' said Mrs Holder, almost irritated. 'I do know who I allow into the house. I know the sort of people I'm dealing with, let me tell you, and there are more than a few I've had to show the door.' She also had her pride.

Maude capitulated. Why should this woman have any interest in lying to her? She wasn't a part of the conspiracy at the boarding-house, she wasn't involved in any way. Her testimony was to be relied upon and had to weigh more heavily than what the others said, because they were only trying to confuse her and make matters more difficult. But to claim that Mr Eldmann had been a common salesman. . . . Could she really rely on Mrs Holder's memory?

'You must excuse me,' she said, passing her hand over her eyes. 'It's not so easy to grasp these things after all that's happened. As I said, we had very little contact . . . and memories . . . I'm sure you understand. Please go on.'

'What is it you'd like to know?' asked the woman, not unsympathetically. 'There isn't all that much to tell, you know.'

'What did he look like?'

'Oh. . . . What did he look like? Just like other men really; there was nothing special about him. Not particularly tall, a bit stout, going a bit thin on top. . . .'

'But he was tall and slim!'

She had to shout, because it was Mr Kønig's well-fed and unwelcome image that for some inexplicable reason appeared before her inner eye, more and more clearly with each word Mrs Holder uttered. When would all this end? And why him, of all people? She tried to think calmly; there were an inordinate number of corpulent salesmen with a bald patch on top who had been to England, so why should this oaf come barging his way into her imagination and pushing Mr Eldmann out? He was the one who never passed up any chance to embarrass her in the presence of other people; one word from her and she could get him thrown out. Really, what a way to behave! If it wasn't that she couldn't bear scenes. . . . And now, with the assistance of this hostile landlady's unreliable memory, he was coming along and violating her memories. It was like two pictures, where one imposed itself over the other and dominated it with its contours and its brutal outlines, coarsened and vulgarized it and made its delicate water-colours seem pale and unreal, even abstract. But *why* should this happen? Was it because he had laid his hand on her knee (and with the Consul obscene masculine approval, that time she had seen them exchanging glances)? Although recently there had been other things too: a hand that brushed against hers when he passed her the bread, a low-voiced compliment, an exaggerated heartiness when they met. . . . She felt besieged by him, by his loud voice, by his corpulence, his blustering manner; she found his whole way of being so loud, so offensive, so completely opposed to everything she found attractive in a man. And when she tried to defend herself, like at lunch yesterday, when she had practically speaking tried to drown him out by talking about Mr Eldmann, about the beach trip, about what a lovely time they had had, it was as if no one could really remember what had happened that Sunday. They had got events mixed up, couldn't distinguish any more who had done and said what when, got confused when their individual recollections didn't match and generally given the impression that they would just as soon forget the whole thing (and the fact that she and Mr Eldmann had sought shelter from the rain beneath the chestnut tree had not been noticed by anyone other than Miss Leander). And with that Mr Kønig saw his chance to intervene and unceremoniously take charge of the whole conversation by suggesting a real excursion into the countryside which they must all join in. Just think of the silent forests; how free you could feel there, miles and miles from other people. ('Miles from anyone' – he had looked at her as he said that, as if it meant something special for him and her.) A thought which the others of course applauded loudly, whilst she herself was left sitting there in silent confusion, not because he had managed to twist the whole thing in order to make himself into the centre of attention again, but because by means of his little talk (and his sly reference to the picture, to the dance of the nymphs in the forest) he had made the whole beach trip and its significance pale, and had made her dream about a meadow, a grassy slope where she could dance freely and happily, safe from the pettiness of other people. . . . In this way he had violated her thoughts, and now he was in the process of invading something much more vital in her soul, her memories of Mr Eldmann, of their unstained love, which was her life's most precious possession; and all this because of two or three thoughtless remarks on the part of some indifferent bystanders, together with Mrs Johanna Holder's evidence, which she could find no reasonable grounds for doubting. And what about herself . . . ? No! She was not going to waver! She repeated determinedly, as if she was reciting a spell, 'He was slim and elegant . . . and his hair was beginning to turn grey at the temples, but it was thick! It covered his whole head. And he was musical, and he had a beard as well.'

But Mrs Johanna Holder merely shook her head in incomprehension. Maude fell back in the all-too-soft armchair, exhausted and on the verge of tears, and practically whispered, 'He was a man of learning, a gentleman, so clever and aristocratic. . . . Oh God!' The extent of the destruction overwhelmed her with its full force as she realized that the words she was using hardly characterized anything real, no longer did justice to what she bore in her heart, were no longer adequate to describe their object, because the object itself was no longer constant and unchanging. It was as if she was sitting there muttering a spell that no longer produced the required magic effect; for it was clear from all the evidence that Mr Eldmann *had* been a cheery, stout fellow with a gleam in his eye and a salesman's suitcase.

No! What was it she was sitting here thinking? She *knew*, after all. . . .

'It can't possibly be the same person we're talking about,' said Mrs Holder, not without a certain sympathy. 'You'll see, there must be several people called Eldmann . . .'

'But he left this address!'

'Now, now, don't upset yourself like that.'

Maude fumbled blindly for her handkerchief. She was fearful of destruction, transformation, a disintegration of the order that ruled her life. The demons which had confined themselves to acting upon her senses since the death of Mr Eldmann now ran amok. With the chaos came annihilation.

Johanna Holder had stood up. 'Perhaps we can sort this out after all,' she said, and walked over to the bookcase. 'I think I have a picture of him.' She pulled out an album and leafed through it, a worn but resolute figure in her old apron, and eventually found what she was searching for. 'It's not a terribly clear picture, I'm afraid. It was taken that summer five years ago, just before he left. He's sitting there on the left.'

Maude looked at the figures in the photograph. Three or four people were sitting around a folding table at the edge of a forest, enjoying a cup of coffee from a flask in the harsh sunlight. A cheerful picnic in grey and white. Walking-boots and anoraks. A hut behind them. Wide smiles in honour of summer and good fellowship, precisely immortalized by the lens.

'That one there.' Mrs Holder pointed.

On the left sat Mr Kønig with his arm around an overweight brunette. Or someone who was remarkably like him. It was not easy to tell. Yes, it must be him; that large, intrusive face was one she knew all too well. Although he was half in profile, half turned towards his girl-friend. . . . It was possible she was making a mistake. He had had more hair at that time and seemed slimmer.

'Miss Ellinor was his fiancée; one of many, you could almost say. She often went with us on Sunday trips to the Beacon.' The landlady was obviously dying to ask the all-important question, but restrained herself.

Mr Kønig or not Mr Kønig? It was him and it wasn't. A plump good-time guy on a trip to the forest with his 'fiancée' and friends, a possessive arm around her waist, amorous words in her ear, a picnic (and Miss Ellinor held her arm over her eyes to protect them from the sunlight and exposed her shaven armpits). 'Ready, I'm going to press the shutter.' Then an afternoon nap with a whispering tumble in the summer grass. How appropriate it all was to someone who had lived in this flat. How like him, she thought scornfully. It was only the day before that he had suggested a general excursion, the silence of the forest 'miles from anyone'. Yes, it was Mr Kønig. Everything pointed to that. It was not possible to get any closer. The decision was hers.

'Yes, that's Mr Eldmann,' she said, with the same feeling of being in a dream and removed from it all that she had had on the street before she had dared to go in, when she could still have turned around and gone back, stopped the process of transformation, or at the very least delayed it a little.

'There you are,' said Mrs Holder proudly. 'It was him after all. It was me who took it,' she added, meaning the picture.

'Yes, I must have made a mistake just now,' said Maude decisively. 'I'm sure it's him. Many thanks for going to so much trouble.'

The annihilation was complete.

'Oh, my dear,' answered Mrs Johanna Holder, flattered, 'it was nothing, really.'

· 15 ·

The trip home through the town. The sun had broken through the layer of clouds which had for several days veiled the sky in a grey mist. There was still a smell of fresh greenery from dark backyards, a delayed birth from the shadows in the depths of the town. Spring had been so late this year. The summer which flowed over the landscape around her was like a flood that had collected into itself all the myriads of the spring's fresh streams, which never ceased, just grew and became more and more overwhelming. It made people stop on pavements and streets, giddy with the swelling silence, and turn their faces to the sun as if to be able to feel more fully the violent shock of the growth which was going on around them, everywhere, on all sides, a gigantic chain reaction in the very chemistry of creation itself.

High summer. It was the middle of July and she hadn't even noticed it until now, when suddenly every breath of air filled her with its spice, as she hastened to put as much distance as possible between herself and 82 Strandgaten. Perhaps she had been too preoccupied with herself and her own problems; she had not really wanted to open herself up to the summer. Even now, as her senses became aware of the abundance all around her, she was haunted by the thought of a disaster which she had only just avoided; by the skin of her teeth, she said to herself, by the skin of her teeth. . . . And she found it hard to relax in this sudden bombardment, where the light seemed to illuminate everything and make it unrecognizable for her, as if the transformation was pursuing her even here to this part of the town, where the houses were taller and better preserved, the shops more tasteful, the streets broader. Everything combined to provide a more stylish, ordered, solidly anchored existence than in the doubtful area around Strandgaten. And after all, what importance could be attached to a blurred amateur photograph and Mrs Johanna Holder's confusion about the men she had had as lodgers?

All at once she felt a little dizzy and went into a chemist's. She wanted to buy some sleeping-pills, as she had not been sleeping well recently. Her tooth had been bothering her as well. But when she reached the counter, she found that she had mislaid the prescription from Dr Gøttlich. Oh well, it was just as well really. The ones he had prescribed were too weak. She would have to make an appointment for an examination again. Instead she bought a tube of toothpaste (as recommended by your dentist) and a bottle of aspirins.

Once she was safely back in her own street she felt calmer. There were the well-kept gardens behind their fences that she knew so well, that she had watched every summer since she had lived here, hedges, fruit trees, flower-beds in neat, well-ordered formation, the leisurely sweep of the lawns. . . . A feeling of security returned, a certainty that all was as it should be, as it had always been. That was consoling. The thought of her visit to Mrs Holder with its confusing implications faded into the background when confronted by this serene harmony. And there lay the house, her boarding-house, large and imposing up there on its little rise, looking exactly as it had done the day she had arrived here all those long years ago. It was with a sense of relief and restored self-confidence that she closed the gate behind her and walked up the shadow-dappled drive.

But all of a sudden there he was again. He was sitting sunbathing on a deck-chair on the grass (right in the middle of the lawn he was, like an island, as if he had every right in the world to be there); a corpulent, untidy figure in white shorts that might just as well have been a pair of underpants (perhaps it was a pair of underpants?), which did not belong here on her lawn, in her garden, in her carefully ordered ideas about the kind of behaviour that was acceptable in gardens in this part of town. It just wasn't done to display oneself so blatantly in a state of undress in the presence of respectable people. This was not a beach; and it wasn't the first time either!

She attempted to hurry past without being noticed, but he saw her and called out, 'Oh, Miss **Maude**, could you come here a moment? There's something I'd like to talk to you about!' – so loudly that everyone must be able to hear it, even behind closed windows.

She stopped, then made her mind up; it would look even stranger if she said no.

'Oh, good afternoon, Mr **Kønig**,' she said reluctantly, as she approached his ample white body. 'You're enjoying the sunshine?'

'Oh yes, it's lovely,' he agreed, and sighed deeply and contentedly as if to confirm the fact. The sweat glistened on his red forehead and in the sparse hairs on his chest. On the regal paunch, which was pushed up and forwards by his sitting position, his navel stood out like an old scar. His thighs and calves seemed slender by comparison with his large torso.

'Here, why don't you sit down?' he said, pointing to a folded towel which was lying on the grass just next to the deck-chair. His own dirty towel. What a cheek!

'No thanks,' she answered firmly, but at the same time felt a little guilty and on the defensive. No doubt he had only meant to be friendly.

'You really are a puzzle, you know.' He twinkled up at her mischievously. 'Why is it so impossible to get you on your own for a chat?'

She was not prepared for such a frontal attack here in the middle of the lawn, in broad daylight, in the blazing sunshine, in everyone's hearing (every window had eyes and ears), and she was glad she had remained on her feet. It gave her a feeling of superiority to be able to stand and look *down* on his person, which at this moment was far from inviting; and at the same time it must be difficult for him to sit there like that and talk *up* at her, especially if he was getting any ideas.

'Difficult to get me for a chat? Do you really think so, Mr Kønig?' From her superior position she could afford to respond a little frivolously to his overtures, to play with his words and return them, since he was sitting there trapped in his deck-chair and his unaesthetic body. But at the same time she was trembling in anticipation of his next salvo, for nothing he said could be indifferent now. It was no longer enough to ignore him, to dismiss him as a tiresome, persistent nuisance, for even though nothing about him had changed at all, he concerned her in a completely different way from before, thanks to Johanna Holder's photo, and this knowledge increased both her fear and her distaste.

'You daren't!' He looked at her as if he too was astonished at the thought. 'You dodge away like a hare as soon as I come close. Are you frightened of me, or are you doing it to get me all worked up?'

'Oh, Mr Kønig, really.' She looked around desperately. What could she answer to such preposterous accusations? How could she make her escape from this dreadful man?

'I thought you and I had an understanding.'

He talked as if they had made some kind of deal, entered on some shady conspiracy; he had taken her by surprise yet again and destroyed her superior position, even though she was the one who was fully dressed and standing up.

'You really must explain what you mean.' There was a sincere plea in her voice. All at once she felt so weak, so indecisive; but she couldn't just surrender, not here in her own garden where she knew each bush, each flower-bed. . . .

He laughed so that his stomach wobbled, intruder that he was.

'Oh no, don't give me that, my dear Miss Maude. You know well enough what I'm talking about. Now don't get angry.'

He could read her thoughts now as well. She could have cried over her own helplessness in this undignified situation. But she no longer thought of flight, of letting him sit there alone with his vicious fantasies; something transfixed her to the spot, like a bird in front of a snake.

He saw how confused she was and adopted an expression as if he was going to place all his cards on the table. His voice became explanatory, almost tender. 'There are certain women, you see, who send out signals. Signals, yes. And I have been registering your signals since the day I arrived here.'

'Signals?' The conversation was taking a dangerous turn. This was getting close to the most vital, the most intimate part of her existence.

'That's right, signals. I don't mean words and gestures, nothing tangible, it's more a kind of vibration, a tension in the atmosphere if you see what I mean, a kind of spiritual code between a man and a woman which means that they almost understand each other better than if they had used some other means of communication.'

'And you think that I with my "vibrations" have been signalling something special to you?' She managed to preserve the irony and detachment in her voice, but that was all. She felt her resistance slipping away. She didn't want him to say any more; she knew what he was going to say. She could guess what it was he thought he had felt. But it shouldn't be put into words!

'Yes, that's exactly what I do mean, Miss Maude.' He laughed. Really, the man had no respect. He smelt of sun-tan oil. His skin was gleaming with sun and sweat across his round forehead and in the folds where chest and stomach met. Those dreadful shorts! She couldn't remember ever having found a man so repulsive. No, never.

'And I suppose now you're going to ask me what it is you've been signalling to me? What message I've been receiving?'

She shook her head dumbly.

'Oh come on, don't pretend, it's written all over you!' He chuckled as he sat there, relishing his own gleaming corpulence. Then he suddenly became more serious, almost severe. 'The strange thing about you is that you look as if you don't *want* to grasp what it is that's happening inside you. You're afraid of the consequences of your own wishes, do you know that? It's not so difficult to pick up the signs of a woman in love, you know – the language of romance is easy to learn. Look how you move your hands; it's so soft. Do you know how soft you are? When you serve yourself at table, it's as if you're stroking a stranger's hand. When your glance escapes and darts away, you do it with a smile that promises something altogether different. When your mouth says no, your heart shouts yes and sends its rays to your eyes, your cheeks. . . .'

She could not follow him any longer. She felt a little giddy. She had been standing too long in the same place without a hat in the strong sunshine. The soft grass yielded beneath the soles of her shoes and made the whole garden sway. It seemed already as if everything around her, the lawn, the flower-beds, the trees, even the well-known elegant house front with its rows of windows, its terrace and its stone steps had changed form almost imperceptibly and become alien to her. His voice and the words he used conjured up a different landscape, new but not unknown, where she had no fixed points, could not be certain about anything, could no longer distinguish between true and untrue, right and wrong, good and bad. She laid her hand over her eyes; the sun and the oppressive heat, his voice which provoked all her uncertainty, stronger and more intensely than ever before. . . . How dare he! But she couldn't even get angry, she was just too exhausted, she wanted to cry, wanted to sink away, to vanish. . . .

And he just sat there silently, looking at her seriously now from down below with his eyes screwed up against the strong light. Perhaps he wanted to discover what effect this frontal attack had had on her? At the same time she had an uncomfortable feeling that it was on the contrary her legs that he was studying, that he was sitting there deep in the deck-chair and letting his glance creep up under the hem of her skirt, up to her suspenders. . . .

'You . . . you shouldn't say things like that!' That was the only one of all her protests, all her objections against him that she could manage to put into words.

'But you asked me to.' His voice was unusually mild and gentle.

'But why did you *say* it?' She pouted like a little girl. She wished it was unsaid; she could still feel abysses opening at the thought of his impertinent remarks, which she just stood there and accepted as if she was blind and deaf. She thought how comical this must look to anybody watching, her standing there like a pillar in front of him, sitting there, no, floating there so self-satisfied in the chair, exuding the smell of sweat through the sun-tan oil, in the middle of the lawn, in full view of everybody. . . . She could feel his glance on her legs and thighs, up over her hips and breasts; but she was too weak, too defenceless to protect herself against his aggression. She merely murmured again, 'Why?' And hoped that he would perhaps soon get tired of this game, would release her and not torture her any more, would let her go.

But he allowed his glance to travel up and down for a further intolerable moment before he answered, almost as if indifferent, 'Because I've fallen in love with you.'

Of all things this was the most astonishing, the least expected. Again she was completely overwhelmed and disarmed; apathy, her last resource, was nullified. Who could feel indifferent towards a man who had just said he was in love with you? Against her will she had to revise her view of him. Perhaps she had exaggerated a little as far as his appearance was concerned (but not his boldness!). Perhaps he wasn't quite so bad as she had thought; at any rate he looked serious, one might almost say moved, at this moment as he sat there in the deck-chair. Perhaps his impetuousity was just assumed, in order to conceal the vulnerability beneath the surface? A silent helplessness in the face of his insidious invasion of her peace of mind welled up in her like tears.

'Oh – but what did you do *that* for?' The absurdity of her question made them both smile, and the smile brought her nearer to tears.

'It just happened like that,' he said, once again his cheerful and slightly patronizing self. 'I looked at you, I read the signs, I fell in love. That's the sum of it. And all this time I've been waiting for a decisive signal from you, something tangible which would seal the pact, but it never came. You've no idea how close I've been to making advances to you several times during the last few weeks, at mealtimes for example. How easy it would be to stroke your hand, just the little finger, or to press your knee under the table. None of the others would notice anything, and as for you, you're just sitting there begging for it – that's what makes a poor fellow crazy about you. You sit there so quietly, so meek and mild, and you're just waiting for the volcano to erupt – and on the surface there's hardly a tremor to be seen. But I've got my own seismograph, I can tell you, and it's told me that you're just sitting there waiting for "Mr Right", the one and only, the chosen one, the man who is worthy of you. But you must see that there isn't any "Mr Right", there isn't any fairy-tale prince, there is only loneliness and different ways of filling that loneliness. . . . You *need* someone, Miss Maude. Can't you see that? You need someone like me and you know that, someone who has been around a bit and can teach you a thing or two about life, but who would also know how to value your. . . . Good God,' he broke off, 'you look like a young girl, you should just see yourself now. Hasn't anyone spoken to you like this before? But you're a mature woman too you know, you're over forty, and if you keep yourself any longer now, you'll keep yourself for nothing. . . . Maude!' He had raised himself up a little in his chair and shaded his eyes with his hand as if to be able to get through to her more urgently. 'Don't pretend you don't know what I'm talking about. I'm in love and I want you to be mine, that's about the sum of it. I just had to tell you.'

She watched, fascinated, the gyrations of the large stomach during the course of this long speech. She was careful not to pay too much attention to the words, tried to let what he said slide passively into her mind, where she hoped it would be stored away in a forgotten corner and not be too troublesome later.

He lay back again, relaxing in the deck-chair, and smiled his unfathomable smile. 'Anyway, I've always had a weakness for plump lasses.'

This last remark stirred her vanity. 'And what do you suppose. . . .' She was almost startled at the sound of her own voice, at the fact that she could still formulate a coherent sentence. 'What do you expect me to answer to all that?'

'Answer what you like,' he laughed comfortably from his chair. 'You can't fool me!'

How crafty he was! Suddenly she realized that he was just sitting there playing with the most precious thing there was, with her own feelings and his, in order to get what he wanted, to entice her into his power, to manoeuvre her down on to his level, his Sunday-trip level with sandwiches and flasks of coffee and fumbling in the grass (and suddenly the resemblance to the picture Mrs Holder showed her came vividly before her eyes). How respectless, how despicable of him! How could she take seriously what he was saying, this courtship (for that was in reality what it was, or as good as) as it was being presented here, on the grass, in broad daylight, with her suitor lying in a deck-chair wearing shorts (which really did not cover very much of his substantial frame), and with her, the object of the adoration, standing straight up and down by his legs, unprepared, humiliated, speechless. How could she know whether to believe him or not?

A shadow from a fleeting cloud passed over the garden and restored an air of solidity to the familiar outlines of the house. A newly risen wind caressed her skin and cleared her thoughts. She noticed that the window of her room was open a little: perhaps she had forgotten to close it before she went out, although she didn't think so. . . . But in any case it was reassuring to be back here in these orderly surroundings, where you didn't make declarations of love in broad daylight. There was a man sitting on the broad bench on the terrace. She conjured up Mr Eldmann's figure, but it glided out of focus and took on a chubby, corpulent shape. She was still not free of Mr Kønig, as he half sat, half lay there beside her legs, making the most of the gravitational force of his naked presence. The resurrected Mr Eldmann. Mrs Holder's ill-starred photograph. And yet she said to herself that nothing was proved beyond doubt; of course not. Did you ever hear such rubbish? It just wasn't true. Couldn't be true. What kind of grotesque fantasies was she falling victim to?

And at that moment he said, 'Now that I have laid bare my soul to you, perhaps you would allow me to repeat my invitation to join me on a little motor-cycle trip around the district, just a short trip out and back if you prefer. Shall we say tomorrow afternoon?'

And with that he had given her a lifeline: here was the chance to break out of the spell he had laid on her with the help of a few well-turned phrases and a chance resemblance to a stranger on an unimportant photograph. A motor-cycle trip. A motor cycle did not fit in at all, not in any context. A motor cycle was a foreign body, it was bad form. Her Mr Eldmann, under whatever form he chose to appear to her, would never be able to be connected with such a machine. Even the vulgar version in Mrs Holder's album had nothing to do with any motor cycle as far as she knew. She saw herself in her mind's eye, sitting behind him astride the modern, narrow saddle with her skirt pulled up, wearing a helmet and a body-belt, roaring at full speed through the streets of the town (she had heard him start up in the morning, and just the noise he made . . .). She had to laugh, she laughed out loud, in relief at this welcome breach in the mysterious logic which even more inexplicable circumstances had constructed in order to ensnare her innocent affections. She laughed and cried in sheer relief.

He looked at her in astonishment, whilst she tried, gasping, to pull herself together to be able to answer his ambiguous invitation.

'Oh no, really, Mr Kønig,' she finally managed to stutter out. 'I'm afraid our motor-cycle trip will have to wait. It seems to me to be something of a risky venture, if I may be allowed to say so. But thank you for thinking of it, I'm sure you meant well.'

'Well, really, you take the biscuit!' He stared open-mouthed, floundering, having lost the ascendancy that he was so sure of just a couple of minutes ago. She could not tear her eyes away from his stomach, as it moved this way and that, passive and unresisting, following its own gravitational laws.

'How long do you think you can go on playing cat and mouse in this fashion?'

'Games like that I leave to people who are interested in such matters,' said Maude with maidenly candour, which she suspected would irritate him unbearably. 'But now I'm afraid I shall have to go. I have such a lot to do. Goodbye for the present. It's been interesting talking to you.'

And without giving him time to absorb this new twist in their relationship, she simply walked away, distanced herself with quick strides from the disturbing force field of this male, and left him sitting there with surprise and irritated protest painted on every feature.

Or was he disappointed? Upset? She wondered in a momentary weakness, as she saw out of the corner of her eye that he had twisted half out of his chair, and was leaning his hand on the ground and staring after her. No, how could he be upset? A man like him? Who could sit there in the blazing sunshine and expose what he called his feelings so shamelessly, and still expect a response, perhaps even an acceptance? It would be interesting to know how often these surprise tactics were successful!

From the bench on the terrace the Consul waved to her. She waved back briefly and abruptly, and hurried on round the corner of the house without hearing what he was shouting. He'd probably been sitting there watching the whole episode, she thought vindictively. They had to keep up with how matters stood. The Consul, the man of the world whom everyone looked up to. It was behind his flies that it had all started at the Christmas party. The Viennese waltz. Mr Kønig's bulging shorts. He was an exhibitionist, that fellow. She decided not to go down to the evening meal. But as she came into the rusty yellow shade of the hall, she discovered that all the furniture was standing there unchanged in its habitual place, just as it had stood for decades, heavy and dignified; and she recognized the elegant – if slightly worn – carpet on the wide stairs, held in place by shiny brass runners, the ornate banisters, the white prisms of the chandeliers as they hung, catching and reflecting the occasional glimpse of sunshine that pierced the indoor shade. She saw that everything here was as before, just as it should be, as it had always been, as if one were safe in here from the relentless march of time and the changes, the fear and the doubt it brought with it. And when at the same moment she heard the maid's light steps in the dining-room, and the clink of cutlery, and thought of the strenuous day she had had and the pleasures of the evening meal, then she nearly changed her mind; for the calm and the imperturbable orderliness here in the hall and the adjoining rooms produced a similarly immaculate orderliness in her churning thoughts. From this she knew that she no longer had anything to fear, that the distractions which had for a moment threatened her equilibrium (just fleetingly, for an unguarded, passing moment) were insignificant, just as insignificant as the nervous play of the summer wind on a dark mirroring lake just before a change in the weather; and besides, she was beginning to feel hungry.

On the table under her window stood a huge bouquet of summer flowers in a vase. The corner of a white card stuck out between the fresh colours: the bouquet was from Mr Kønig. She must forgive him his little amorous impulse. . . . A little flowery greeting to celebrate the beauty of a summer day and her own loveliness, from her loyal admirer. PS He had persuaded the room-maid to lend him the key without any idea of what he wanted with it, so she didn't need to worry that he had compromised them.

Asters, lilies, dark red peonies. . . . That was a different sort of language from the one he was using on the lawn a while ago. Motor-cycle trip! She snorted.

But later, as she was lying resting with the counterpane loosely over her legs and feet, watching the sun playing with the breeze in the curtains, she couldn't help thinking of the squat motor cycle, standing straddled over its broad-based stand in the shade behind the house and exuding its powerful smells into the afternoon heat (it had been most considerate of him, though, to open the window a little so that the smell of the fresh flowers didn't completely fill her little room).

Gleaming and powerful it stood there with all its intricate mechanisms, two nickel-plated exhaust-pipes, its broad, grooved cylinder block, the large shiny light, like an eye, like a bald head with the handlebars sticking up like horns on either side; a goat, a fat, oily, hairless billy-goat, that was what it looked like. Just like its owner, she thought, and could hardly help laughing. She could see Mr Kønig's body, glistening with oil, in the deck-chair; for there was something about the machine's heavy, compact, latent power, even when it was standing still, which could be reminiscent of Mr Kønig's broad torso, once no doubt muscular, but now running to fat, the prominent petrol-tank on his stomach which projected so self-confidently, the narrow, shiny cylindrical springs around his legs with their thin knees and ankles, almost without hair.

My admirer with a four-stroke engine.

It was so reassuring to identify him with the motor cycle; in that way he could be kept at a distance, so that it was less dangerous to be pleased by the flowers.

But then she came to think of his grotesque declaration of passion out there on the lawn and decided to renounce the companionship of the evening meal after all. That would teach him a lesson.

## · 16 ·

Late that night there was a knock on her door. Her heart stopped, then began beating wildly. It was *him*!

She was sitting in front of her mirror in her night-gown and had just brushed her hair out (it was beginning to get long again after she had, on an impulse, had it cut a little too short in the spring), gathered up a handful of it and registered to her sorrow that it was growing thinner, when she heard steps approach and stop outside and the sound of someone knocking on her door. . . .

What on earth . . . ! Should she open? Or pretend she was asleep and hope he would go away again?

She had already seized her dressing-gown and with a glance in the mirror ascertained that she looked younger with her hair down and her eyes opened wide in amazement, at the same time as she searched for words for the reprimand she was about to give him, when she heard a voice outside, a woman's voice.

'It's me!' A tearful whisper.

Miss Leander.

'But, my dear. . . .' She looked in horror at her friend's miserable, tear-stained face as she opened the door. 'Come in, for goodness' sake! What is the matter?'

Everything that had happened during the last few days had pushed the thought of Miss Leander and her dubious condition entirely into the background. Now Maude suddenly remembered that in a way they were in the same boat; they were both laying claim to being Mr Eldmann's heirs, if one could express it like that, and it was really a matter of judgement as to whether she should regard her friend as a rival or an unfortunate sharing the same fate.

Right now, however, there was no doubt. Maude put her arm around Miss Leander's shoulders and pressed her cheek comfortingly against her warm, moist one. All at once it seemed natural to her to express her sympathy and pity by means of physical closeness; the very strangeness of the situation (Miss Leander here in her room so late) seemed to demand an extraordinary reaction, and at the same time the memory of the close, sisterly intimacy they had experienced together the first time she had confided in her was revived.

'Come here,' she said, and made Miss Leander sit down on the bed. 'Now tell me what it is that is worrying you.'

'I think it's started to kick!' The words came rushing out in a single long moan, almost indistinguishable through her tears.

'To kick?'

'The child! I felt something. Here. . . .' She placed her hand beneath her breast, tentatively. 'Just as if. . . .'

Of course. Her tummy upset. It was Thursday evening, four days after their conversation in Miss Leander's room, and since then she had completely suppressed all thought of the embarrassing situation her friend imagined she was in. Of course it was a phantom pregnancy, but nevertheless it must be unpleasant to be tormented by it like this. Poor little thing.

'Do you think. . . . Could it have been that?'

She was so helpless, so appealing. What on earth should she say? wondered Maude uneasily. To start with she was no expert on pregnancy, and in any case this was something quite different; a broken heart you could perhaps call it. Poor girl, she must have been terribly in love! And at that moment Maude became aware that the thought of Miss Leander's love affair (the importance of which was of course exaggerated by her imagination – for the brunette with the shaven armpits on the photograph was proof that any connection between them must have been a long time ago, but never mind that) was breathing fresh life into her own memories of Mr Eldmann. It was as if the poor girl had become a go-between, a pitiful intermediary for their fading relationship; although of course she could not allow the thought of their amorous contact to assume *too* concrete a form. There was an inherent contradiction in all this, but she overcame that by transposing their unthinkable alliance to an abstract plane on which even the pregnancy, a foetus beneath Miss Leander's heart, a living proof of Mr Eldmann's life force, a seed sprung from his sperm, became acceptable; in fact it became a welcome insurance against the distressing consequences of a failing memory and against the misinterpretations of her own unpredictable impulses.

So her voice was full of genuine concern as she asked, 'But isn't it a little too early?'

'That's what I thought too.'

When did a foetus actually begin to kick?

Side by side they sat on the soft bed and explored each other's ignorance of life's most essential mechanics; two virgins (even though in a technical sense only one of them was) who had not given up all hope of reward, the victory of the meek and an ultimate release.

'But how old is it then?' Maude saw her chance here to gain fuller access to her friend's most precious secret and seized it. 'When . . . when did it *happen*?' As long as she maintained a clear distinction between dream and truth, fantasy and reality, there was no risk in asking such a direct question.

'I'm not all that sure. . . . Two or three months ago perhaps. . . . Perhaps around Easter. . . . I've never been all that regular.' Miss Leander was crying again, in despair that she couldn't keep track of the simplest facts in her life's tragedy. 'We didn't take any precautions. We were engaged after all!'

'But wasn't there . . . wasn't there' – Maude blushed involuntarily – 'any time that you remember specially? When he was especially loving or good to you?' Maude had vague memories of having read in a book somewhere that a woman could only feel pleasure at the moment of conception. Or something like that. It had seemed logical to her (and so right, so exactly in tune with her romantic ideas about union with a man) at the time she had read it.

'He was always so tender and kind to me. You can't imagine. . . .' It was as if they both found the comfort they needed in the thought of how tender and kind Mr Eldmann had been, and Maude took hold of Miss Leander's hand and pressed it, as a sign that she knew what her friend meant, and as an encouragement to her to carry on talking about the impression of Mr Eldmann that it was in both their interests to retain.

'That first evening when we danced, at the Christmas party you know, he said that I was talking "the language of love" to him, a language he understood intuitively. He had registered "signals", he said, and as soon as he said it I realized that it was true, that I really had been fancying him for quite a long time. He was such a handsome man! And he danced so well. . . . It was the first time I had ever danced so close with anyone.'

Maude could hardly conceal her disappointment and irritation at the drift of Miss Leander's account. So that was how she had imagined it. Did she really think that Mr Eldmann's courting would have been so banal and transparent? She felt positively overwhelmed by indignation on Mr Eldmann's behalf and on her own, and when she thought about it on her friend's behalf as well (though she was fully aware of the apparent illogicality of this thought process), exposed as she had been to such vulgar tactics of persuasion.

'Oh, aren't they all alike, these men!' she burst out spontaneously; no doubt the next thing would be motor-cycle trips and picnics in the country! But no one was listening to her. Miss Leander had suddenly grown quite still, and when she turned towards her in order to seek comfort in their joint resigned wisdom Maude saw that she had become quite pale and was sitting with her hand clutching her stomach whilst she breathed convulsively through her open mouth.

'Are you unwell?' It took a moment before the suspicion of what was wrong struck her with full force (for this pregnancy was just a figment of her imagination, she must not forget that), but then she was carried away again by fellow feeling as she caught a glimpse of her friend's pale, frightened face.

'There!' she gasped. 'There it was again! Like a stitch!'

'But can it be possible?' thought Maude aloud, in dismay. 'Three to four months?' Suddenly she found it both absurd and irritating that Miss Leander, who worked at a library (it's true she was an archivist, but nevertheless . . .), couldn't have found out some information about these things. Fish, lizards, rabbits . . . what stage had she reached? And when did the creature start to move?

'There it was again!' She repeated the words on a note of rising panic. Maude felt a wave of nausea in her own stomach.

'Now, now, you mustn't let it upset you so.' She tried to comfort her, put her arm around her friend's shoulder and leaned towards her, just a little, in order to give herself reassurance as she took on the role of comforter. Miss Leander sniffed gratefully and squeezed her hand; barriers between them collapsed.

'See if you can feel anything.'

And suddenly, as if it had happened in no time at all, Miss Leander was half undressed; her blouse buttons were undone, the zip on her skirt was pulled down, and she had seized Maude's free hand and placed it resolutely on her stomach, straight on to the warm flesh.

The shock of the sudden intimate gesture and the contact with the warm, living body made Maude tremble.

'Is there anything? Can you feel anything now?' Her friend had snuggled up close against her now, protected by the motherly arm. Maude could feel her warm, sobbing breaths mixed with her own excited breathing.

How frightened and helpless she is, just a little girl really, she thought. Her whole being vibrated with sympathy, with desire to help, to share the tenderness and goodness she felt she was filled with on account of this remarkable closeness which was perhaps not quite right, which would perhaps be misinterpreted by others, but which was in reality a sincere proof of their friendship, of the comradeship between them, so elevated that it was impervious to criticism. Therefore she did not move her hand away.

'You were the only person I dared come to,' confided Miss Leander, with her face against her neck. 'I knew that I would be safe with you. I just couldn't cope with it all on my own.'

'Of course,' said Maude, moved. Her hand lay on the other woman's soft belly as if paralysed.

'Do you think it might be *that*? Can you feel anything now?'

Dutifully Maude commanded her own hand to search, to feel cautiously around Miss Leander's middle, over her stomach where it swelled out modestly, unrestricted by the tight waistband, tactfully around the navel. . . .

'No, I can't feel anything. I think it's too early.'

She noticed that she was whispering, and that they were in this way sharing the shame and the strangely resigned humility which had remained like a cloud after their grief, and which she had seen change Miss Leander from an efficient, pleasant and independent career woman to a sobbing, formless object, an organism with no other perspective and no other goal than to observe its own cellular divisions, the only, synthetic memory of an illusion of love; and all this had happened in the course of one month.

'I can't feel anything.' She had to repeat it in order to be able in this way to bring to a conclusion this little excursion into forbidden territory, to underline that she regarded this sisterly consultation as terminated. She did not, however, move her hand away; for this abject surrender that had reduced her friend to a bundle lying in her arms and begging for help and comfort, the same disintegration of acceptable behaviour which she herself had contributed to (and had become a part of) by listening to her pleas and offering her person and not merely detached assistance, a hand on her skin instead of friendly advice, a hint, a sensible word of caution – this complete inversion of the rules of what was proper and what was not proper, the possible and the impossible, gave Maude a strange feeling of freedom of action in relation to the friend who had surrendered herself to her there on the bed. Impulses and thoughts which only a few minutes ago would have been suppressed by the strictest inner censorship were now liberated, in this chain reaction which their mutual sympathy and common helplessness had set in motion. Her hand on her friend's stomach identified her more strongly with the suffering which had been confided in her, and made it into an expression of her own torment and longing; and the friend who now sat so close to her, so stripped of all formal identity, so abandoned to the new physical contact between them, also became a part of herself in this way, a poor fellow human whose loneliness and dreams she shared – yes, more than shared, felt as her own (for at this moment it was not just a question of a phantom pregnancy, but more, much, much more). In addition to all this, the warm proximity made her nervous heart swell, become strangely full, so that she almost had to gasp for breath.

So therefore she remained sitting with her hand on her sister's diaphragm, which quivered (or so it seemed to her) beneath the disordered clothes, and felt her warm breath on her neck, and heard her now and then make noises like a baby or like an animal, and thought strange thoughts about this woman's body which she was sitting and hugging so closely to her own: the skin, tender and untouched like her own (despite her day-dreams), the soft breasts which rested their twin weight so freely on her arm, the hair beneath her stomach which she suddenly saw so vividly in her mind's eye, dark and curly, endearingly untidy like her perm that was growing out. She allowed herself to be filled with boundless devotion towards this defenceless body which lay there, given over to her care, and so very similar to her own.

So when her hand, almost involuntarily, recommenced its wandering over Miss Leander's inviting expanses of skin, and the amateur medical examination began to take the form of a gentle touching, almost a caress, the reason was not first and foremost because the unaccustomed familiarity through new physical contact awoke new sexual awareness in her, but rather because she felt the stirrings of an urge to take care of her friend, to give her all the love of which she was deprived and which she, like all women (and herself not least), required, because they were robbed of it by men, unworthy, brutal men and immodest fantasies about men (just think of the Christmas party!).

And once her embarrassment was overcome, and she could let herself be carried along by her tender impulses, by her modest urges to sensual experimentation which were directed at herself as much as at her sister, and noticed her answer, her fumbling response, and heard her whisper close to her ear, 'Oh, Miss Maude, I feel so safe with you, it's so good and safe with you!' – then she felt a joy greater than any she had known, at the thought that she with her delicate advances had managed to give her friend (and herself) that feeling of devotion and trust which she was sure was the very essence of love, and which – of this she was sure – Mr Eldmann had wanted to convey to them both in just this way. And thus the symmetry was re-established, and their – Mr Eldmann's and her – heavenly–earthly connection was consummated; since by letting her friend share in what she knew was the expression of true love, which she had been carrying within herself all this time without any possibility of communicating or assuaging it, she had automatically taken his place and carried out actions that she had always attributed to him. Even at that moment, as her sister's breath sounded louder and louder in her ears, and her hands, which were the medium for his intimate caresses, became more assured in their movements, she could only connect the whole affair with their secret pact of love. She floated in her friend's warm, unresisting physical presence like someone who never again wishes to rise to the surface; for they had reached a point in their joint exertions from which a face-saving retreat was no longer possible. Yet this was immaterial so long as she was aware of her function as an intermediary, and felt her friend's body mirror her own longings precisely; she was grateful, so boundlessly grateful, to be allowed to sacrifice herself in this way.

Mr Eldmann the deliverer.

She groaned in ecstasy and devotion to him and let her tongue pass over her sister's tear-stained eyelids, licked her salty lips and thus sealed the harmony she had conjured forth with the aid of her high ideals, which ignored all that at first sight seemed inadmissible, and located their ambiguous actions in a context far removed from that of everyday life. It lifted their exalted desire into a sphere where no petty doubts could cloud its purity, from which it seemed that a higher, an almost unearthly and sublime correctness illuminated their untidy, impossible ménage in the bed.

## · 17 ·

Two days later, on Saturday afternoon, just after lunch, Mr Kønig invited her on a trip into the country the next day, and almost to her own surprise she accepted. In reality she had no desire to go with him, in fact she was near to feeling both fear and revulsion at the thought of being completely on her own with this man; but the whole question and the way he had phrased it seemed to fall into place at once in a structure, a logical pattern over which she had no control (especially as she had been sitting during lunch and looking at the picture over the fireplace, the dance of the nymphs, the lascivious glance of the faun . . . ).

Once again she had been ensnared in the strange driving force of continuity, the magic of transformation − for it was the pattern of events unfolding that was decisive, she suddenly felt, the quantity of time which divided one occurrence from the next and enabled the chemistry of change to operate, unstoppable, irreversible. . . .

After all, a trip to the country was something quite different from charging around on a motor cycle (and if he had mentioned the motor cycle, then she would perhaps have managed to escape yet again, but no); a trip to the country with Mr Kønig suddenly became something almost acceptable. Indeed, behind the thought there lay fulfilled expectations, a realization of something, a confirmation. And it was not only because the blissful nymphs in the picture could sway so wondrously carefree in their dance in the forest clearing; it was Mrs Holder's picture as well, the plump Mr Eldmann (for he it was!) behind the wobbly camping-table with his arm around 'his fiancée', a picnic in the grass, 'miles away from anyone'. Finally it was Mr Kønig who came panting up the steps behind her, reached her before she could escape and almost pushed her against the wall with his importunate bulk before he asked (and as he asked, as she understood what he had said, she realized too that she had been waiting for this). There was a curious symmetry about it; his resemblance to Mr Eldmann on Mrs Holder's picture, Mr Eldmann in the country, his mysterious 'deputization' at the boarding-house − all this must have a deeper meaning. It must be thus it was ordained. And on top of all that, it was sweet of him constantly to surprise her with flowers.

In any case, she said yes – and regretted it immediately; but one could not go back on one's word, one didn't do such things, and in any case she could not rid her mind of that ambiguous picture and the thought that he had said he loved her there on the grass only a couple of days ago. 'I love you,' he had said; she could remember it quite clearly as he stood there now so close to her at the top of the stairs. Yes, it fitted in so well with a trip to the country, a trip to the forest, with Mr Kønig who was identical with Mr Eldmann in the pictures, and furthermore was large and red-haired and had glasses. There was a symmetry, an orderliness about it which she could not evade; it was so important to her to have her affairs in order.

'Perhaps we could go to the Beacon,' he said.

The Beacon. That was where he used to go. She became almost gay. 'Oh yes, can we do that? It's so nice there.'

'Splendid,' he said, pleased and happy with her willingness. 'Do you think you can arrange some food? I'll see to the drinks.'

'Of course.' She could just talk to the maid. It would be quite straightforward.

'We'll set off early in the morning then, so that we have plenty of time.'

'Well, not too early.'

'You're not such a lazybones as all that, are you?' He was teasing her now. She was just waiting for him to tell her he loved her all over again.

'What if it rains?'

'What a pessimist you are. If it starts to rain, I'll build us a shelter of pine branches with my own hands. We could have a fine time in there, I can tell you! When I come to think about it, actually that's not such a bad idea after all. . . .' That round, reddish, moonlike face of his was beaming with glee. Was he thinking of raping her there in the forest? Standing there with a hand on the banister wearing his usual English tweed (which she had disliked to start with), he looked actually quite passable, she thought. Just you take care, my little chubby prince. . . .

But she said, 'Don't get carried away now. It had better be a trip in all innocence, otherwise I'm not coming!'

'A little trip to the pine forest in all innocence, as requested.' Even the vulgarity was a part of it. Already she could feel, with a shiver and a little sting of irritation, his plump arm around her waist after the picnic had been consumed. That cursed photograph. Did she really have to agree to this? But it was too late now, and she was excited about the next day too. She liked the thought that powers greater than herself were ruling the course of her life.

Later, as she was giving instructions to the maid, she deliberately spoke so loudly that Mrs Sebastian, who was just passing by in the hall, would have to hear it. She wanted them all to know that she was going on a trip into the country with Mr Kønig. So they would have their way, those who had wanted to push her at him (and she would have the pleasure of sacrificing herself). Then there would be no doubt about who had attracted his interest – and by so doing, had won the competition for Mr Eldmann's posthumous attentions.

## III

## *The Dance*

· 18 ·

Such ripeness!

It was nothing short of sinful, the way the weeds broke through and threatened to overwhelm the summer flowers in their beds with their thrusting life, their corrosive green, their unbridled abundance.

Those poor, delicate flowers. . . . It moved her to see them like that, surrounded, even weighed down by these unattractive, intrusive green plants – and how green they were, how incredibly, unnaturally green! – which shot up everywhere; here a fleshy leaf, there a sturdy stalk. It was impossible to halt this crazy proliferation; they oozed out their green sap, spreading a numbing scent of depravity. . . .

Those poor, poor flowers. How threatened they were by such unbridled zest for life.

The gardener. . . . She uttered a silent, mild rebuke as she stood between the rows of phlox and dahlias.

But when, half angrily, she grasped a tall, slim weed and pulled, she was amazed at how easily it released its hold and came away, and she felt secretly moved by the sticky wetness between her fingers as they held the crushed leaves, and let the other hand crumble the clods of earth that hung heavily from the tough root hairs.

Kønig. Mr Aleksander Kønig. King Alexander. Tomorrow they were going on a trip to the woods. . . .

But what had happened to her garden? The grass was growing waist-high on either side of the narrow path leading to the bench. The summer-house had been besieged and conquered by ivy, which in its turn had been routed by a climbing rose. Moss was dripping from the decaying bowl of the fountain. On the bench lay a leaf and some down. Glassy green sunlight filtered through the foliage and fell like dust on everything that grew.

When did she last walk down here?

On the green branch of the apple tree, a couple of green clusters of flower bases signalled their determination to turn into fruit.

Miss Leander. She had advised her against visiting the doctor, but who knew whether she would not go there anyway? That poor nervous little thing, so lost in her own misunderstandings; how she needed her help and comfort. Maude felt a tender surge of sympathy in her breast. *She* knew what was wrong, and she was the only one who could help, by means of the invocation. Their seance. It gave her a feeling of security to think of that little episode in her room (so far away now, almost like a dream, but the thought of it brought Mr Eldmann closer). It made her invulnerable.

She thought of her loud instructions to the maid just a few minutes earlier, and of Mrs Sebastian who had been standing listening. That would pay her back for her ambiguous remarks in the lounge. That would show her (even though what she had said had been intended mainly as a reference to Miss Leander, of course). She was triumphing over everyone; they could not hurt her any longer. Even when she thought of her impulsive promise to Mr Kønig to go on a trip with him, of the photo, of the cheery Mr Eldmann, of his plump arm around her waist in the green grass, the feeling of security remained. She thought of the enchantment she had experienced together with her friend during the short moments of their joint quest, and she knew that Mr Eldmann was there with her. She was protected; an angel was watching over her steps.

How the trees were lavishing their green abundance on the shaded bench over there, as it stood at rest with its dry maple leaves and its down. She sighed, overcome by the peaceful picture.

But she could not sit down. Instead she walked over to the poplar, which was standing pointing clear to the sky, turning its shiny leaves in light and wind; right up to the poplar she went, laid her hand on its pale trunk and felt her closeness to it. She loved trees. She was filled by the lonely person's blind love of trees, identified with the tree, even though you would not think there were any points of similarity between this young, slender tree trunk and her own heavy, sweet, woman's body, so formless and decrepit compared with the erect symmetry of a poplar. . . . But a friend, it was a friend nevertheless, a grateful creature of God opened up to this beautiful day. And she wet the dry bark of the tree with the point of her tongue.

She stood there in the heat of the afternoon, which filtered down to her intermittently as she stood with her feet planted on the soft grass, caressed by lush growth, thrilled by this pagan fecundity. Everything was so overwhelming, so boundless, so much stronger than she was.

A trip to the forest with Mr Kønig, Aleksander Kønig, a plump arm around her waist, his hand and fingers, Mr Eldmann's lascivious face behind the picnic table, an exposed shaven armpit, tumbling in the grass with her 'fiancé', with Mr Kønig, with his red face close to hers. . . . The ambiguities, the transformations. The way in which familiar shapes continually arranged themselves into new patterns from which there was no escape. Time passed and eroded everything lasting, everything she believed in as fact. She saw it now, understood it well, this logic, this new 'order' which linked one occurrence to the next, one suggestion, one piece of circumstantial evidence to the next – and all in spite of her resistance and her fear. It was a chain of dreams on a foundation of reality, a flight of fancy immortalized in pure transformation, the hidden and the revealed, indissoluble connections which bound her and her lover. She imagined she could see them now, and she was not afraid.

The high grass garlanded the path and increased her feeling of being in safe hands. The munificence of the season. The late spring tide of her own juices. She walked so slowly, unwilling for it to end.

Behind the fence she saw the dog. It came running towards her, wagged its tail, barked, jumped up and begged with its inviting pink tongue. It wanted to be scratched and patted. She waded through the grass towards it, feeling leaves and stiff stalks scraping against her defenceless calves, saw the dog putting its paws against the netting and stretching its belly expectantly, saw its little penis, so touchingly protected in its hairy sac, so innocent, almost beautiful. . . . Here then, boy. Come on . . . there, there. What overflowing tenderness on such a lovely day!

Tomorrow she was going out with him. How pleased he had been when she said yes. Even though she couldn't say she liked him, at least not particularly, she felt almost a kind of indulgence towards him. He was so clumsy, so often went too far, didn't know where to draw the line (but he was entertaining, that she allowed, even charming at times), lacked any real refinement in his whole being. Just a little salesman who belonged to the rented rooms around Strandgaten, she thought a little condescendingly. But she could remember his voice quite clearly saying, 'If it starts to rain, I shall build you a shelter with my own hands. There you will be safe. I love you.' He was a romantic when all was said and done. The chubby face (on the picture) so dangerously close to the open armpit. She was both dreading and looking forward to the following day. Thank goodness she had her sacred bond, her pact with Miss Leander (just think of her shy touch, her quick, helpless breathing!). She felt her heart beat fast.

The warm dog's tongue was licking in between her fingers. Come on then, boy. Come on. Who's so fond of Maude today then? Are you so fond of Maude? Are you, Mr Kønig? Will you protect me against the rain? Do you really love me, Mr Kønig? Mr Aleksander Kønig?

How wonderful to be worshipped. The dog licked her hot cheeks. She looked at the sac which it carried so gracefully under its belly. How orderly everything was in the animal kingdom; so clean and harmonious. Even a dog's organ was almost beautiful.

The heady perfumes almost made her faint.

## · 19 ·

She had to insist on them taking the bus up to the Beacon. He couldn't understand that she refused to mount the motor cycle, teased her a little, laughed indulgently, then looked at her almost in irritation as she stood there in her suit, wearing her good, solid walking-shoes and clutching the picnic basket as a barrier between them, determined not to let herself be talked round.

She was just as irritated at him as he was at her. Couldn't he understand how wrong it was to drag the motor cycle into this, to interfere with the plans laid down for their trip? How could he be so insensitive to the proper way of going about a trip to the country? And a glance at the object of their dispute, that awe-inspiring (and unspeakably vulgar) machine which stood there shining and four-square, exuding its unfamiliar odours of petrol-station and mechanics, strengthened her objections. That was the last straw, the last wisp of self-respect which stood between her and humiliation; if she agreed to that, she would be lost, and chaos and the obliteration of the order which ruled her life would be inescapable.

On the bus he once more attempted to assume a jocular tone, but the fact that they were suddenly sitting thigh to thigh, since they both more than filled the narrow bus seats, made his jocularity a little forced, and made her turn away from him and devote her attention to studying their fragmented mirror images in the glass of the window. It wasn't a bad profile he had, she had to admit that. But mostly she let herself be mesmerized by the pale oval of her own face, in which the shadows formed by eyes and mouth were filled with a wild, luxuriant vegetation which constantly changed. It was summer around her, summer within her.

Still she could almost feel the prickling in her neck from all the glances that she knew had followed them down the drive, and her relief and happiness grew with every curve and twist in the road which showed that they had reached the first hills and were already at a safe distance from the distractions of home. Out here in the open air everything would be simpler and clearer, but at the same time unrestricted by preformed notions (except for those hinted at by Mrs Holder's photo) and therefore riskier, she thought with a little thrill of mischief, conscious of the constant pressure from his warm, plump thigh – for which he could not be blamed so long as these blessed seats were constructed in the present fashion.

From the bus terminus there was a well-trodden, signposted path which led the last kilometre to the Beacon and the small viewing platform from which you could see the little town below, in miniature detail at the bottom of the broad bay. It was a strange, abstract model, a projection of reality which after all was only half an hour's bus ride away.

Up here Mr Kønig was in his element. Looking excessively sporty in his double-breasted hiking-jacket with matching knickerbockers, he took command at once, working out exactly where they should leave the path in order to find the best route to make their way to a spot 'away from the public thoroughfare', where they would in addition be 'more sheltered from the wind', which, it was true, could get up in a few moments up here and could be a nuisance. He passed comments on the landscape, on animals and plants as he led her with brusque gestures through dense undergrowth and treacherous thickets, and behaved in general quite as if he was at home in the forest. And that was just how it should be, thought Maude as she followed him along his carefully chosen paths which led them here and there through the pine forest. She had to struggle a bit to keep up with him quite often, in her uncomfortable suit jacket which she hadn't worn for a good two years, and which had now got too tight and constricting around the bust.

It hadn't rained for 'years' (it must be about three weeks), and the dry spiciness of the air which hung between the tree trunks made her skin prickle and glow. Apart from the bird-song, their own heavy breathing and occasional comments were the only sounds to break the summer Sunday stillness.

Would they soon be there? Where was he taking her? Half anxiously, half exhausted, she realized that she would never be able to find the way back on her own if. . . . But she stopped herself, banished such thoughts, because he had said that he loved her and because the most dramatic thing that could happen on a forest trip was to find an arm around her waist and perhaps let herself by persuaded into a little frivolity in the grass after they had eaten. She was sure of that. An angel was watching over her footsteps.

And Mr Kønig marched on with head held high, humming now and then a snatch of a tune she had never heard, English no doubt, held the branches for her – the most awkward ones at least – and was as polite as he could possibly be. Now and then he sent her a merry glance, the old fox, so cocksure he was, almost nonchalant, now that he had her in his power here in the wilderness.

At last they came to a clearing where he stopped and threw out his hands. 'Have you ever seen anything so lovely?' It was clear that he knew the place. No doubt this was where he used to come with his 'fiancée' and friends, she thought, in a sudden flash of cynical irony. But at the same time she felt a strange fulfilment. She had to struggle against an impulse to sink to her knees here on the soft grass, so green and so tempting after the long march across the crisp, dry forest floor. Whether it was tiredness or capitulation she wasn't really sure; but she just wanted to surrender herself to the endless silence that suddenly pressed down upon them at that moment as they stood motionless and hardly dared to breathe in the glorious peace of this spot. There was a silence and a calm which removed her even further from her old conceptions of what was permissible and what was not, and made her speculate passively as to whether he would do anything to her here, in the grass, right away, or whether he would perhaps wait until they had eaten. And she realized that right now in this wordless moment, when they had both moved so far away from the strict order of the boarding-house, or of any other place to which they were bound by the orderly pattern of life, she could feel neither disgust nor terror at the thought of what must come.

But when he had found them the best place, spread out the rug and with a grunt of well-being sat down beside her, and made as if to snuggle up close and put his arm around her waist under cover of a vulgar little joke that he delivered with a flourish which showed that it had been used often, she became nevertheless a little frightened and moved away a bit. After all, such sudden invasions of her soft and precious flesh, such unsubtle physicality could not be tolerated, not even here in the forest (and especially not when they had only just sat down, such inelegant haste!). Had he no sense of tact, this odious little fat man?

However, when she saw how crestfallen he was and how disappointed, just like a scolded dog, Maude's anger evaporated; for it was just because he was fond of her, so very, very fond of her, poor thing; he loved her above all else, that was what he had told her, and that was why he acted as he did. She glanced across at him furtively, at his dejected countenance, large and red amongst all the fresh greenery, quite an attractive profile. Perhaps he should grow a little beard? It was a face that she recognized from a photograph, from a dream of irrevocable transformation, and she felt an emotion that she could not name streaming from her breast towards this face that had told her it loved her so much.

There was a ramshackle hut on the edge of the clearing. It was only now that she noticed it. Just as on the picture. Of course! she thought, of course! It seemed that there was nothing in the way any longer. . . .

For a while neither spoke. Then he leaned back on his elbow, peered across at her, smiled teasingly, sure of himself again, and said, 'Since when did you start playing so hard to get?'

What did he mean? And how familiar! No doubt he was bold enough here in the forest, 'miles from anyone'.

'What do you mean?'

'Oh come on, don't play the virgin,' he said almost impatiently. 'Everyone knows that you were having it off with a fellow at the boarding-house this spring; Eldmann he was called, wasn't he? Someone said he was engaged, too.'

How dare he? She could hardly breathe. She felt her eyes glaze over with the tears that wanted to spill out. What a callous brute! The impudence of the accusation was bad enough, but to utter Mr Eldmann's name out here in the forest, when they were sitting so close beside each other on a rug so far away from all rules and all regularity, was dangerous. It meant that a new kind of link was established. By taking Mr Eldmann's name in his mouth, Mr Kønig (whose profile she had already registered as acceptable) had instantly acquired a closeness to her beloved that could not be explained away or disregarded as having originated in her own head and having no existence anywhere else. The magic of a name. A name whose bearer's existence was uncertain, flexible, problematic, a name that could bestow its enchantment on anyone who took it and used it (like all names, to a lesser extent, to a much lesser extent). What would happen if the name were repeated now, if he understood how to use it, and took possession of it?

'What was he like then, this Eldmann? I've been told that you used to flirt madly with him before he upped and died.'

'Oh please. . . .' What could she reply to such an outrage? Every time Mr Eldmann's name issued from that mouth, something was irrevocably distorted and displaced. She felt all her defences crumbling away. It was impossible to keep things under control. Now past and present were indissolubly mixed together.

'But, my dear. . . .' He had seen how upset she was. He came closer. She sat there powerless.

'But, my dear, I didn't mean it like that. It's just that I'm so jealous, you see. I can't bear the thought that you've belonged to someone else, this Eldmann. . . .' He was completely serious. He was really jealous. He had a right to be. She couldn't even be cross with him any more. Now he seized her hand. 'Were you really so fond of Eldmann then?'

As he said that, she felt an arm around her shoulders, and a force that was imperious and solicitous and irresistible drew her closer to the coarse tweed. She thought, almost with relief, almost cheerfully, that everything was turning out as it should anyway, since she was here with him on a picnic in the woods, and since he had such a large, hungry face which had forced its way into her consciousness, and since she all at once felt more intimate with him, not because she felt she knew him better (and really she wasn't sure that she liked him all that much), but because he had used Mr Eldmann's name in connection with her and with himself and what they were going to do here in the forest. So when he repeated the question, but softer and more confidentially now, whether she had really been so fond of Mr Eldmann, so extraordinarily fond of him and still thought of him, with his face so near to hers that she could feel his breath on her skin and the warmth of his body, she nodded in answer and let herself be persuaded to yield to the strong arm. She leaned heavily against him and passively allowed his experienced fingers to open the buttons of her jacket and squeeze her soft roundness, as if such compliance once and for all emphasized, or rather proved, her love for Mr Eldmann, gave weight to her admission. It was as if such an offering up of her modesty, through a third person, had become necessary in order to make up for something they had omitted, to make good a little imperfection, the importance of which Mr Kønig (who had implicated himself in the affair by taking Mr Eldmann's name in his mouth, and now had to be convinced) demonstrated by whispering over and over again, 'How lovely and round they are! How wonderful you are! How big and beautiful they are!' – whilst he sat the whole time and stroked and squeezed her ample fullness, pressing his cheek against hers, red and hot.

If it's all that important, she thought, she would make the sacrifice gladly (it was woman's lot in life to sacrifice herself). If it brought him (and therefore Mr Eldmann) such great happiness, then she would not mind agreeing to this (as long as she was dressed, please note, as long as her actual self, her skin, her body, was protected by material, by layers of outer clothing, a blouse and finally the intricate construction of a bra, so orderly, so practical, so reassuring). She followed his hand's, his fingers' exploration of the contours of her bosom and felt a little embarrassed, but also flattered; although it was a bit comical too, she thought, to see how charmed he was, how fascinated by these round breasts which she herself almost forgot now and then. No, that wasn't true, she didn't forget. When she heard his voice whispering how big and how desirable they were, heard the fever that lay behind the words, felt the impatience of his reverent touch (things that would have frightened and repelled her if they had happened elsewhere, in other circumstances, but which after all were within the realms of possibility here on a picnic in the woods), then she felt a shy pride kindle within her, the same self-absorbed pleasure she felt when she looked at her own body in the mirror, when she was combing her hair after a bath for example, and realized how attractive woman was, what a priceless treasure she was preserving for the right man (who could never, never be worthy of it, she now realized, and who would always be dependent on the indulgence of the woman, on her understanding of his searching, his torment and his imperfection). For this reason she could almost let herself be swept along by Mr Kønig's breathless adoration of her loveliness – for she was lovely, his greed for her proved that beyond any doubt – and enjoy his enjoyment of herself. All this steadily increasing bodily involvement with this man simply made her more beautiful and more unattainable in the eyes of both. She could even feel a strange sort of gratitude – even though *he* was the one who was grateful and had reason to be, he expressed that clearly enough – because he was doing this to her and thus emphasizing her eternal, seductive femininity; and also showing her how unique she was, how majestic and sovereign, and at the same time how vulnerable, tender and feminine, and he let her feel the pleasure of that. In that way he enticed her near to the essence of the nervous, complicated woman she was, and linked up her surface existence with her secret one; and in a moment of ecstasy she saw herself dancing, floating over this meadow here at the Beacon, 'miles from anyone', in freedom, in perfect harmony, in loose, flowing garments which drew attention to her attractiveness and charm.

And therefore she allowed him to press his mouth against hers, after they had looked deeply and seriously into each other's eyes, this short distance apart – it happened as if by agreement, slowly and in a considered fashion, without hesitation or misunderstanding – and force her lips apart and even let his tongue slide into her mouth, now beneath and now above her own tongue, then far back towards her throat so that for a moment she was afraid she wouldn't be able to breathe, whilst his breath thundered in his nostrils.

A kiss.

He was kissing her. He was licking the inside of her soft mouth with his warm, thick tongue, there in the midst of the sunshine, here in the middle of the forest where nothing could be right or wrong any more. A lark trilled indifferently from its privileged look-out post high up in the sky. It was so strange and so intimate that for a moment she was frightened and had to seek comfort in the thought of Miss Leander's shy, light brushes of the lips up in her room, on the bed, and of their common disgust at nauseating male sexuality; but then finally she understood that this mixing of spit was basically a tribute to the eternal feminine (and, besides, permissible on a picnic trip) because it demonstrated her humility, her willingness – at Mr Kønig's instigation – to act out her devotion to Mr Eldmann, who now, behind closed eyelids, could scarcely be distinguished from the corpulent male who suddenly (or so it seemed to her, indeed) was lying half on top of her and bestowing on her an oyster kiss which went on for ever. So much was she prepared to sacrifice.

But when he changed his position and attempted to push his thigh up between her knees, she became a little frightened and pulled away from him and his clinging embrace, sat up and straightened her clothes a little, then her hair, shocked and dazed. She was upset that he had had to destroy the brief rapture which had flowered between them, behind closed eyes, with his impertinence, his lack of restraint and moderation. With his latest manoeuvre he had suggested an inadmissible untidiness in their forest relationship, a disorder which went so much further than a naked armpit and a little thoughtlessness in the grass after coffee, which penetrated even through her vanity and left behind it a fear that she had let things go too far, that 'that' which she could not even properly put into words, but which she feared and guarded against more than anything else, had suddenly lurched all too close, so close that it became a part of the pattern, of the symmetry which lay behind all her thoughts and deeds, and therefore became ineluctable. In the same way, his impertinences at mealtimes, the secret correspondence of signs, coincidences, indeed this picnic trip itself were all links in a logical chain which was a part of her imaginary world and her unspoken wishes and at the same time reality, a force so strong that she was powerless against it.

And this too she found it natural to hold him responsible for, at least at this present moment, as he sat up again with a stupid expression on his face, clearly struggling to find something suitable to say, something that could smooth over and make light of what had occurred, and indeed preferably put the clock back a couple of minutes, back to the moment when she was lying soft and receptive on the rug beneath him and her passive acquiescence had made him misinterpret the situation so fatally.

'I'm sorry, Maude,' he said finally, looking down at his knees, whilst she sat there stiffly, sizing him up and thinking how strange it sounded when he pronounced her name: Maude, M-a-u-d-e. . . . Like an oval, a lazy circle which slowly filled, opened up and then emptied and closed again; a melodious sound, a sound rich in promise. It was a beautiful, eternally feminine name she had. She was grateful for that.

'I shouldn't have done that. I apologize.'

He looked quite dejected, the poor man.

'I let my feelings run away with me. Dearest Maude, I'm so much in love with you, can't you understand that?'

He placed his hand on hers, humbly; with just the right degree of humility to suit this awkward change of mood, and her new position with regard to him, she thought. For when he shortly afterwards put his arm around her once more, and tentatively drew her back into his warm field of gravity, it was no longer him but her who controlled the course of events. He was reduced to begging for the slightest favour, and this suited her admirably; but at the same time it made her perhaps a little more generous than he had strictly speaking deserved. It was all because the sun was blistering down on them on the rug, and she was reminded of the fact that she was on a picnic with him and that a little compliance in the grass was part of the arrangement so to speak, as she sat here with her picnic basket and patches of sun on her cheeks so close beside Mr Kønig, her would-be seducer with the large, red, crestfallen face.

At any rate she accepted his cheek against hers once more, and his tongue in her mouth, and let herself be caressed by a frivolous breeze whilst the sun made dancing patterns over her eyelids. She had not sufficient presence of mind to be frightened or suspicious when he started to tell her, in between long kisses and passionate stroking, that she was driving him crazy, that certain (unidentified) needs were pressing and that she *had* to help him with something, until finally, all at once, it began to dawn on her what he meant. But by then it was too late; for he had already seized her hand and at the same time done something to himself, to his clothes, and she could feel movement, a trembling beneath her fingers, of something alive and warm, a life which burned and pulsed independently of both of them, down in Mr Kønig's crotch.

She knew what it was, of course; but nevertheless she was taken aback, almost panic-stricken, for she had never been able to picture the male organ to herself without a feeling of nausea, of mild consternation and resentment that it was *possible*, as if she intended to hold the Creator responsible for having created his male figure in a way which was so offensive to her delicate sense of aesthetics. Such an inordinately *conspicuous* organ – she shuddered – even though you normally couldn't exactly *see* it.

But now it was too late to do anything, she thought, almost paralysed, whilst, half choked by his tongue, she registered with every fibre of her body what it was he was intending to do with his unmentionable member and her hand. A retreat now, when such things had been set in motion, would involve an embarrassment on both sides that would be more crushing than any of the other consequences which might ensue in this undignified sequence of events. (She thought of having to sit there and watch him button his fly, and the mere thought made her so agitated that she involuntarily put her free arm around his neck and hid her face in his shoulder; a movement that he naturally misinterpreted, and he set about his unmentionable activity with even greater enthusiasm.) But at the same time she thought with sober relief that it was at least slightly more 'orderly' to get involved with him like this, at half an arm's length – just the thought of having him up between her knees with all his messiness, and her underwear. . . . So she made up her mind to get it over with (for she was already aware of the kind of exercise he was driving at), and could feel how his impatience pressed against her hand with ever increasing urgency. It was not unlike a dog's snout, she thought, and almost had to smile as Mr Kønig at that precise moment began to utter sounds which in fact were not unlike a dog's panting. Some of her unwillingness and confusion melted into tolerance, even benevolence towards him, which resembled the tenderness she had felt a short while ago. For she understood that all this was necessary because he was so fond of her, so fond, so fond of Maude, and therefore – and also because he had made himself into Mr Eldmann's representative, so to speak, by taking his name in such a well-calculated fashion – it was her duty to fulfil the harsh demands made by love. Even his warm doggy snout stirred an impulse of tenderness in her breast, for it was also fond of her and needed her to take care of it; she stroked it a little of her own volition, patted it gently (as she had patted Peik yesterday) and thought that it was not really so terrifying and 'messy' as she had feared, so she carried on stroking whilst Mr Kønig's grunts rose higher and higher, and thought of her conversation with the peeping Tom on the beach. 'She knew what to do with her fingers, that little miss, she was all over him. . . .' And a moment later something happened to him, to the unpredictable part of him that she was holding in her hand. Seven or eight timid strokes were enough; the tension which had swollen in her inexperienced grip reached the point of climax and then burst, and she felt wetness on her fingers. And when it happened she wasn't even surprised, just felt a thrill of distaste. For she knew that this was exactly how it happened; she had read about the emission of sperm; she was not in the least ignorant about such things. Everything was as it should be, a little different from how she had imagined, it was true, but as it should be nevertheless. She was grateful for that, for it gave the whole episode a structure, a beginning and an end. It was over, it was done, she had done her duty, and behind her tightly shut eyes she wondered embarrassed when he would like her to let go.

Soon afterwards they were lying peacefully on the rug, hand in hand beside each other (she had put a stop to anything else), staring up at the sky, and he told her once more how lovely, how wonderful she was, how much he loved her and how grateful he was that they had at last come together and now belonged to each other. But for her part, Maude was wondering, downcast, whether she really did now belong to this pushy fellow who had enticed her to go too far – for this was not a part of her ideas about what a picnic entailed – here in the midst of the thick forest so far from the behaviour of civilized people. She found that her attitude to him had scarcely changed after this major concession (which still made her tremble and feel numb over her whole body; the emotional turmoil, the shock of this bold attack).

More than anything she felt a little lonely, used and abandoned as she lay there with the hem of her skirt modestly covering her knees, dizzy beneath the suction of that deep, boundless blue, whilst everything around her, even the forest's impartial, dignified calm, and particularly Mr Kønig's self-satisfied declarations of love strengthened her feelings of melancholy abandonment.

He was lying there so serenely, so pleased with himself, on his back with his hand in hers. She had dried her hand thoroughly on the grass, but could still feel the sticky wetness between her fingers, and she thought she could still detect the faint, pungent odour of his sperm, like the smell of a flower-bed whose flowers are choked by weeds. He was once again Mr Kønig, her impetuous admirer with no manners.

A little while went by.

Suddenly she noticed that he was breathing deeply and regularly and realized that he had fallen asleep. For a long time she just lay still and felt relief changing her dejection into a feeling of calm satisfaction, even with a flash of impishness: he had fallen asleep, her little libertine; now he was lying there motionless and harmless, asleep in the grass. She had to look at him. She turned her head.

The dry warmth burned her cheeks. Over her the swallows swooped in their airy spirals. She thought: have I really changed? Has everything changed? But she could find no answer, just the feeling of bitter-sweet disappointment mingled with the shame of what had just happened. But so what – it was over, completed, done with; a sacrifice she offered up gladly. Good heavens, it wasn't so much really, just to be kind and stroke the dog, that was all; so soon buried and forgotten. . . . And there he lay, asleep in the grass, and they were completely alone here in the forest, no one could see them. . . .

Cautiously she raised herself up on one elbow and looked at him closely. She studied his calm profile. It was quite attractive, almost noble as he lay there so still, almost innocent, his cheek so becomingly touched by the shadow of a stalk. Now he was hers. Forgotten was the humiliation of a few minutes ago. Now he was lying here in the grass asleep, an attractive man when you studied him closely, a man she didn't need to be afraid of any more, a man on whom she could bestow all her disinterested devotion, where he now lay. She lay there enjoying the sight of him for long, silent minutes; and even a muffled snore from her prince could not distract the elf-like flitting of her senses around his somnolent perfection. In this condition, the whole man became an object for her restrained infatuation, and she could even see the recent transgression in a more conciliatory light. It was only a case of the man's helplessness, his lack of tact and finer feelings when it came to showing a woman his devotion, the urgency of love which could not be denied, and which no doubt was not so different from the urgency she herself felt as she sat and looked at her unthreatening seducer, traced his body with her eyes, slowly and in detail, from the soles of his feet to his scalp and back, and registered the large nostrils, the open hands, the belt which cut into the softness of the stomach, the wet patches on the fly, a knee-strap which had come loose, the sports socks, the perforated shoes with thick soles, so polished and shiny. She felt a yearning in her breast, a tingling through her whole body which she could not decipher, until it occurred to her almost incidentally, that the need to go to the toilet had made itself felt even whilst they were sitting on the bus. She got to her feet cautiously and stood there for a moment a little dizzy and confused, alone in the middle of the meadow, stunned by the silence which no bird and no breath of wind disturbed. Then she slowly walked a few steps towards the edge of the forest, but changed her mind and stopped, lifted up her skirt, pulled down her underpants (he wasn't going to wake up, was he?) and squatted down, a fallen, generously endowed goddess, in the mild sunshine of the meadow, so near that she could still see him where he lay. And for the first time since she was a little girl, Maude peed in the grass.

Later she served him rolls, and they drank coffee from a flask, and afterwards a bottle of beer which made her sleepy. Perhaps she did doze a little, with her head resting on his arm, whilst he held her hand and entertained her with stories of his studies in England – no doubt he was exaggerating a bit, but not so much that it mattered – and afterwards he told her about the confectionery business, about his travels, about former friends; and she was happy because he seemed so cheerful and content and did not try anything.

Not until just before they packed up. Then he approached her in a different way, in a nonchalant, comradely fashion, as if intimate actions had become a matter of course between them; so she had to pull away from his hand and whisper, 'No. . . . No more! Please. . . .'

And at once he became amenable and agreeable again, and apologized profusely, at the same time as he praised her round breasts yet again, and in the end won her gracious permission to mount an assault on them once more (for now her suit jacket was properly buttoned), and stick his tongue into her mouth; but only for a short while, for she was determined to get home and banish this Sunday morning into the past.

But she seized the moment, nevertheless, whilst he was standing with his arms around her, pressing her close to his body, to get him to promise not to speak familiarly to her whilst anyone else was listening, particularly any of the residents at the boarding-house.

On the bus on the way home, down over the gentle slopes with all the twisting bends, she sat and felt his thigh pressing on hers as she looked out of the window at all that was rushing past, the countryside, a house, walkers by the wayside, and felt his presence here amongst other people as an unnecessarily painful reminder of the compromising disorderliness of what they had got up to there in the forest, although she tried not think about it. Such things were best forgotten. They had had a delightful picnic, and that was that.

Through the mirroring surface of the window she could see them, his self-satisfied features, her own face broken up by the wayside flora, wilting and dusty. That's just how it is, she thought, and felt herself all at once to be so disillusioned, so clearsighted. It had all been a waste of time; here she was as before, a half-virgin full of fanciful ideas, forty-seven oppressive summers old, sitting here with her *Liebhaber* whom she couldn't even say she particularly liked, exhausted and humiliated after having pursued the spectre of love with him. And as she stroked her face as if to cool her cheeks which burned from too much sun, her skin felt soft and wizened, like the outer leaves of a summer rose in August.

'It's going to start raining, you'll see,' he said, making the most of a bend in the road to let her feel the weight of his majestic presence.

That's all we need, she thought, and sighed involuntarily. An appropriate finale. The perfect ending to the fairy-tale. She would never again go out for a picnic with a man. The journey home was the worst.

'You're so quiet,' he said. 'Don't you think we had a nice time in the forest?'

'Oh yes, it was really nice,' she said. 'I'm probably just a bit tired. . . . So much fresh air, you know.' She made herself smile at him. He had deserved *that* at least, even if she didn't exactly like him, and especially didn't want him so close to her here amongst all these people. But he was fond of her, and he was no doubt doing his best.

'Did you have a better time with that other chap? Eldmann?'

'Better, what do you mean? He . . . actually we never went on a picnic together.'

'But was it *better* with him? You know what I mean. What did you *do*?' Almost in a whisper.

She understood what he meant, and it amused her a little that he was so jealous. It was only because he was in love with her, so dreadfully in love with her, the poor thing. And she had to think of how peaceful and attractive his face had been as he lay asleep in the grass, how tender and generous she had felt towards him then, and how difficult it was to summon up the same feelings now, as they sat here all too close to each other and bumped up and down on the narrow bus seats. He was holding on to her hand tightly, squeezing it in a way that was positively uncomfortable (her red-faced faun). And now he had insulted her once more by bringing Mr Eldmann into this charged atmosphere which had evolved between them (and thus brought new disorder into her relationship with him), and furthermore had asked her questions that related to her most secret life as if it were the most natural thing in the world; questions she could not answer because any kind of answer at all would determine the way he saw her. The very fact that the words had been uttered at all meant that a new factor had entered their relationship, a new expectation, new demands, new fear; the unthinkable was becoming a part of the 'order', the mysterious pattern that governed her actions, that organized everything for her with its 'logic'. She had to watch out for the dangers that lay in wait everywhere, the snares that were laid by ambiguity (it had been a close thing today, when he took possession of Mr Eldmann's name and thrust his thigh between her knees . . .); the conspiracy that was only waiting for a fatal mistake to topple her.

She could not answer him, could not summon the strength to express the turmoil she felt in so many words. She felt so tired, inclined to abandon herself to a fate which she knew could only involve the very worst. He was sitting half turned towards her (that face which had slept in the grass, so alien here in the bus), tense, egotistic, sure of its rights. She whispered, 'But, Mr Kønig! How can you say such things? We are neither engaged nor married!'

'I had to say it!' His voice was pleading. How he could change from conceited *Liebhaber* to humble beggar in just a couple of minutes. How insecure he must be, deep inside, she thought.

'I know you were sleeping with him. I have heard. . . .' Here it was as if his voice broke, he was so upset; and she realized that he was speaking the truth.

'Yes,' she whispered. 'I did sleep with him.'

'But why . . . why do you have to treat me like. . . .' He was positively squirming. 'Promise me that you won't torture me like that any more! Promise me!'

He knew no bounds; he just said it straight out, was so uncouth, so indescribably insensitive, and yet. . . . But she did understand how important this was for him, and what new sacrifices might soon be demanded from her.

'No longer, please. . . .'

He was begging like the dog. She had confessed and he was sitting there like a dog and begging to be patted, to be scratched.

'No, dear Mr Kønig,' she said gently and patted his hand. 'Not much longer now.'

And she was not far from feeling a little pity for him.

## · 20 ·

The Inspector was the only one who could help. Her last chance.

It had suddenly become clear to her in the midst of all the confusion after what had happened last night. A solution, if one was to be found, must lie with that smart young man with the calm voice and the becoming spectacles. She had confided everything in him. If only he was able to draw the right conclusions. There was no way out: she had to go and talk to him.

Despite that, she regretted her decision as she stood outside his office after having knocked, hastily, breathlessly, without really wanting to do so, but aware nevertheless that this was something she had to do.

What was she going to say to him?

Her first impulse had been to tell him about what had happened the night before, but now she realized that that was pointless. What had it got to do with the Eldmann case that Mr Kønig had asked her in a whisper at the table if he might come up to her room that night? Although it had a great deal to do with the Eldmann case, it had everything to do with the Eldmann case. Now it was Mr Kønig's face, flushed with desire, that looked down on her from the large picture, Mr Kønig decked out as a faun. And the dance on the light meadow was no longer a well-controlled game that permitted only the slightest hint of Eros; it had turned into a dubious sensual dalliance which bordered on the provocative. The beautiful nymph's half-exposed, rounded breasts awakened unpleasant associations in her mind, and the whole scene suddenly appeared so brazen, so unambiguously sexual, that she was amazed that they had not protested long ago and had the picture removed.

He had even been wearing his reading glasses when he asked her, though she could not see why he should be doing that as they were sitting at table, if it were not to make her uncertain (that description of Mr Eldmann she had been given on the beach by the refuse collector: large and flushed, with a beard and glasses – she remembered it with fear and trembling). And in the lamplight his hair, that thinning circle around his shiny pate, had a clear glint of red. None of the others seemed to find it remarkable that he was sitting whispering to her like that. After the picnic they had become a 'pair' at the boarding-house, like the Consul and Mrs Sebastian, or even come to that like Mr and Mrs Moser. It was as if such irregularities were disregarded as if by some kind of common consent, and this tacit, approbatory acceptance of their affair was for Maude the same as a challenge to her to give in to his vulgar demands. They were all expecting it. She would have to be extra vigilant. So she answered indignantly, 'But, Mr Kønig, that is not possible. You know the rules!' – and hoped that the threat was averted once more. A breathing space, a short reprieve. . . .

And when there came a knock on her door late that evening, after she had gone to bed, she decided not to open the door, and lay quite still – until she realized from the pleading, whispering voice outside that it was Miss Leander. She had come to confess to her (with an apologetic, tearful face; oh, how that irritated her now!) that she *had* gone to the doctor and that he had examined her and taken a urine sample and that she would know the result in a day or two; but that it was as good as certain already, for her breasts had grown larger, and she had put on weight, and besides she was so very sleepy all day long.

And after this of course the intimate feeling between them was ruined, despite the fact that they had again sought absolution in each other's arms, each of them for their small (and not so small) trespasses; for by means of her visit to the doctor's, her urine sample and her symptoms, Miss Leander had given her phantom pregnancy a substance, a concrete reality which made it impossible to link her sad tale of love with Mr Eldmann, who quite categorically did not run around with other women and impregnate them. The consequence of this was that the touch of her friend's skin, of her pointed breasts (Maude had to look at them, had to feel them too; it was incredible how they had grown these past weeks!) was far from summoning up the ecstasy of ideal love and the image of its personification, but on the contrary made her think of Mr Kønig, his groans (which in fact had sounded not unlike her friend's helpless little cries) and his warm dog's snout – but not even accompanied by fear and nausea, or at least not only that – and in the grip of this hallucination she bestowed on her friend an oyster kiss which went on for ever.

And when Miss Leander late in the night had said she must go, and they had stood close together by the door, whispering goodbye, she had suddenly grasped Maude by the hand and said with a serious expression, 'You know, sometimes I think this new man, this Mr Kønig actually looks a little bit like Mr Eldmann. Especially last night when he was wearing glasses. . . . They're not really very similar, but nevertheless there is something about him which makes me think of it. . . .'

'Yes, you may be right about that,' whispered Maude back. 'I have thought that myself at times.' And with that she knew that it had got out, that it was not just something that was going on in her own head, but that 'order' was showing signs of cracking everywhere; and that only the Inspector could help her. He was the one who knew all the facts; only he could weigh up all the possibilities and draw the right conclusion. He was her last chance.

She raised her hand to knock again – perhaps she had not knocked hard enough first time – but still she did not know what she was going to say to him, what excuse she could find for disturbing him in the middle of his work, how she would persuade him to inform her of the result of his investigations. All she knew was that he was the only one who knew the answer.

The door was opened by a youngish woman with thick, black hair and a sallow complexion.

Was the Inspector available, by any chance?

Did she have an appointment?

No, but he had said that she could call at any time if there was anything she wanted to talk about.

What was it in connection with?

Maude hesitated. The Eldmann case.

The woman looked puzzled. She was not informed; she was a subordinate, a little secretary, a nobody.

In connection with the death at Clem's boarding-house.

Aha. Now the woman remembered. She would inquire of the Inspector. Just a moment. Perhaps she would sit down for a moment? And could she have her name?

She showed Maude to a chair in the waiting-room and then went to the door to the inner offices.

Her hair was the most attractive thing about her, thought Maude; but she envied her the privilege of being able to call on the Inspector whenever she liked. It was precisely such things as that which gave women a power of attraction which was far in excess of that with which they had been endowed by the hand of nature. She was already a little jealous of this young woman who collaborated so intimately with her Inspector and involuntarily threw her a suspicious glance as she returned and announced that the Inspector would see her now, if she would just like to go in.

As she walked the six or seven steps across the floor, over towards the padded door, she thought again with a mild feeling of panic that she had still not worked out any strategy, made any plans about how she was going to worm out of him the information she needed, and she bitterly regretted that she had acted on an impulse to come here. But as soon as she stood in the Inspector's safe, sound-proofed office, and saw him sitting there behind the desk, friendly and welcoming, smiling in recognition behind his glasses, she knew that her fear was groundless, that she could simply tell him everything as it was and he would understand. At the same moment she suddenly remembered (and could hardly restrain a cry of joy and surprise) that she still had that significant piece of paper in her handbag, the paper with Mrs Holder's address on it which she had found in Mr Eldmann's waistcoat; and she realized that this gave her the best excuse in the world to come here and take up his valuable time.

'And what can I do for Miss Maude this morning?' he asked gallantly, but with no particular interest, she felt.

'It . . . it's about this.' She opened her handbag, pulled out her wallet and found the piece of paper after a little feverish fumbling. She held it up.

'You told me I was welcome to come if. . . . Well, if I came across anything he – I mean Mr Eldmann – had left behind, anything which might give a clue.'

She passed him the paper across the desk. He took it, looked at it curiously, and then seemed to lose interest.

'Where did you find this?'

'It was lying in a book he lent me,' she lied impulsively. '*November Rain*. A marvellous book!'

How good it was to think of their secret communication now, here in the Inspector's presence, in the holiest of holies of the law, where nothing in the world could upset the inviolable order of things.

'There's an address written on it,' she said, as he did not do anything. 'I thought that perhaps it might give some kind of indication . . .'

'It was perfectly right of you to think like that,' he interrupted in a kindly voice, 'and I'm most grateful to you.' There was something he was dissatisfied with, she could see that clearly.

'Isn't it any help to you?' His disappointment had transferred itself to her own voice.

'No, not really,' he said, and ran his hand over his forehead. 'You see, we've already checked this address.'

He had already spoken to Mrs Holder! This fact, totally inconceivable as it was, spread like a fever through Maude's consciousness. She could feel how all her efforts to keep ahead of the unfolding of events were losing ground, coming to nothing. She had pinned her last hopes on the Inspector, expected miracles from him, hoped for assurance that she was the one who had been right, that Mr Eldmann had been a mature and civilized gentleman, a teacher at the town's high school, of medium height and slim, with thick black hair that had begun to turn grey at the sides, a noble profile, polite and attentive, reserved and romantic. . . . But she understood that the Inspector too had become the prisoner of the facts, that the wheel of change had turned imperceptibly and moved them all with it, that nothing in the past was capable of being unambiguously established. The long chain of evidence proved that everything was possible, did not exclude any possibilities. To believe that one could hold on to anything was an illusion. Identity was a result of pure coincidence.

'So you found nothing of any interest at this address? I thought that perhaps he had lived there . . . or . . .'

He looked at her as if he had forgotten all about it. Then he thought about it. 'Yes, he did live there, you're quite right; about four years ago. At that time he was calling himself a salesman. There wasn't much more to be discovered there. Although his landlady did have some photographs which will be able to help us with the identification when we get that far.'

'Photographs?'

'Yes, a couple of private snapshots. There's no doubt that they are of him. But apart from that, we're completely stymied. We've been through all the lists of missing and wanted persons, but we can't find any Eldmann. Well, of course it's quite probable that he operated under a false name, but the description doesn't fit anyone on our lists either. And the name August Eldmann is not to be found in one single official card index, not on any census list.' He sighed in exasperation. 'He certainly didn't leave many tracks, your – er – fiancé.'

'What are you going to do now, then?'

'We shall continue with our investigations, of course, but I have honestly no idea as to whether we shall get anywhere. It's like looking for the proverbial needle in a haystack. It all seems just as if he had never existed. But he did of course. Oh well . . .'

Maude was suddenly frightened that the audience might be over, and asked quickly, 'Can I. . . . Do you think I might see the pictures of him? The photographs you mentioned? Perhaps I might be able to think of something or other.'

'Well, why not?' he answered indifferently. 'You have done your best to help us. I'm afraid I only have one of them here. The other one is being examined in the laboratory right now.'

He got up from his chair and went over to a filing cabinet, searched through the index, pulled out a drawer and picked out an envelope which he brought over. Maude thought that every move he made was so reassuring, so safe and correct, so sure; here from this sound-proofed office he presided over life's small accidental contradictions, he organized the patterns that must be obeyed by existence itself. Without men like this, the whole world would collapse into chaos, she thought, and shivered.

'Here you are. It's not very good, but at least you can see that it is him.'

He passed her the picture. It showed a smiling, corpulent man in sporty attire, a thick, double-breasted jacket and knickerbockers, who was standing leaning on the handlebars of an old-fashioned motor cycle. It could easily have been Mr Kønig, if it had not been for the slim moustache on the upper lip. He was slimmer, of course, his whole figure was more supple than she knew it now, his face was younger, thinner, but it could easily have been him. It had been taken several years ago, after all. Perhaps he had had a moustache at that time as well. . . .

'Well, do you think it's a good likeness?'

'Yes, I think it's him,' she said a little uncertainly. 'It's not so easy to say, he's much younger here on this picture, but it must be him.' She wondered, a little surprised, almost frightened, whether it was *relief* she felt. She understood suddenly that *she* was much closer to solving the mystery than the Inspector was. She remembered the conversations she had had with the clerk at the mortuary and the refuse collector on the beach, Mrs Holder's evidence and the picture, even Miss Leander's little hallucination last night; all the threads were gathered in her hand, and through her they led to Mr Kønig, because she had recognized him, and only for that reason. She could hardly resist the urge to tell him that the man on Mrs Holder's photograph was walking around as large as life at the boarding-house, indeed she was as good as engaged to him; but she could hear how absurd it sounded to her inner ear. He's called Aleksander Kønig and lives at the boarding-house. He has a motor cycle. We went on a picnic together last Sunday, in a clearing out near the Beacon. We're going to get engaged. . . . (And if the Inspector had asked, she would with pleasure have told him everything about their picnic, right down to the smallest detail; he was a person in whom you could confide everything.) But you couldn't say things like that. It was madness. And yet. . . .

'The other picture isn't much better,' he added, almost apologetically. 'It's from an excursion, a trip into the country or something like that. He's sitting together with a group of other people drinking coffee out of doors. But you can't see his face so well.'

'Oh, I see,' she said tonelessly. She felt something growing within her, the urge to break out of this vicious circle of tentative suspicions and half-truths. It would not take much: a little break in the chain of suggestions and the tension which had built up would be short-circuited; a little hole in the dike. . . . It sounded easy.

'It's strange, you know. . . .'

He looked up, so strong and reassuring behind his glasses.

'You know, this man.' She pretended to be studying the picture. 'Actually he has a remarkable resemblance to a gentleman who moved in to the boarding-house recently, a Mr Kønig.'

'Really?'

'Yes. . . .' Her courage failed her. The words she chose sounded so ordinary. She felt that she could not manage to raise her sensational revelations above the level of an everyday occurrence; she had not the power to suspend the false 'order' to which everything was subject. The only thing she could hope for was to capture his attention, so that he did not shelve the case. So long as he was working on it, there was still hope. She continued blindly, 'Mr Kønig is a commercial traveller in textiles. He's a lively sort as well, incidentally, and' – she could feel that she was blushing – 'he's also a bit of a ladies' man. He invited me out for a picnic last week, up to the Beacon. . . . He has a motor cycle as well. It's actually amazing how strong a likeness there is!'

'Well, that is a strange coincidence,' he interrupted her indifferently. And she had been prepared to tell him *everything*! She felt betrayed, ruined. She was dead tired, just wanted to go away and sleep, sleep herself away from it all. Cry.

The telephone on the desk shrilled. He gave a short, concise order. Then he put the receiver down and got up.

'Well, thank you for coming.' He came round the desk, over to her chair (so slim and attractive in his well-fitting suit, long, narrow trousers, young, strong thighs . . .). 'But you will really have to excuse me, I have a meeting.'

With elegant courtesy he helped her to her feet whilst she stammeringly tried to express her helpless disappointment. 'What . . . what will happen now? What will you do?'

'Well – we shall carry on with our investigations, of course,' he repeated almost casually as he led her to the door (a strong but friendly grip on her arm); 'but you must see that I can't promise anything. However, we shall do our best, and you will hear from us as soon as we have any concrete results.'

'Thank you,' she whispered with emotion towards the door as it closed behind her. 'Goodbye, Inspector.'

She could see him in her mind's eye, sitting there in his hermetically sealed office, behind his massive desk, as on a throne, an unimpeachable authority who divided right from wrong, justice from injustice, order from chaos. So long as he was in charge of her case she was not utterly lost. So long as he was involved in the problem of Mr Eldmann's identity there was a chance that order would triumph over chaos. And she would have the opportunity to meet him again. Such a tall, attractive young man.

All her hopes were bound up with this.


'Perhaps you should grow a beard,' she said. 'It would suit you.'

They were walking in the garden after supper. He had invited her with due courtesy. None of the others thought it was strange that they went out together in the gathering darkness; on the contrary, they positively encouraged them to do so. All this talk at the table about the 'lovely evening' (even though in actual fact it was rather oppressive), the Consul who had to mention 'the magic of the gloaming', Mrs Sebastian's knowing glances. . . .

He laughed. 'Actually I did have a moustache once, a long time ago, but I shaved it off after a while. Everybody said I looked like Clark Gable.'

They returned to the terrace. He persuaded her to sit down on the bench and at once attempted to make familiar with her charms beneath her summer dress, but she stopped him. It really wouldn't do to let him carry on exactly as he wanted to! What about her honour, her self-respect? They could hear a soft hum of voices from inside the lounge.

He was altogether too active, she thought reproachfully, so vital, so full of energy, so unashamedly *there* (as now, when he had laid that great head on her shoulder and was breathing warmly and heavily against her neck). How different it was when he was asleep, with that large red face at rest in the grass, an ageing faun in heavy repose; she had felt such tenderness for him there in the forest, the whole of him, even that unpredictable part of him which had caused such struggles, such embarrassment (and towards which he was now trying to direct her attention once more). It was as if she knew him and was at ease with him when he lay there still, without moving, breathing peacefully, with shadows playing over his skin. She had nothing to fear then.

'No, not that!' She pulled her hand away determinedly.

'But you promised . . .'

'Later,' she whispered. 'When the time is right. You must be patient for a little longer.'

## · 21 ·

One week later Mr Eldmann was laid to rest.

Notification had arrived from the police station that it was not considered necessary to postpone the funeral any longer owing to investigations into the affair, as it had been more or less ruled out that the deceased had any living relatives.

All that meant was that the authorities were anxious to get him into the ground as quickly as possible, without placing any more strain on public funds, the Consul boomed over the dinner table. He also had a couple of things to say about the efficiency of the investigation; the case was a long way from being cleared up.

'Thank goodness he left enough money for a decent burial, anyway. That's the least we can do for him after all the upheaval,' said the manageress. She had already decided what kind of arrangement would be the most satisfactory, for the bereaved as well as for the deceased. She was keen on organizing any kind of occasion.

Maude hardly had time to prepare herself for her last farewell to the earthly remains of her beloved, for Mr København was courting her so energetically these days. His substantial figure pursued her everywhere; he positively laid siege to her as he gradually became bolder. One afternoon, with an inventive excuse, he tricked her into coming into his room (Number 11!), where he repeated his suggestions, his indignities, and almost suffocated her with the physicality of his 'love' (for he was both big and strong), and even though she defended herself as well as she could, and called him a bandit, he would not leave her in peace until she had relieved him of some of his uncontrollable urges. She noticed to her surprise that this process no longer filled her with such nausea (even though she was of course terrified that someone might come in and surprise them in the middle of the exercise – the door was not even locked! – and even though he took the liberty of running his hands over her body wherever he pleased – or almost – the whole time whilst it was going on). It was as if the contact with the little living creature that quivered and swelled down there beneath her hand and required her ministrations filled her with a deep understanding of the bestiality of man's erotic drive (hadn't he even begun to want to lick her recently? to lick her skin like an affectionate dog?). It was as if by tolerating all this she underlined her own femininity towards him. For was it not a woman's lot to have to give and give, to be soft and submissive and to make sacrifices even of her own self? So she repressed her own pricklings of dislike and counted the moments until it was over. She felt almost more pity for him than for herself. She knew where all this was leading (and he was certainly impatient enough to get there!), she knew what was the supreme sacrifice that they were all waiting for, the last, irreversible transformation that would restore the harmony, fasten off all the loose threads and make the many pieces of the puzzle fall into their allotted places. But at the same time she reprimanded herself for thinking in this way. It was unforgivable, it was morbid. She was even frightened of herself and her compliance with such impulses. She forbade herself to think like that! Where did she get such fantasies from?

It was as if only one way led out of this delusion: almost in desperation she got Mr Kønig to promise that he would attend the funeral. She lied, saying that she would miss him, would need his support in this difficult time, whilst in reality she glimpsed in this a last chance to break out of the circle of half-truths, of fantasies, of interconnected coincidences that threatened to lead them into disaster.

Mr Kønig at Mr Eldmann's bier. There was something improper about the combination, something almost indecent which she felt would be able to explode the surface appearances and lay bare the naked facts – although she could not say that she knew any longer exactly what the facts were. But the Inspector would no doubt be present at the funeral. He had investigated the case, he had seen Mrs Holder's photographs (and identified Mr Eldmann on the basis of that); no one was better acquainted with the details of the case. Their last hope of salvation was linked to the Inspector's perspicacity, to his ability to see how it all hung together.

On Friday morning they set off in two large taxis, those amongst the residents who wished to follow Mr Eldmann to his last resting place. It was brilliant sunshine, the kind of weather which almost forced you to be in a good humour despite the heat in the black car where Maude sat in the back seat, squeezed in between Mr Kønig and the manageress and wearing her only (and now pretty old-fashioned) black dress and black hat, staring longingly at the gardens they were driving past, where the water-sprinklers were sending refreshing spurts over the thirsty lawns.

She could not imagine a funeral service in sunshine. When her mother had been buried, the rain had been pouring down, and it had seemed so right, so appropriate, that it had almost cheered her up, comforted her in her sorrow.

In the graveyard chapel where the service was held she caught sight of the Inspector – the representative of the authorities, since this was rather a special case – right over by the door, and her heart did a little leap of joy. Fortunately Mr Kønig did not seem to have noticed anything, as he stood there beside her singing the second verse of 'The Day Thou Gavest' reverently and sonorously, with a face which seemed even more voluminous in this solemn moment. She tried to catch the Inspector's eye, make him aware of them, but he would not look up.

In the interval between the singing and the sermon all was still except for Miss Leander's stifled sobs (distracting in more ways than one!) and the light footsteps of the organist over the gallery: he had fifteen minutes' break. The sun projected the red, blue and yellow pattern of the stained-glass window on to the white wall opposite. Mrs Sebastian dropped her hymn-book on the floor and the Consul cleared his throat. It was cool and airy in the chapel.

But by the grave she managed to catch his eye, and nodded, full of seriousness as required by the occasion, but also filled with new hope, for now he surely *must* notice Mr Kønig, who was standing just behind her (so close that she was the whole time worried that he would 'get up to something', lovesick as he was), and recognize him from the picture. But the Inspector simply nodded briefly back and looked away.

She felt her hopes falter and disappear as she feverishly wondered what she should do in order to direct his attention to Mr Kønig, for it was certain that he would be forced to recognize him when he studied him closely. Whilst her head was whirling with desperate schemes, all equally hopeless and unworkable, she suddenly felt a tickle in her throat, and before she knew what she was doing she was doubled over, coughing uncontrollably, whilst Mr Kønig supported her, with his arm protectively around her shoulders, offering her his handkerchief. She even took a step forward towards the open grave (they had just lowered the coffin and the vicar had raised his hand and was in the middle of reading something), so that it looked for a moment as if she was about to fall in, before he rescued her. At that moment she looked up and caught a glimpse of the Inspector standing on the other side of the deep pit, so stylish in his well-fitting dark suit, with eyes wide open and a look of astonishment on his face; and she thought that *now* he could not avoid realizing who the man who was standing holding her really was! But the coughing fit passed, the Inspector resumed his formal expression and looked away, the vicar carried on with his speech after a momentary pause, and Miss Leander cried quietly into her handkerchief.

Nothing had happened. The Inspector had seen Mr Kønig, there was no doubt about that, but had not recognized him. The whole thing had been an embarrassing incident, and nothing more. Birds trilled in the blue, blue sky, the sun beat down on her back and shoulders and made her body ferment beneath the funeral clothes. What weather! What a glorious day!

She was lost.

She stared down into the grave, at the ornate, varnished coffin lid (everything in connection with the funeral had been so tastefully arranged, the manageress had really made an effort; after the burial there was to be a meal at the Crown). She tried to imagine her embalmed beloved attractively laid out in this elegant wooden box, beneath the flowers; but the fact that Mr Kønig had not let go of her since her little upset (and was making the most of his chance to knead and stroke her upper arm), and that the Inspector seemed impatient to leave the whole ceremony, distracted her. Nothing about the coffin, or about the whole funeral ritual come to that, had anything to do with Mr Eldmann. But what did have something to do with him, in a most disturbing way, was Miss Leander's broken sobs, which kept on reaching her ears through the vicar's monotonous mumbling: the urine test had been positive. Miss Leander had come along late last night and confided in her what the doctor had said. She was completely beside herself. She had to get rid of it. There was no other way out. She had an address (little Miss Leander had got hold of the address of a quack) – if it wasn't already too late, if the baby wasn't too far on. The poor woman had broken down completely, but Maude had refused any contact with a body which had suddenly become alien, inimical, a passionate female body which carried within it the inflammation of conception. What sacred pact could exist between them now that the proof of her friend's fall was incontrovertible?

Finally she had excused herself because of a headache and persuaded her to return to her own room. The spell had been broken, it had perished beneath an avalanche of hurtful (and unpalatable) facts. Everything was over between them.

The result of all this was that she could find no answer to her searching in the open grave, however desperately she tried to concentrate on what the vicar was saying. She was incapable of feeling anything for Miss Leander's incautious lover (for the bereaved woman's tears left no doubt that it was he who was being buried), the author of her misfortune, who was now so incontrovertibly documented with doctor's pronouncements and urine tests. At the same time Mr Kønig's hand carried on its most peculiar flirtation with her left arm, camouflaged as a sympathetic gesture. And the sun blazed over their bowed heads.

Earth fell on the coffin lid. The last words of the ritual; then the ceremony was at an end. The Inspector had a short conference with the vicar and then exchanged a few words with the manageress, shook her by the hand and hurried off without vouchsafing her and Mr Kønig a glance.

All was over. Mr Eldmann was buried; the last yardstick for life's ordered regularity was effectively removed from the surface of the earth. The Inspector had not intervened; on the contrary, he had looked relieved when everything went according to plan. It had obviously been high time to get him buried and finished with. She thought she could see that on the faces of the others too. Their expressions registered sorrow, of course, as was both desirable and proper; but through the sorrow she glimpsed a satisfaction that it was now accomplished, that life could at last continue without any troublesome stowaway, without any force which could delay and postpone the oblivion of what had to be put behind them, without a double vision of what was to come. To postpone a funeral is to transgress against the formal etiquette for the relationship between life and death, to keep the dead alive, to prevent the wheel of time from turning full circle.

She looked out over the level, grassy cemetery with its dusty grey paths, the serious ornaments of the gravestones against the background of luscious green, the mighty lime trees along the wall which shielded it from the noise and bustle of the street. The late summer fruitfulness penetrated all her senses; it dripped fragrantly from open pods, hung juicy and heavy from ripe boughs, completely overwhelmed the small, timid monuments with their cleared patches of earth, most of them overgrown and neglected. It positively lifted her up, carried her as on a powerful shoulder, filled with potent sap, enveloped in fragrance, as she carefully stepped along the gravel path in her best shoes beside Mr Kønig, dreaming of floating over green meadows clothed in light veils, dancing for her sluggish god of the forest, revealing her ripeness to his eyes (a more prosaic wish to get out of this tight dress was also making itself felt), drinking in her own loveliness.

(At that moment he turned his face towards her to say something, but she didn't see him, didn't hear him, was aware of nothing.)

What a day!

August. The heavy, ripe, fruitful month when nature is gorged on itself, when all growing things threaten to burst their bounds; a flower, a sap-filled plant, even the blades of grass. Had the grass ever grown higher? Had the thick leaves ever been so green and tempting? Had the flowers ever spread their petals so wide to all sides as they did today? Their poor, defenceless petals. Her secret symbols. Her aphrodisiac.

She felt how the summer warmth urged the blood faster through her veins. What prevented her from giving herself over to her own femininity here, in the cemetery, in all that soft green grass? That was what they were all waiting for after all, with solemn satisfaction, those who were walking along in front of and behind them, impatient to carry on with their interrupted existences. Now it was all down to her, Maude; one surrender and everything was fulfilled. If only fate had seen fit to rid her of people's voices and glances; if only the lime trees had grown a little more thickly and been able to protect her against the machinations and manipulations that lay in wait, if only the swallows had united to give their consent as they wheeled up there in glorious freedom beneath the sky and presided over all her earthly intentions. . . .

She knew that she had witnessed Mr Eldmann's last journey. They had stood there, scattered and motionless, around the open grave and seen the coffin lowered. Dust to dust. Ashes to ashes (that vicar had not spoken clearly at all – she had hardly heard a word!). Dry lumps of earth which fell on the lilies. With that everything should be finished, she should feel sorrow and emptiness at a loss so great, so irreparable. . . . But Mr Kønig was walking along beside her on the narrow gravel path, holding her arm and talking in a low voice about how brave he thought she had been at the graveside, during the vicar's sermon, how hard it must have been for her; and the sun burned down on them, and the grass was growing tall and dark green and his fingers were squeezing pleasurably the soft fullness just above her elbow. She leaned a fraction closer to him and knew, dazed by sunshine, that this was how it had to be, that everything else was accomplished, that this was all that remained. But his size, his corpulence, his insistent presence, his activeness nevertheless made her restless and dissatisfied. It was as if something was still missing.

In the dining-room at the Crown Hotel she was given a seat just opposite one of the high windows which was opened because of the heat and which now and then admitted a breath of aromatic afternoon warmth (which caressed her swollen ankles beneath the table). From where she sat she could see out into the garden, where a wind was stroking the yellow mane of the willow tree and the sun was casting a cascade of hues over the cement-grey wall opposite. She thought with her head singing a little after the glass of sherry they had had before the meal that the large table was so tastefully decorated; the manageress really did know how to organize things properly. After the steak, the Consul said a few words in remembrance (a crow flew lazily across her field of vision and was gone over the roof-tops). With the dessert they had a glass of port. The Consul and Mr Kønig were already discussing something in loud tones, and Mrs Sebastian laughed out loud, exposing pale red gums. Afterwards, coffee and liqueurs were served in the lounge.

In the taxi home Maude suddenly felt that she had to laugh at everything Mr Kønig said, and this no doubt was part of the reason for his sudden decision to put his arm around her, despite the fact that the manageress was sitting in the front seat and every now and then made a remark about something or other and glanced back at them in order to hear their opinion. She just let it happen, and rested her head against the reassuring material of his dark suit, closing her eyes and letting the wind from the open window blow through her hair. She felt the gentle swaying of the car and the sounds from the street blend with the dying vibrations of the summer day until she almost fell asleep, indifferent to what he was doing and what the manageress might be thinking; although she seemed perfectly agreeable as she sat there, glancing at them over her shoulder. Even the manageress.

Then they were home. All too soon. She stood at the gate, a little unsteadily, and tried to fix her hair, which was coming down. Behind her the car doors slammed and she heard steps approaching.

'It really is a lovely afternoon, despite everything,' said the manageress with a sigh. Her funeral arrangements had been a triumph.

'That's certainly true,' agreed Mr Kønig, holding the gate open for them.

'A lovely afternoon,' repeated the manageress. 'It seems a shame to go indoors.'

There were only the three of them there. The others had left before them; or perhaps they were coming later. Maude was not really sure.

'How mild the air is. It's the sort of day when one ought to be going for a walk.' It was a hint, a definite hint.

The manageress began to walk slowly up the path whilst Maude and Mr Kønig stood there, hesitating. They really had to go for a walk in the garden after that.

'Well, perhaps we should take a stroll in this lovely weather?' he finally ventured. 'Over to the summer-house?'

'Yes, if you like,' she answered, feeling herself surrounded by layer upon layer of unreality. An angel guided her steps along the path.

They sat down. He cleared his throat. After all, it was broad daylight. He pushed two fingers into his waistcoat pocket, searching for something.

'I've stolen something from you,' he said teasingly. 'A memento I shall keep for ever.'

She saw that it was a hairpin he was holding in his hand. He had no doubt found it in the taxi. There was fulfilment in this too.

So she resigned herself herself obediently to his boldness on the bench in front of the summer-house where they could not be seen by anyone, and performed her duty, her little finger-dance for him, purposefully, with shy familiarity now. She even let him play a little with stubby fingertips up along her silk stockings right to the top (but no farther, not just yet, you must be patient for a little while longer, just a little while, little piggy), and whisper that she was so 'incredibly sexy' in that black dress (which fitted her quite well, she must admit, despite being a bit old-fashioned) and that he had wanted to 'have' her during the whole funeral service.

And afterwards, when he held both her hands in his one hand, and kissed her fingertips, gratified and content, and asked her if she would go out to a restaurant with him and have dinner and dance the following evening, she said yes. It was time for her monthly indisposition, but she said yes anyway.

She awoke that same night, shaken by a disturbing dream, and realized that she had to go to the toilet. The long corridor was dimly lit by the dawn, unreal like a picture on a linen screen. She shivered. Her heart was pounding so much that she had to struggle to keep calm.

She carried out her errand, even cast a glance in the mirror over the wash-basin, but the impression from her dream did not fade: the feeling of him so close to her. She had discovered such an appetite for him, his plumpness, his liveliness, she could see him before her eyes as he walked around the boarding-house, bespectacled, red-haired and blustering (and with a fine, noble profile which somehow did not go with the rest); it was as if his presence filled her to the brim. . . . She realized how dangerous this could be for her, what a threat it was to all peace, all order and calm. She didn't even like him particularly, he was the opposite of everything she valued in a man, and had always done; except for one moment in the grass, when he was lying asleep with shadows playing across his face, so calm, so serene in sleep. It was essential to keep hold of this, and she knew what she had to do. . . .

But the dream pictures would not release her. She remained standing outside the closed door of Number 11, bashful, gasping, wearing nothing but a night-gown; she could hear his breathing in there, so peaceful and regular. She pressed her tongue against the dry wooden frame. She had seen him tearing the flowers to pieces, those poor, poor flowers, and her own longing had surged so that she was almost beside herself. She knew that it could not be long now, and she knew what she had to do to save everything which was valuable, pure and orderly in the world. Everything which was more important to her than life itself.

## · 22 ·

Dr Gøttlich had his practice in a villa in the neighbourhood, only five minutes' walk from the boarding-house. The same solid bourgeois district. That was one of the reasons why it felt so reassuring to consult him.

Maude sat in the dark, old-fashioned waiting-room, twisting her fingers nervously. It was early Saturday morning, the day after the funeral, and a sudden impulse just after she had woken up had made her come here, without saying a word to anyone, straight after breakfast. Dr Gøttlich was the only one she could seek help from. Only he could preserve her from the crazy fancies that pursued her day and night. She shivered when she thought of the various things she had said and done in the last few weeks, the things she had let herself be persuaded into according to an idea that she was following the essential dictates of love, even though she knew very well the whole time that she had given her love to one man, once and for all, irredeemably, and that this one and only had passed away and she had remained as a lonely widow, with no other comfort than her memories and her unshakable devotion to what had once been, as was right and proper.

But it was as if a thousand things had conspired to sabotage this simple certainty: the circumstances surrounding Mr Eldmann's death, confusing information which had collected (though was it that significant?), suggestions which didn't make sense when you thought back, new events which had thrown an ambivalent light on what had happened previously as well as on the present, chance statements. . . . And not least Mr Kønig himself, his boorish presence, how he managed continually to set things up in order to make her lose her composure, and thus entice her into participating in the demolition of everything she believed in and held to be true and right, a process which she herself at times had found pleasurable; oh, how ashamed she was when she thought of it now!

It had appeared so clearly to her early this morning. As soon as she had woken up, she knew that Dr Gøttlich would be able to help her out of these terrifying delusions that threatened to overwhelm her completely. In fact, she found it almost strange that it had not occurred to her to visit her doctor before. Just think how much torment and ignominy she could have avoided! Dr Gøttlich had helped her over depressions before, listened to what she had to say and given her something soothing. Perhaps the whole thing was not as serious as she had imagined? Perhaps it was just an unfortunate mood; after all, she had had such mood swings recently, and it wasn't surprising if her nerves were a little on edge; and in any case she was at the dangerous age.

For just the fact of sitting here in Dr Gøttlich's waiting-room, with its old-fashioned furniture, assuaged the fear that she had felt a little while ago and made her feel more in control of the situation. After a little while she could even smile at her feeling of shock and powerlessness this morning; all she had to do was to tell him everything exactly as it was, confide everything in him and ask him to give her something to calm her nerves. It was no more difficult than that. Yes, she felt distinctly better already (and at the same time remembered her restaurant date with Mr Kønig that evening and had to admit that she was actually looking forward to it; just think to be going out for the evening for once!).

A new patient came in quietly, nodded silently and sat down on Dr Gøttlich's creaking leather sofa. It was a woman, in an advanced state of pregnancy, with pale features and an unhealthy skin.

How she must be suffering, thought Maude, and smiled at her involuntarily, out of pure sympathy with her suffering, with her sacrifice. But soon after she became restless and just wished that Dr Gøttlich would hurry up and finish with this patient who had been talking to him for an inordinately long time; for it was her turn next, and really she always felt a bit uneasy at the sight of pregnant women, because it was such an *unaesthetic* state, so deforming, so brutal a strain on the body, and because the whole thing always called up such strong and painful emotions, was so dramatic, and made her think of a number of things she would really rather leave alone. Just at this moment that woman made her think of Miss Leander and her unfortunate 'accident', of the fact that her poor friend would now have to seek the aid of a vulgar quack doctor. That was the way things were: conceived in sin and brought forth in sin. She shuddered. She felt so sorry for Miss Leander, thinking of how much she had changed for the worse recently, and how pale and unkempt and miserable she looked.

She had filled out as well, and was no doubt in the process of losing her good figure (she thought of her own trim, rounded form – no decay there, just luxuriance and rising sap . . .) – and now she was reduced to an illegal, painful and by no means risk-free operation into the bargain, in order to salvage what was possible of her reputation. No, it made her so depressed to think of Miss Leander, who had squandered the riches of her femininity, that gift which it was to be a woman, and who now was forced to pay so dearly for it; and this woman, this other patient who was sitting there opposite her on the sofa and reminding her of all this – she must also be weighed down, broken by the heaviness of her fate.

But when Maude looked more closely at her, she realized that the woman did not look unhappy at all; on the contrary, she was sitting there with a satisfied, almost a beatific expression on her pale face. How was it possible? she wondered, and felt positively disturbed by this violation of what was so clearly the correct way of thinking. Was it possible to be happy in circumstances like that, in that condition, with an ugly, inflated belly, a condition whose origin was humiliation and whose conclusion was pain? She could not understand it. It offended her sense of what was seemly, it almost shocked her; and what shocked her most was that if it was possible that this woman was happy and contented, then there was also a possibility (even though it was a purely theoretical one) that Miss Leander felt something of the same contentment, a deep, 'feminine' contentment (for it could not be denied that pregnancy and childbirth belonged to the 'order' of the female role, the eternal feminine) – despite her lamentable transgression, her sin, and that perhaps in spite of everything she had gained from this experience, as a woman, because she had 'lived' (she had whispered last night, 'I wouldn't have it undone again, at least I have this, at least I have lived', but Maude had of course not been able to believe her, not then). And this word 'lived' suddenly struck Maude as being of the utmost importance, because she could not say for sure what it entailed; and she was all at once uncertain as to whether she herself could be said to have 'lived', despite the fact that she had always kept to what she knew was right, was best, and had never done any harm to anyone.

So the fact that this woman was sitting there with a peaceful expression on her face, enthroned in her unmistakable contentment, suddenly placed a question mark against Maude, against her very self and her conduct of her own life. And this made her both uncertain and alarmed (even though it cheered her up a little to think that she was going out to a restaurant this evening, a dance restaurant), because she had never doubted these things, and because – in more practical terms – these doubts undermined the very purpose of her visit to the doctor's.

So when Dr Gøttlich's face finally appeared in the doorway, and she was called in to his consulting-room, she was so preoccupied with justifying her own life and actions *vis-à-vis* Miss Leander that she was for a moment a little confused as to why she had actually come. But it was not very long before she had regained her awareness of her various worries (really she would have to watch out! How could she let herself become so forgetful?); so that when he said 'Now, Miss Maude, what can I do for you today?' she answered immediately that she had been nervous and under the weather recently and didn't really know what the reason was, just as she had planned, and waited for him to begin asking questions. This was how things normally proceeded between them. She had boundless confidence in Dr Gøttlich ever since she had once had to let him examine her for cystitis (she had overcome all her panic-stricken shyness and laid herself open to him, and after a few moments had felt herself lifted on a wave of contentment, almost transfiguration, at his professional touch; he was so clever, so full of wisdom, the only person who with objectivity and sureness could handle her disorderly nether regions). Nevertheless, she found herself becoming a little distracted as he asked her whether she had had any particularly upsetting experiences recently; for it suddenly occurred to her as he was sitting there behind his old-fashioned desk, with his large, stern face leaning over towards her on the other side, that he had taken on a remarkable similarity to Mr Kønig. Her heart missed a beat in fright, for it was an unmistakable resemblance; she could not understand how it was that it had not occurred to her before.

He repeated his professional question, and added, 'Of course, I did hear about the gentleman who passed away. It's always upsetting when such things happen in one's nearest circle . . .'

She interrupted him, 'Yes, that's true of course, but actually I had very little to do with poor Mr Eldmann. We hardly knew each other, he never said very much, kept himself to himself.' She was completely absorbed now by this large face with the stern glasses, the round, almost bald pate. And whilst she spoke, her thoughts were diverted yet again, this time by a faint, gnawing stitch in the pit of her stomach, a signal that her period was approaching. (But there was no danger, it could be several hours, even a whole day before it came. She thought about her date with Mr Kønig. If she was not unlucky, she should just about manage it.) And this reminder of her own blooming femininity – for menstruation was also a trial, an ordeal which woman had to bear, and therefore a privilege – filled her utterly with its overwhelming significance and combined with Dr Gøttlich's mysterious likeness to Mr Kønig to make her thrill with excitement. She was going to go out and dance, *dance* with her breathless satyr, her lap-dog who worshipped her so, her secret lover; this in itself was a response to the urging of her blood, to the demands of life, of which she had been reminded in time.

She said, 'No. I really don't know what it can be, there's nothing in particular that I can think of. . . . Perhaps it's just that I've been sleeping so badly at nights recently. Perhaps you could give me something to help me sleep?' For it was clear to her what it was she must do, what final sacrifice was being required of her in order that all mysteries should be solved, what had been left undone should be remedied, and all distracting details should fall into place in the pattern that was the only solution, a sacred, divine order.

The tablets he had prescribed for her were too weak, and in any case were almost used up. They would not be able to serve her purpose. She knew now that *this* had been the true purpose of her visit to Dr Gøttlich, an intention that had lain buried beneath indecision and doubt, but which nevertheless had directed her footsteps here, where the solution of her problems was at hand. She knew what she had to do.

'The last ones you had were not strong enough, then?' He had already got out his prescription pad.

'No, they're not much use any more, I'm afraid.'

He wrote a name, a formula, with the scratch of a fountain pen. 'You must under no circumstances take more than two of these.'

'No, of course not, doctor. And thank you very much!' She could hardly restrain herself from snatching the prescription out of his hand, she was so impatient.

'Perhaps we should take a look at you whilst you're here, in order to make sure that everything's all right?'

She didn't really have time, but his tone was so authoritative, and the thought of an examination made the blood rise to her cheeks. It was only a matter of listening to her heart and measuring her blood-pressure, and possibly an X-ray; but she enjoyed revealing herself in her underwear to Dr Gøttlich. The thought of her little bit of exhibitionism even gave her a titillating feeling of being just a tiny bit unfaithful to Mr Kønig – a transgression she would make up for, oh yes, she would make up for it many, many times over in just a few hours. She promised herself that as she popped the precious prescription into her handbag.

'We'll just have a little listen first then,' said Dr Gøttlich, and adjusted his stethoscope as she submissively opened the buttons of her blouse.

At the chemist's she was given the sleeping-pills with instructions that a half to one tablet was the normal dose, which suited her perfectly. Everything went precisely as planned.

Outside, there was a moist warmth in the air, with a layer of clouds which clung to the shoreline and the hills but did not portend rain.

So it'll be fine tonight.

On the way home she bought a bottle of advocaat.

He's going to get a treat tonight, she thought with pleasure as she put the bottle in her shopping-bag.

Tonight he's in for it!

## · 23 ·

And the evening came and Maude and Mr Kønig were dancing.

She had put on her red dress and he was wearing a suit. The dance band was playing a slow waltz, the lights were dimmed, and he held her so closely that she could feel his erection against her stomach through her clothes. He was not all that tall, not so tall as the Consul, but he was still a head taller than her. They had eaten, they had drunk wine, the orchestra was playing a slow waltz, and Maude was conscious the whole time of that slight pressure which indicated love's first little impatience. But it did not alarm her, it didn't even make her embarrassed and uneasy, not tonight, for everything was prepared, and she had the courage to unite the momentary distractions of the flesh with the eternal harmony of the ideal. It was precisely at that point, where the two intersected, that she would experience fulfilment and make him identical with the longing she carried within herself. She even thrust her broad pelvis against his thigh, not demonstratively hard, but hard enough for him to feel it; and she felt how the pressure made a glow, a quiver vibrate deep in her belly. Readiness for what was to follow.

She thought how elegant he looked as they were dancing, with his large, red face at peace, so stylish in his dark suit. She leaned backwards and studied him: he was dancing with the slightly exaggerated suppleness of a corpulent man, as a carnation (taken from the flower arrangement on the table in an impulsive flourish) shone dazzlingly against the discreet stripes of his jacket lapel.

The same suit.

'It really suits you, that red dress,' he said.

'Thank you.'

The orchestra played a slow waltz; Maude and Mr Kønig danced, and he tested her gently resisting body with his thigh.

It had been an excellent dinner; they had drunk wine (the Lantern Restaurant was well known for its wines), he had stroked her silk-clad knee beneath the table and she had looked into his eyes (it was not so dangerous here at the restaurant; here she was safe, and later she knew exactly what she must do). Now they were dancing, and she followed his movements attentively.

She almost felt a little pity for him, for this face, so calm, almost elevated in its seriousness now that the orchestra was playing and he was holding her in his arms. But the impatience beneath his stomach lived and swelled, demanded attention; and she felt suddenly that they were dancing far too close and almost felt a little cross with him because he could not control himself better, here at such a superior restaurant. Then she forgave him just as quickly, for it was their first dance, and also their last. She thought: my dearest Mr Kønig, you are dancing with a tear in your buttonhole. . . . And he did cut a fine figure in his suit with the discreet stripes, the suit he normally wore when he came here; she had to lay her head against the material of his jacket and let him stroke the hair on her temples with his chin. She was a little in love, after all.

The lights were dimmed. Other guests were sitting at tables eating, with glasses; a waiter hurried forward in answer to a nod. There were very few who were dancing. The orchestra was playing a slow waltz. It was a good-quality restaurant, a respectable place, and she was grateful for that. It was reassuring to look at the tasteful interior, the well-dressed guests, to have wined and dined well, to feel yourself surrounded by quality, by elegance, by 'order' in its most sophisticated form, to hear good music played by a good orchestra whilst you sharpened your fleshly appetites under cover of dancing. It gave a kind of absolution to the moment.

The orchestra took a break and he escorted her back to their table. She was in no hurry to sit down again, but stopped him on the floor, looked him up and down and said, 'I like that suit you're wearing very much.'

'Thank you,' he answered, a little surprised, but also self-satisifed.

He was rather vain, almost affected, she thought. 'But didn't it once have a waistcoat? It looks to me . . .'

He looked at her, surprised. 'Well, yes, it did actually. How did you . . . ?'

She interrupted him. 'Where's the waistcoat now, then?'

He looked bewildered, almost shamefaced. 'I've lost it. It no doubt sounds ridiculous that it's possible to lose a waistcoat, but I sent the suit to the cleaners a little while ago, and when it came back the waistcoat was missing.'

'I see.'

'It was a strange episode. I moved heaven and earth, but the waistcoat had vanished without trace. In the end the cleaners had to give me compensation . . .' He seemed almost nervous now.

'I know,' she said, smiling, and pressed his hand to reassure him (how little he knew of what went on in a woman's thoughts!). 'I like the suit as it is, anyway. I just wondered.'

'You do ask about the strangest things,' he said, looking relieved that the subject seemed to be exhausted. 'I can't make you out.'

He held her chair as she sat down. Then they were sitting face to face and his knee was touching hers beneath the table.

'No, it's not easy to make you out,' he murmured, and then smiled as she allowed him to lay his hand on hers. A glow. A restlessness. How slowly, how tentatively things were moving between them, even now when the decision was made. She caught his knee between her own and squeezed his fingers hard. They smiled to each other. She didn't like his face so well when it exhibited feelings and emotions; it was as if it became formless, grew larger and redder, and his expression became so much more 'disorderly'. It was better when they were dancing; then he looked so serious, almost devout, and there was something almost noble about him despite that little piece of impudence squirming below his belt.

'Tonight, then,' he whispered, and let a groan of longing (or was it more simply prosaic impatience?) escape with the words. Their table was standing in the corner, in the half-darkness, secluded. He had his knee between hers. They smiled at each other, knowingly, securely. His large face was alive with adoration, with desire, his mouth opened and closed, he swallowed, his Adam's apple jumped up and down; but it would not be very much longer now, just a couple of hours perhaps, perhaps even less.

'First you must tell me if you come here often.'

'Oh.' Again he looked taken aback, a little uncertain. 'Occasionally, yes, not very often of course but . . .'

'Do you wear that suit then?'

'Well, yes, I might do. I can't say that I remember particularly what I've been wearing. But I have no doubt worn this suit here before.' He reached out for her and smiled awkwardly. 'Why do you ask about that?'

'Well, I have to get to know you,' she said. 'No woman with any self-respect would accept an invitation from a man she doesn't know.'

'And do you think you know me now, then?' He had become so

gentle, so accommodating; no doubt he also felt that it was only a question of minutes, of a few half-hours.

'A little better,' she said mysteriously.

'Well enough?'

'Just about. A virgin has to be particularly careful . . .'

He stared at her wide-eyed. 'Are you . . . ?'

'Hush!' she said, laughing. 'Don't let's talk about it! But I shall consider your tempting offer.' She had to add the last sentence because he looked so thunderstruck. It was the final acquiescence. When she looked down, she could see him in her mind's eye whilst they were dancing, so serious and elegant, with a solemn, immobile face. Now she could hear him summon the head waiter.

'Champagne!'

Champagne – how trivial. A man about town celebrating his latest conquest. But what difference did it make? It was all part of a ritual to which she had submitted herself, and of which she was now directing the finale. For that matter she could just as well have let him drag her off to a cheap hotel like a helpless whore; but everything was made ready in her room, it had to happen in an orderly fashion, exactly as it was prescribed by the structures of improbability, the triumph of spirit over appearances. She was nothing but the means, the medium who was the focus in which all threads and all intimations were gathered together, and which through her would work their way through to their diffuse, fragmented whole, their final form, their 'order'.

'My fiancée would like some champagne!' she heard him boom out to the waiter who brought the bottle.

My fiancée. That was sweet of him. But she did not look up. She could allow herself the luxury of this little game, considering the gift she had bestowed on him. She would prefer to avoid seeing the doglike devotion in his formless face (but it would soon be over!).

'Cheers, my dearest.'

He held out a glass, and she drank, looking down at his waist where his jacket was open, and the shirt and belt held his substantial stomach in place.

'I'm sorry the waistcoat is missing. You were right, there should be a waistcoat with this suit.'

How sweet and confused he was, just because she was a virgin.

'Think no more about it,' she said. 'You'll see, that waistcoat will sort itself out. I have a surprise for you.' She seized a flower from the table arrangement and pulled it apart, petal by petal. Its innocence blazed like a flame between her fingers before she let it drift down into the glass of champagne.

'You are a wonderful woman!' she heard him breathe, as she concentrated on the stripes in his suit material. Perhaps he was beginning to understand.

They sat as close to each other as they could get with the rectangular table between them. He held on to her hand the whole time. His knee was thrust up between her thighs now. She could feel that the time was drawing near. She was not nervous about it, although the red face was still far too large, formless and unfamiliar. It would soon come to rest, become like the other face, the face of love. It would not be long now, then it would be time for her and Mr Kønig to dance. She was not nervous.

The penetration?

No, she was not nervous.

He raised her hand to his lips and kissed her fingertips. He loved her, he said, now he said it, she had heard it before, but it was only now he said it. She loved him too, but she could not say it, not yet, not until they were at the end of the road.

'My room or yours?' he whispered as they stood outside on the steps and breathed in the darkness which filled the sleeping house.

'My room,' she answered. Everything was ready.

'Then I'll get ready and be there in ten minutes.'

It was like a farewell when he pushed the key into the lock, but she let him embrace her in the hall. She could only feel his warmth and the material of his suit, could not see him. Then they tiptoed each to their own room. Two doomed lovers.

She bustled around her room putting everything in place, putting the finishing touches to it, humming to herself. 'Now she's got it coming to her, now Maude's got it coming. . . .'

The last little details: two glasses and the advocaat. She poured it out: one glass for him, one for herself. More for him than for her, it was right like that: the man's role was the hardest, the most demanding, the woman's role was to give.

The bottle of sleeping-pills. She shook out four. Was four enough? No, it was best to be sure: five. Six. She placed them neatly on a piece of paper and began to crush them to powder with the handle of her nail file. It was easy. There wasn't much powder at all. Should she take some more?

She took two more. Best to be quite certain. Then she tipped the powder into his glass and stirred it well with a hairpin. It wasn't possible to see any difference in consistency. Satisfied, she put the glasses on the bedside table. She had fulfilled her arrangement with the dead.

But now she must hurry. He could be here at any moment!

Quickly she got undressed (a glimpse in the mirror, pale and blooming ripeness), put on her night-dress, the most transparent, most attractive pale blue one, and over it a light négligé (mustn't give him everything all at once), then shook out her hair over her shoulders. A spray of perfume. . . .

Then she lit two candles and put out the lights. There. Now he could come.

No, wait! The waistcoat!

She ran over to the wardrobe, pulled out the lowest drawer and took it out. It was creased and looked a little the worse for wear, but it was his. His. She laid it on the table and tried to smooth out the material with her hands. Midnight blue with discreet stripes. He had good taste, her fiancé, who was soon to become her lover and then her one and only beloved. Mr Kønig. She stroked and stroked the striped material. Soon the lines would run together. Soon it would be accomplished. She would make up for what she had previously omitted. What had been begun would be finished. A symmetry would be sealed: love. She herself had made all ready, and she was not nervous. She would gladly make a sacrifice, any sacrifice for this which was the only thing in her life. 'We have all been born into the world in order to realize the ideal of love.' What a beautiful thought. Where had she heard that? Read it? In *November Rain*? She felt like crying. The champagne was still prickling beneath her skin, in her body's most tender places. She had drunk three glasses. She drank so rarely. She didn't like people who drank. She had always heard that things went badly with people who drank.

Her mother.

She sat there thinking about her mother, how she had fallen that summer day and had been driven away in an ambulance. She remembered the dream she had had that night. That was the strange thing about dreams, that they could come back after so many years. . . . She thought about the strange man who had been found dead in a garden in the neighbourhood one morning. And about the police inspector who had gone around all the houses asking questions. That same summer. Everything had happened that same summer, the summer when Daddy had gone away and left them. She remembered it so well. How it all came back to her now!

She stroked the striped waistcoat with trembling hands. His waistcoat. Soon it would be accomplished, uplifted into her own God-given harmony. Now he could come. She was ready. She felt not the slightest fear, not even for the penetration which was supposed to be so dreadful. It was supposed to hurt; she had read so much about it. . . .

But, after all, it was no more than something to be got over, a physical formality, the least of the sacrifices she had to make. Now Maude had it coming to her!

Maude. . . . She tasted the name. Now it sounded greedy, like a chasm that opened and was filled, an ambition to surrender to her own boundlessness, to open herself and embrace everything, the whole world. . . . The eternal feminine. He would come any moment now. Everything was in readiness. She had made her agreement with the dead, the dead who were near and with her when she was aware of love, who were with her now. . . . How she longed for peace, for the stillness afterwards, when no mysteries, nothing inexplicable existed any longer, when everything would have come together into an imperturbable, harmonious whole through her sacrificial act.

Now she could hear something! His steps out in the corridor!

Quickly she sat down on the bed and didn't even have time to get nervous before he was there. He came in without knocking. Closed the door carefully behind him. Whispering. Like a thief. He was wearing a striped silk dressing-gown and slippers. His face shone, newly shaved. He had combed his thinning hair. There was an air of victorious well-being about him.

The whole thing was so unreal: Mr Kønig in dressing-gown and slippers here in her room. Candlelight. And she herself – here she was sitting on her bed with her hair down in a night-dress and négligé, showing a leg, a knee! Her first impulse was to beg him to go. It was all impossible after all, she could not go through with it; his presence in the room, a shocking, offensive foreign body. But suddenly he was close to her, his hands were stroking the silken cocoon which she had spun around her body, and his voice was whispering how lovely she was, how deeply he loved her, what a happy man he was; and then things fell into place again, for this was also a part of it, the fact that she permitted a couple of small tender excesses was all part of a natural, sensual escalation that could not be omitted. She let it happen, she even made little concessions, squeezed, patted and pressed herself so close, as closely as she could, against his corpulence;

she made small noises, did things she knew instinctively that he would like, for she had also become a little restless and impatient.

But still one thing remained, one detail.

'Take off your dressing-gown,' she whispered. 'I have a surprise for you!'

He seemed unwilling, but had to do as she said. She didn't let him get out of it, teased him, was a little unkind; it wasn't too much to ask when all was said and done. So there he stood, ignominiously half-naked, in his slippers and his wide underpants, and she jumped up and fetched his waistcoat from the table with a laugh.

'Here you are, here's your waistcoat. Try it on.'

He just stared at her open-mouthed. 'Do you want me to put this waistcoat on?'

'Well, it is yours. The one you said you had lost.'

'Are you crazy?' He laughed a little uncertainly at her eagerness.

'Go on, put it on!'

'All right.' Perhaps he realized that it had a greater significance than was apparent on the surface. With a dumb look on his face he put it on.

'There you are. That's the one! It fits!'

'Well, I don't know about that. . . .' He was struggling with the buttons. It was a little tight over the stomach.

'Of course it fits! You've just put on weight a bit.'

It was the right waistcoat. There could be no doubt about it.

'Isn't it the one you lost, then?'

'Well. . . . Yes, it is similar. . . .'

It *was* the one! She was filled with inexpressible relief and exhilaration. Transfiguration. Now nothing more stood between them.

'Yes, it might well have been this one,' he muttered, examining the material. 'It looks like the same cloth.' He looked at her hopefully, as if he had at last realized that in the final analysis it all depended on his acceptance of the waistcoat as his own, whether she would give herself to him or not.

'It's the one all right.'

How sweet he was, really, standing there struggling to make the tight waistcoat fit, with his fat stomach and his ridiculous underpants. She laughed at him. The time had come. 'Come over here, I've got something good for you.'

He sat down, meek after the demonstration, realizing no doubt he had become a part of a process which could not be reversed and that he was not directing developments any longer. She passed him the glass of advocaat. He wrinkled his nose, obviously not feeling much like drinking anything now; instead he let himself sink down towards her inviting softness and buried his face in her silken bosom.

'Come on, drink it anyway,' she whispered. 'It's the best drink there is a for a woman – when the man drinks it!' She giggled. She could be so coquettish when she wanted to.

They both laughed, and he drank. She barely sipped at her glass. He took a large gulp.

'All of it now!' she commanded. 'Drink it all up . . .'

'. . . and I'll grow big and strong!' He threw her a merry glance and emptied the glass of thick, yellow liquid.

Then she was lying beside him, waiting.

He had undressed her in the golden candlelight, laid his hands on her as reverently as a priest, as irrevocably as an executioner, had penetrated the shield of her clothes, the last illusion of order and decency in her relationship to him; and let her feel how his hands shook as he traced new paths across her skin. She had cast herself towards him, suddenly so frightened, exposed, repentant. It was too overwhelming after all, too violent, too humiliating. It had all come too quickly. She felt that her skin was shining phosphorescent white with its dark patches in the dimly lit room. She couldn't, she *could not*; she threw herself against him. He had misunderstood, been greedy, had wanted at once to go too far; but she had pleaded with him, begged for a postponement, just a little while, a very short while, she was not quite ready yet! And when he had raised himself up on his elbow and looked at her, his face was at bursting point, swollen and unrecognizable, and she fought against a panic-stricken fear which made her want to burst into tears, holding her hands over her breasts even though shyness was not the issue any more. A storm that was rising within her threatened to break through all the barriers of what she had previously known; and she knew it would have to happen soon now, in a few moments. And without knowing why, whether it was a feeling of powerlessness, revulsion or the fact that she loved him which prompted her, she thrust her hand with all her force against this face and scraped downwards over the smoothly shaven skin with her nail so that it left a trail of blood; he swore in surprise, then laughed and pulled her towards him.

And now she was lying on his arm, waiting. She had wiped the blood away with her hand, wetted her finger with spit and licked up the drops of warm saltiness, and thought that now they were one, one blood; and he lay still, just stroked and patted her, called her a romantic, and embraced her gently and carefully, just as he had done before, that time beneath the tree, when they had both stood there so irresolute and helpless under the weight of their passion and let themselves be caressed by the transparent finger-like leaves of the chestnut tree.

She lay waiting. She had let one hand resume its little gymnastics with him, its 'five-finger exercise', and could sense the result, the dance beneath her fingers. She lay waiting, lay and watched him, longing for the moment when it would be accomplished, when that perfect peace would spread over the face so full of blood and emotions, of life; then she would be able to love him, really to love him. And she could see that the moment was approaching, for he was calmer now, and heavier, as if floating in his massive immobility, just lying there enjoying her manipulations, and she thought: a man who is asleep always has an erection. For she could feel his potency swelling and increasing under her hand, and she loved him for this most significant inconsistency of life: a man who is dreaming. . . . And she laid her face next to his and whispered, 'Darling, do you ever dream about me?'

And at the sound of her voice, he turned, drugged with sleep, and made as if to answer; but suddenly he opened his eyes wide as if he was seeing her for the first time, or seeing something else, farther away, something beyond her. He whispered in amazement, 'About you . . . ?', let his head fall, and was asleep.

She had done it!

It was difficult to believe it was true. Now he was lying there asleep. Now he was hers.

Now you are mine!

He lay with his head turned away. His breast rose and sank almost unnoticeably. His dark organ lay pointing upwards across his white stomach, erect and powerful, gleaming like metal.

Now he is mine!

This was the miracle which united the living and the dead, the profane and the sacred. Now the transformation was complete. Now she could without disturbance consummate her dreams about a love which was not of this world.

He lay on his back, lay motionless, breathing almost imperceptibly. She let a hand pass over his face (so peaceful, almost beautiful now). He slept. So it was time for her last, her most important sacrifice.

She straddled him, finding the right place without difficulty. She had read about the various positions; she was by no means an ignorant woman. She sat enthroned in triumph, and the life beneath her on which she rode thrust so gently but inexorably through seal upon seal within her; and she felt all her coldness, all her arrogance, all her ignorant, helpless innocence burst with the yielding resistance, and it melted within her, turned to a river, a flood, to fire, as she rode there so high on the man's last spark of life. And like an echo of an old, cast-off thought that there would never be the chance to think again, she whispered over and over to herself like an incantation: *The old story; the old, familiar story*, whilst her breasts swayed back and forth between her plump arms. For she had read about the ecstasy of the flesh and recognized its symptoms. And when it was there, when she felt her volume grow to an indescribable pitch, when her body burst its bounds and madness lashed her onwards, when it seemed to be only seconds before she must die, be torn apart by a rage and a greed that had been unleashed and could no longer be controlled, then she grasped his neck in both hands and squeezed with all her might, dug her nails into the soft flesh as if to annihilate this force, as if to bring to an end with her own hands what had been begun and to present to eternity the sacrifice that it had demanded of her. And at that very moment she was delivered; she was overtaken by the last, blind flash of nothingness, went under in a torrent of blood, and the fall seemed never ending.

Then she was lying crying, covering his body with her own, and the final cramps shook her and departed, and the last spurts of fire sprang up and died, leaving behind a heap of ashes; her life was played out, used up; and she covered his dying, formless body with her own and sobbed like an animal.

Later she was standing on the floor beside the bed and looking at him, looking at the sleeping face on the pillow beneath the golden sheen of the candles. His mouth hung open and his eyes were sunken beneath the shadow of the brows. Her lover of a summer's night. It was finished.

His breast no longer moved. She thought: Are you dreaming about me now, dear Mr Kønig? Two dark stripes could clearly be seen on the thick neck.

She could wake him with a kiss whenever she wanted to.

His sparse circle of hair had become ruffled during the struggle, and a few greying, reddish wisps were plastered over his temples which showed white against the pillowcase.

The black dew of night in his hair.

His eyes swam like half-moons in the shadowy darkness. He was a good-looking man, and now he was hers. He slept. She could wake him up with a kiss if she wanted to, but it was best to keep him like that, like the sleeping prince in the fairy-tale, so noble, so beautiful. Only then was he really hers.

She stood naked on the floor beside the bed and watched the sleeping man whose breast no longer moved. A little while ago they had been dancing together, she and Mr Kønig. Beneath the majestic stomach his member hung limp and innocent, like the dog's, she thought suddenly, just as orderly, just as unthreatening: the mark of love against the paleness of his thighs.

A strange odour hung in the air, an odour of the ride, of the wild dance, a peculiar odour like musk: her own odour, her own musk. Maude's musk. Oh, my beloved! How the candles flickered and made the shadows over his sleeping face come alive!

A drip of warm moisture distracted her. It ran down her inner thigh and fell with a plop to the ground. Ugh, she thought. How unpleasant. But she did not move her gaze.

More drips followed. A gnawing pain suddenly made her aware of what it was: her period. What a nuisance. She'd better go and wash herself and find a rag to wipe the floor. What a mess!

But she remained nevertheless standing by the bed, watching Mr Kønig sleeping without breathing, his calm, stern features on the pillow; his mouth hung half-open, his eyes swam like half-moons in the shadows beneath his brows. He was paler. The paleness of dawn was mirrored in the drawn skin of his temples. The dew. . . . One of the candles had burned down.

Drips were falling on to the floor beneath her. Dear God, she thought. I must wash myself. I must find a rag and wipe up this mess. But she remained standing there on the floor beside the bed, watching Mr Kønig. There was plenty of time to wash and clear things up before they came.

For they would certainly come. When he did not come down to breakfast in the morning. They would talk about it, wonder why not. Then the maid would come. Then the doctor. Then the Inspector.

She thought about the Inspector. Tomorrow he would come, and she would have to tell him everything: that they had been engaged, Mr Kønig and she, that he had taken her on a picnic, that they had danced close together; every little detail, if he would listen to her. She was almost looking forward to it. Now he would certainly listen to her!

She glanced down at the little pool of brown blood that had collected between her feet. Dear God in heaven! Must go and wash! Can't receive people like this! What a mess! She thought about the Inspector who was going to come.

But Mr Kønig was lying there on the bed, so calm, so beautiful; her fiancé, her only love. What a noble profile. What an elegant man!

But she must see about getting herself washed. It wouldn't do to receive people like this. . . . She must also get the room tidied up. What would they think about her otherwise? She looked down at her thighs. Oh, Mummy! But she didn't move. Menstruation, a sacrifice, a privilege. How proud she was of being a woman!

She must wash and tidy up the room before he came.

Like a fairy-tale prince. She couldn't take her eyes off him.

She thought of the Inspector, of his understanding look behind his glasses. He would listen to her. This time he would listen to her. She would tell him everything. He was like a father. She remembered her own father (despite what Mother had said). She thought about Dr Gøttlich, his stern glance, his professional touch. She felt so little with Dr Gøttlich, little and naughty. It was quite different with the Inspector. Peace and order ruled with him. He understood her. He was like God the Father. And soon she would tell him everything.

The fairy-tale prince.

Her blood. (Oh, Mummy!)

She must get washed. Find a rag and wipe up the puddle on the floor. What would he think of her? But she didn't move. Just stood staring at the furrow that ran along his cheek. At the hair that was plastered to the night-white temples. At the eyes that had retreated under the shadow of the brows. How beautiful he was! What a marvellously beautiful man!

How she longed to see the Inspector's understanding face and hear his calm voice saying that everything was all right now, that he would take care of matters personally, that she didn't need to be worried about the slightest thing, that nobody would have anything to blame anyone for, that all had been for the best. If only she could get the floor cleaned up and get herself washed!

Dawn was near. The windows were growing lighter. Soon he would come. The Inspector. Her Inspector. If she just got herself cleaned up. Got herself washed. Tidied up.

She would be able to tell him everything.

He was like God the Father himself.